ANOMALY ONE

RICK KRUSKY

MWPR Inc.

ISBN: 978-1-7361545-1-9 (Paperback)
ISBN: 978-1-7361545-0-2 (Ebook)

Published by MWPR Inc.
Los Angeles, CA 91602

www.mw-pr.com
www.rickkrusky.com

PRAISE FOR "ANOMALY ONE"

"A fast-paced and compelling read, right from the first line. I was immediately pulled into a rich and mysterious new world full of alien creatures, nefarious plots, beautiful royalty, and grimy underworld action."

— Ken Daniells, Amazon review

"The structure flows. The story flows. The curiosity builds. It's like a gradual, never-ending cliffhanger—in the most positive way. I have rarely had a formless blob come to life from a piece of paper as vividly as if it were next to me—this book did that."

— Jon Le, Amazon review

"This thrilling, fast-paced, and surprisingly emotive sci-fi novel is perhaps one of the greatest bookish surprises I've had all year. Both pacy and plot-driven while also remaining character-focused throughout, Anomaly One is a unique and compelling sci-fi novel with a huge range of appeal."

— Ellie, Goodreads review

"Starts with a bang and never lets up. Great characters and a believable set of alien beings."

— David A. K. Aspelund, Amazon review

"Highly recommended! Krusky shows great insight into his characters and tells the story in a way that pulled me along night after night."

— Steve Wagner, Amazon review

"Best sci-fi book I've ever read. Rick takes you through an incredible journey of the cosmos while exploring your deepest imaginations of alien races and other alien worlds."

— Amazon review

"Krusky built alien races, cultures, and worlds that were relatable and compelling. I kept turning pages until the end."

— Glemmert, Amazon review

To my mother and father, both taken from me
far too early by the callous grip of cancer.

THE EVOLUTION OF AN EMPIRE

ANOMALY ONE

RICK KRUSKY

a·nom·a·ly | noun

a deviation from that which is
conventional or expected

Part One

THE CONGLOMERATE

CHAPTER ONE

Chakeena attempted to lift herself, winced, then dropped back to the unfamiliar bed beneath her, the filth of the coarse sheets detectable and foreign to her, far from the opulence she'd been immersed in for the entirety of her twenty years of life.

She strained to see, her ebony eyes squinting to fend off the glare of a single ceiling light swaying above. Matted from fever and the fallout, her ink-black hair clung in damp strands to jutting cheekbones and lay limply over her pale, papery skin—her body a frail remnant of its former elegance.

Beyond the musty walls could be heard a shout, then another—each an agonizing assault on her throbbing head. She wrestled to orient herself as her eyes gradually adjusted, the jarring harshness of the light letting up bit by bit. And then, as it all began to come back to her, the terror set in.

She'd been taken against her will—kidnapped, abducted, whatever the hell you want to call it. There were alarms, blasts, blood, and... The monsters! Large, ugly, argued about everything. She gasped. Her heart rate spiked, a shortness of breath ensued. She let out a fragile "help" heard by precisely no one...

Over the last few days Chakeena's health had worsened, but this time the doctor had been far more concerned. He'd assured her she'd be okay, but it was his eyes that had given it away. For they told her in no uncertain terms that she would not return from this bout, that this was it for her, short of some sort of a miracle, something which she'd foolishly begun to believe in of late.

The staff had been reduced at the palace. It was what the doctor had learned from the lab—the news of the gene and the unprecedented developments. Contact with others had been restricted and more closely monitored. She'd been moved from the main residence into one of the many guest quarters on the estate which, truth be told, had been just fine with her. But then the monsters, the alarms, and now this...

The room was stale and stunk like a rotting animal. An ache in her arm yanked at her attention. She looked down. Bruises and open wounds had formed and begun to fester, symptoms of the final stage of the disease as it consumed her body from within.

A creak of the floor alerted her to the nearing footsteps. Her eyes darted for some sort of protection. But there was nothing, no one—a situation in which she'd rarely found herself if ever. The futility of it fed the apathy; the apathy further fed the futility, a vicious cycle with all roads leading to the same pointless place. So there she lay, alone and at the mercy of whoever—or *whatever*—it was that approached.

The footsteps ceased. The door squeaked open to reveal an anonymous figure—vaguely human, the silhouette suggesting a female. A pair of enormous goggles gripped its elongated head, partially obscuring its stone-gray eyes. A surgical mask veiled its face. A lab coat cloaked its narrow frame, draping clear to the concrete floor.

Any visible bits of skin were a chalky white, its species undetectable. It glided toward her with weightless grace and an unapologetic air, pushing a wheeled tray burdened with cold metal instruments and medical equipment, then stopped beside the bed and towered over her.

Chakeena managed a whisper, dry and barely audible. "Where am I?"

It did not answer. May not have even heard. Certainly did not care. It instead went straight to work: removed a monitor-band from the cart, wrapped it around Chakeena's atrophying arm and fixed it to a display unit—the gauges instantly springing to life.

It picked up an infusion bag and hung it from a hook above the bed, ran a section of clear feedline and connected it to an awaiting syringe, then boldly sunk the needle deep into Chakeena's vein, her ability to recoil now reduced to almost nothing as well as her ability to speak.

What is it? thought Chakeena. *What is she doing?*

It is a supplement, it thought back, tilting its oblong head toward her. *Do not attempt to remove.*

Chakeena's elegant eyebrows tightened over her gaunt expression. *What?*

The telepath maintained its gaze and repeated itself. *It is a supplement. Do not attempt to remove.*

Chakeena gaped in shock. Its mouth had not moved. She was certain of it. *A telepath?* Of course it was always possible she was merely hallucinating and—

You are not hallucinating, it thought back, its mental tone

5

as emotionless as the empty eyes peering through the magnified lenses.

Silently guiding its cart, it circled the bed with mechanical precision and repositioned itself at her opposite side. It readied an extraction assembly with its lanky hands—a slim siphon needle tipped with a glinting point—and inserted it into Chakeena's arm, then fastened the conduit to a collection unit on the cart. The device powered up and began to pulse, each beat drawing a measure of the Princess's blood down into a row of glass vials.

I don't understand, thought Chakeena. *You're helping me and killing me too?*

I am not killing you. The disease is killing you.

But... My blood. You're—

The blood must be drawn before you die. It is of no value if obtained after you expire.

Chakeena just stared, struggling to comprehend.

The telepath saw the uncertainty. Sensed it. Attempted to clarify. *The supplement will vitalize the blood. It will not help you. The disease has taken its course. It is irreversible.*

A tear appeared in the corner of Chakeena's eye and trickled out. The fact was, it was fitting. She'd always felt alone. Always empty. Always a stranger. So for her to die without even so much as her mother at her side or one of the very few people she considered friends was *indeed* fitting.

And what of Kaiden? What of her chance at whatever that had held for her? A chance at life? Love? Yes, it was the perfect end. Chakeena Anastasia Amana, heir to a meaningless estate, princess to a faceless Empire, bearer of a purposeless existence, would die fatherless, faithless, friendless, and heartbroken with her final breath being

drawn in a cold, dark, lifeless room with this cold, dark, lifeless bitch—if you'll pardon the lapse of decorum.

She closed her eyes and resigned herself to the
inevitable.

How long? she implied at the telepath, her breathing
now heavily labored.

Without a hint of hesitation or even so much as a glance,
it merely replied with: *You shall die any moment now.*

CHAPTER TWO

A sun too distant to fathom lit the edge of Vietrus Prime, the planet from which all species in the sector had evolved and the center of the spacial infrastructure known as the Conglomerate.

Surrounding the planet sprawled a mesh-like webwork of through routes and way stations connecting the thousand-plus off-planet cities that made up the metropolitan aggregate.

Overpopulation was ultimately the reason for the expansion, leaving the outer-sphere the only remaining territory in which to settle. So settle they did by the billions, though not without an enormous amount of bureaucracy and heated dissension.

It began with the matter of rights, a subject complicated enough when it came to land. But applying those same policies to the outer-sphere, and eventually outer space, is where things really got messy.

And on top of that, and completely aside from the technological feats required to pull off such an endeavor, civic and government agencies bumping heads with monarchial laws led to much political strife. But over the course of some ten thousand years, everything and everyone eventually found their place, including an unworldly young man named Kaiden.

Leaving the limits of his teeming city behind, Kaiden banked his jetterboard into the interchange and leaned into the curve, the wisps of space dust streaking by forming into twisting airstream funnels in his wake while the flickers of lane-lights blurred into luminescent veins beneath him. As he came out of the corner and leveled the board, the crush of the curve's g-force eased from his spine and taut facial flesh.

Before him extending as far as could be seen stretched a glowing path encircled by the unbounded heavens themselves. It was a synthetic expressway of sorts—translucent and turquoise—its topside reserved for pedestrians and portable travel units with its underside designed for more conventional autocrafts.

As he soared in the direction of his destination, redistributing his balance to compensate for the forward thrust, the surrounding space took hold of his attention—a brilliant blood-red backdrop dotted by a trillion stars glittering brightly in the night. It was a sight to see and far cry from the bustling streets of his home so he eased off the speed and took in the magnificent expanse for a moment before shooting off again down the expressway, the flitting glistens of oncoming traffic lighting his way.

The need for spacesuits was a thing of the past. Sure, if you went beyond the boundaries you'd need one. But environment pods encircling the Conglomerate had been installed long ago, providing not only conditions to support off-planet life—with oxygen, gravity, regulated temperatures and the like—but comfortable conditions at that.

Trailing behind Kaiden glided Boomer, a companion of canine descent with unusually large eyes and uncommonly keen ears, his chocolate-brown coat slickly sheathing a body bread for reduced air-drag. But for one who spent so much time at Kaiden's side, he yet lagged tonight. It was the silhouette of the sparkling city that had caught the young pet's eye, calling him again and again for another look. And on this night, a night with fewer travelers and a brighter moon than usual, his curiosity could not be contained. He spun his slender frame and snuck another peek, maintaining his speed as he did, then whipped back around and instantly caught up to Kaiden, the repulser cushion generated by the governor on his collar keeping him a comfortable distance above the path.

Kaiden's thoughts had drifted. But a single yelp of a siren snapped him back to the present. He braked the board, slowed to a stop and glared ahead, his sapphire eyes firmly fixed on the scene. "What the…?" He paused. Subtly shook his head. Swept a strand of his blue-black bangs from his oval face. "How the hell are we—" He suddenly buckled, his hands involuntarily dropping to his abdomen…

It was the pain again, like a knife jabbing deep within. It would not last, but he steeled himself for the nausea that would surely follow just as it had with every instance since the phenomena had begun. There was no feasible reason for it, or at least nothing pinpointed by the medicos. Yet continue they did at regular intervals, each increasingly intense and always accompanied by the same impressions and irrepressible urge to…

His head hurled forward as the onslaught inundated him, a whirlwind of overwhelming emotions compounded by an instant mosaic of disorienting images: *An audience. An opera house. The Empress. A faceless girl. Pain. And... Blood! Lots of blood...*

He swayed as his equilibrium failed him. He dropped to his knees, hands pressed to the path to stabilize himself. His neck wrenched as the images continued their assault: *A crimson overcoat. A pair of dying eyes—black and pleading. Even more blood. And...*

But as fast as it had come, it let up. The impressions moved off like receding flood waters. The nausea subsided. The whirling in his head slowed as the ungraspable bearings gradually settled. And then, it was gone.

He lifted a hand to his head, took a moment and a couple of breaths, then carefully stood and reoriented himself.

The scene on the path remained. It was a problem. He lifted his wrist and tapped his timepiece, noted the result, then looked to Boomer who hovered motionlessly at his side, his attention locked like a vice on his human.

"We gotta go," said Kaiden. He leaned into the board and shot off!

As they neared the commotion, more details came to view. There was a laser barricade holding back a crowd of onlookers and a pair of law enforcers firmly standing guard. To the left sat a parked turbocraft and two skyway-bikes, their emergency strobes blinking brightly in unison. And to the right, the reason for the inconvenience: a man flat on his back.

One of the officers broke his stance and approached, his manner stiff and haughty. "Have to wait until the situation is resolved."

"How long?" asked Kaiden.

"No idea. Ambulance is on its way."

"I have an engagement," said Kaiden, his tone remaining reserved despite the inner urgency.

The officer gave an indifferent glance and shook his head. "Still have to wait."

Kaiden stared the officer down and maintained his composure. "It's for the Empress."

"Sorry," said the officer. "No exceptions." He adjusted his belt and sauntered back to his station beside his partner.

There was a groan from the man on the path as he rolled to his side and balanced his substantial weight on an elbow. He examined Kaiden for a moment, glanced at the craft, then cleared his throat and spoke. "Young man."

Kaiden's glare remained on the officer now making small talk with his colleague.

The man caught his breath, tried again—a little louder this time. "Young man. Did I hear you say the Empress?"

"That's right," said Kaiden, his response detached and distant along with his attention. "And if I don't get going soon I'm—"

"You're going to be late," said the man. "Yes, I *get* it."

There was sufficient command in the statement to register. Kaiden turned and looked down, looked the man over. He had a stocky build blanketed by a royal-blue coat and matching trousers. His cuffs and collar were edged in golden piping. He wore scuff-less boots to his knees with a silken aviator scarf loosely slung over his neck—exceptionally groomed from head to toe and *clearly* a man of wealth. In fact, apart from whatever physical issue was afflicting him, and maybe a little too much in the weight department, he was flawless in every respect—everything about him starkly contrasting the scene and compromised position.

The man grunted and lifted himself enough to sit, the

glow of the path casting itself on his sizable frame and head of silver hair.

Kaiden instinctually reached to assist but the barricade said otherwise with a warning-zap to his hand. He yanked it back, inspected his palm. Quietly cursed to himself.

"You alright?" asked the man.

"I'm fine," said Kaiden. "But maybe *you* should take it easy."

"Oh, it's nothing," said the man. "Just a short spell. I'll be fine soon enough." The man studied Kaiden some more, then brushed off his coat and raised a hand in the direction of the craft. "Can you pilot that?"

It was a calm question in an almost encouraging tone. And with it came a glint in the man's eye. Kaiden looked at the machine. "I think I could manage it," said Kaiden. "Worked at a raceway on Vietrus for a while. Part of a pit crew."

"Splendid," said the man. "Then what are we waiting for?"

Kaiden's narrow brow tightened. "Really?"

"Really," assured the man. "You'd be helping me. And maybe it would help you too?"

Without waiting for a response, the man directed his attention to the officer in charge. "Sir," he blurted.

The officer looked up, made his way over.

"My friend here will be taking over," said the man. "You can be on your way now. No need to hold all these good people up any longer."

"You sure? Ambulance is on its way. Be here any—"

"Oh, not to worry. I'll be fine," said the man. "Feeling better already, in fact."

The officer queried with a curious look.

The man gestured that it really *was* okay.

The officer shrugged it off and walked away, ordering his partner to disengage the barricade. He directed the onlookers to be on their way, then called it in on his communicator, cancelling the ambulance. The crowd dispersed as the officers mounted their bikes and sped off down the expressway in perfect formation.

As the whir of the engines dissipated in the distance, the man heaved himself up and stood, his hand cradling his paunchy midriff. "My name is Magnus, by the way. And you are?"

"Ryder. Kaiden Ryder."

"Ryder, huh?" Magnus smiled. "I like it. Good name."

He pointed to Boomer. "And who's this?"

"That's Boomer."

Magnus straightened his coat and looked Boomer over. "Is he fast?"

Kaiden nodded.

"Well, I suppose we shall soon see." Magnus grinned and worked his way over to the craft, stopped and tapped a panel on its side. The door slid open with a swish. He tugged at the scarf, dabbed his forehead with it, then climbed aboard and into the open cockpit, stopping to steady himself before settling into the rear seat, the squeak of its vintage leather straining under the heft of his frame.

"A Spitfire, huh?" Kaiden moved in closer, admiring the craft. "These are rare."

"Oh yes," said Magnus as he belted himself in. "And fast too."

Kaiden extended a hand and rested it on the machine, a craft designed for speeds not even authorized in this sector. The bulge of the hood scoops flared like a pair of seething nostrils before tapering down to seamlessly join the fuselage and the streamlined rudder assembly, its gleaming chrome side pipes peeking out from the stabilizer section, all fitted atop a G2000 Prophecy turbine running the entire length of the craft. Not an inch wasted—a virtual jet engine with seats and the propulsion to match. Flawless design, the epitome of aerodynamics, and not a speck of dust in sight.

"Well, Mr. Ryder," said Magnus. "Whatd'ya say? Let's get you to where you gotta go."

Kaiden climbed in and tucked his board beneath the dash. The door swished closed. He wrapped the seatbelt around himself and clamped it closed as he inspected the instrument panel before him and its array of switches and analog gauges.

"How's it look?" asked Magnus.

"Reminds me of the old Mustangs. A *real* turbocraft. Not like all the pods these days."

"Precisely," said Magnus, a hint of a cough resident in his throat. "I knew there was something I liked about you."

Kaiden leaned a hand on the ignition pad. It lit up red, announcing its objection with a dissonant blip.

"Override security protocol," said Magnus.

A panel lit up displaying the words: *voiceprint recognized.* The ignition blipped and turned green. The engine roared to life. The manifolds gulped at the artificial air as the turbine's whine rose in pitch before settling at a loping idle, the scent of exhausting terra-fuel forcing on Kaiden the memories of his youth. He wrapped a hand around the wheel and engaged the airlifts with the other. The craft creaked as it lifted under the groan of the motor. Boomer, seemingly in tune with it, hovered alongside as it inched its way across the path before stopping at the edge.

"How's she feel?" shouted Magnus.

Kaiden found Magnus in the mirror. Smirked. "Like a beast."

"Like a beast indeed!" Magnus dropped a hand on Kaiden's shoulder, a reassuring firmness in the grip. "Then what are we waiting for?"

Kaiden eased the steering column forward and upped the throttle, skimming the craft off the edge and slowly circling it around to the underside. And as he lowered the Beast into position, the awe-inspiring scene came to view. There were symbols, lights, a string of glowing dots, and a constant stream of traffic whipping by.

He aligned the rumbling craft with the onramp, perfectly poising it to enter the stream.

"Well done, Mr. Ryder," shouted Magnus over the deep drone of the turbine. "Well done, indeed."

Kaiden merely nodded.

Boomer, maintaining his position at its side, readied himself for takeoff—the tractors in his collar now activated by the underpath's guidance system.

Kaiden dropped a hand to the throttle and watched for a break in traffic. And when the time was right, thrust it forward.

They roared off into the night!

CHAPTER THREE

Chakeena and Empress Amana made their way through the palace's labyrinth of ornately decorated hallways, each of the many staff encountered stopping to stand firm with heads bowed until the Empress and her daughter passed.

Chakeena—long, slender, spitting image of her mother—slowed as she entered the royal atrium, its arching ceilings as high as a dozen men displaying the etchings of her ancient ancestors.

Her layered chiffon gown sewn by the hands of a seamstress she'd never met and never would draped down her delicate figure and swept in vain the immaculate floor beneath it.

A single emerald stone set in gold swayed on a chain held by her neck as she strode between the lines of staff flanking her route, her manner remaining aloof until one of the servants suddenly caught her eye.

Chakeena stopped, her dress gently settling to the floor. "Mia," she said to the young lady. "Your sister. Any word?"

The servant stepped forward, eyes held downwardly,

lightly clasping the sides of her burlap robe in a subtle curtsy. "Oh yes, Princess. Just yesterday, in fact. I'm happy to say she's been blessed with a daughter."

"And you a niece it seems," said Chakeena, shadow of a smile sprouting on her otherwise sullen face. She grasped the servant's hands and lightly squeezed them. "That's very good news. Congratulations."

Mia's eyes brightened as her glance lifted. But her years of training tugged them quickly back to the floor. "Thank you, m'lady. So nice of you to say. Grace to Ijo."

"Grace to Ijo," muttered the staff in unison.

The Empress watched from aside, her stance regal and reserved, unmistakable pride in her eyes as she took in the exchange. Chakeena turned to face her, a knowing nod indicating she was ready, and they resumed their journey through the palace.

The pain on this particular evening was more bearable than usual, just one of the many symptoms of the disease. *Mortiferum* was its name. Many had it. And those who did had never been cured. But while most contracted it much later in life, Chakeena had never known a day without it. Ever. And as much as she'd resisted it over the years, it had ultimately come to define her in ways that she to this day resented.

As she and her mother arrived at the transport-tube they were greeted by two security staff who assisted them in and promptly set the coordinates. The tube—a cylindrical craft, transparent, higher than wide, seatless—silently lifted through its shaft and departed from the palace's gaping skylight bringing to view the entire Empire, its foundation situated on a single dedicated terraplate the size of a small city. Chakeena looked out to the sea of structures wrapping the estate, then further beyond the webwork of pathways to the silhouette of Vietrus.

Visible from almost anywhere in the palace, the planet yet seemed unreal and out of reach to her, serving more as decor than a destination. Many tutors had taught her much about it but she'd never actually visited, though just why anyone would want to be bound by such a place was beyond her. True, from a distance it was intriguing—its entire surface lit up at night by the lights of the unending cities— but up-close images and newsfeeds revealed an awfully ravaged and overcrowded environment.

As they drifted toward the Imperial Opera House, Chakeena's gaze shifted to the crowds below. Those who saw the craft smiled. Many placed a hand on their chest as a gesture of allegiance to her mother. In turn, the Empress held out her hands, fingers interlocked, fists closed—a symbol of unity and common purpose.

"They're good people," said the Empress.

"They admire you," said Chakeena. "And you deserve it."

The Empress smiled and embraced her daughter. Seeing this, the crowd erupted into cheer as the transport-tube neared the opera house and descended toward the private entrance.

As the long doors of the tube slid open, Chakeena and the Empress exited, additional security forming around them. "Your opera coat, Princess," said one of the staff. Chakeena turned and let another of the servants hang the garment over her exposed shoulders. The silken lining slid on her skin as the coat eventually engulfed her, its concealing nature further taking shape with each button fastened. It was plush, pleated, a rich ruby-red with a luxuri- ously oversized collar snugly embracing her neckline—the fit not unlike her life: pretty and protected yet unmistakably prison-like.

Though few had seen this area of the theater, Chakeena knew it all too well. It was the Empress's private quarters where they could retire to when desired. There was anything and everything one could imagine needing, but Chakeena needed only her favorite window which is where she spent the better part of her time.

Security moved with them through the room to another transparent vessel that, unlike the transport-tube, did not leave the building but instead traveled through a shaft bringing those in it to their chosen level. They entered and it began its descent.

Chakeena sighed at what would come next, for she knew all too well what awaited them at the officials' level. And this is where it got tough: putting on and maintaining an air of interest in a room of those who could not possibly be more uninteresting. But this was her life. This is how it was and always had been. This is what she had to endure to support her mother and the Empire. So she took a moment to mentally prepare for it and the greeting they were about to receive, then grasped her giant collar and snugged herself deeper into its welcoming hollow.

As the vessel arrived, a group of the most senior officials of the evening were revealed perfectly lined shoulder to shoulder ready to receive the Empress. Some were familiar to Chakeena, others were not—but all were submissive in stance, if only somewhat, and all equally cringeworthy.

A crowd of lesser representatives behind the receiving line filled the room to its furthest reaches, the hall extending some forty meters in all directions and twenty meters high, a shimmering chandelier half the size of the ceiling suspended above.

The doors to the elevator tube slid open and the Empress and Chakeena stepped out, a harmonious blast of horns sounding to their left officially announcing their arrival. The echoes of the blasts reverberated through the hall, a rolling surf of sound surging in waves from wall to wall, floor to ceiling, slowly dying down with each cycle completed. And when they'd at last waned to nothing, the Empress extended her hands high above her as she spoke: "Good evening, All. I'm pleased you could make tonight's affair. Thank you for attending. I hope you have an exceptional time."

The room erupted in applause.

With her daughter at her side, the Empress formally greeted those in the receiving line, adjusting gestures to suit each of the official's specific cultural customs.

Chakeena watched the interaction, noting in the eyes of many the same yearning for power by way of her mother that had always followed her—their ulterior motives obnoxious and obvious. In fact, some even hungered for *Chakeena's* influence, which was nothing new either, though she *had* seen a steady increase over the years as she'd aged. But now that she was undeniably a young lady, it had reached an all-new and unwelcome height.

With security at their side, Chakeena and the Empress moved forward and into the crowd, guardsmen encircling them as they advanced. Chakeena's mind and striking black eyes wandered the room noting the evening had indeed yielded an impressive turnout—her raven hair, sleek as lacquer, trickling down the back of her opera coat. And although she maintained the semblance of a smile while greeting those introduced, she could not ignore the pain—ever present and utterly unsympathetic to the agony it inflicted.

21

After what seemed like hours of social necessities, a security team at last escorted Chakeena and the Empress to their private viewing balcony, a velvet-lined box high above the arena's audience with a snow-white sofa in its center and matching pair of chaise lounges on either side. The Empress stood at the window and gave a wave to the throngs below before seating herself beside her daughter.

A butler in formal dress approached with a silver tray in hand and offered them each a pair of opera glasses. Chakeena accepted, plucking it from the tray and placing it on a beveled ledge before her. The Empress politely declined with a wave of her gloved hand, then thanked the butler and excused him.

Chakeena sunk into the sofa's cozy upholstery and took in the enormity of the theatre—the vast space beyond it casting a crimson hue on the tens of thousands below, the comfort of her mother at her side, the privacy provided by the isolated box, and the anticipation of an evening of beauty and art. A sense of relief swept through her as she gazed into the expanse and buried her hands into her cashmere-lined pockets. What would ensue, she hoped, would surely be more pleasant than what just had.

The network of lights suspended above the theatre slowly dimmed as a wash of quiet crept over the audience replacing sound with silent anticipation. On the stage stood a rotund female of a foreign species, the glasslike floor beneath her casting a bright teal glow from it. As it blended with the evening's skylight it produced a violet halo about her. She closed her eyes, slowly inhaled, and paused for a moment. And as she let it out, her voice began to fill the space, growing in volume—the lone sustained note building in intensity and eventually changing pitch. A melody developed, wandering into a delightful pattern that echoed throughout the arena, adding to the already exquisite environment.

The music took hold of Chakeena. It was refreshing, relaxing, somehow calming to the tormenting pain. She dropped her glance to the large body amidst the shifting colors. And though it *was* certainly better than the reception's pomp and the officials' pursuit of further power, it did not hold her attention for long. Her thoughts drifted...

She recalled a time when a young man had approached her at just such a performance. He'd traveled from afar to attend and hadn't known of her. He'd taken a fancy to her, and she to him. The Empress, away on official business, had left Chakeena to do as she pleased. After the performance, he and Chakeena had found a quiet place to talk. She'd had little experience in such matters, so was uneasy. But things had been going surprisingly well until the pain presented itself. She'd never forget the look in his eyes as she explained her situation to him. His fancy quickly faded, extinguishing the fleeting flame and turning them into cold, hard ice. Her eyes in turn dimmed even darker, and her heart dipped to an all-new depth...

The voice faded in and the stage once again came to view. The colors continued to change—still exquisite, yet somewhat less so now. She looked to her mother, the gemstones on her headdress sparkling in the night. The Empress reached over and took her daughter's hand. Chakeena smiled and savored it. But as comforting as it was, it yet failed to soothe what she now felt in her chest. Not a symptom of the disease—a symptom of something else entirely, but just as chronic. It was a symptom of the boy, the unpleasant memory thereof, and the pain therefrom.

"Are you enjoying yourself, my dear?" asked the Empress.

"Yes, Mother. It sounds lovely."

"It does. And such a beautiful evening."

"Quite," said Chakeena. But her attention was now far more inward than out. For it had been several minutes since the last wave of nausea, and though the intervals between them varied slightly, they nevertheless always came. The unceasing rhythm was not unlike that of the great water-bodies on Vietrus she'd learned of so she readied herself mentally for the inevitable. If only her "ocean" could still itself, calm itself, let up long enough to allow her even an hour of peace, what she wouldn't give for that. She turned to her mother, pallid lips pressed to the Empress's ear. "Mother, may I retire to the private quarters during inter-mission?"

The Empress leaned in and whispered back. "Pain?"

"Only a little. No more than usual. Just a few minutes and I'll join you with the others."

Though there was never a time when the Empress was unaware of her daughter's condition, facing the effects never failed to tear at her in a way only a mother could know. And it never got any easier. She looked lovingly at her daughter and nodded, the indelible ache in her eyes impossible to hide.

"Thank you, Mother."

Chakeena placed a hand on her mother's lap and directed her gaze back to the performance.

On the stage now standing behind the singer stood four unfamiliar creatures striking their instruments in unison, sending forth and throughout the arena an array of reso-nant tones. Just how they managed to produce such sounds was beyond Chakeena. A legato feel with seemingly no attack, regardless of the force of the blows. The soothing textures strengthened and began to surge, building to a final crescendo then diminuendo before softly dissipating to nothing.

Plaudits gushed from the crowd. Genuinely affected by the performance, Chakeena joined in, then stopped and sat back—bracing herself as her own surge began to build in her belly.

CHAPTER FOUR

The pitch of the turbine rose as Kaiden eased on the throttle and leveled the craft for the oncoming straightaway. Whipping by them was an endless stream of machines heading back in the direction of the city. He glanced to his left, observing how effortlessly Boomer retained his position with them as they soared along the underside of the expressway, then looked up into the mirror where he found Magnus resting in the back. He tightened his grip on the steering column and peered down at the scene below, taking in the layers of fluorescent lanes teeming with activity, then drew back on the throttle as he maneuvered the Beast lane by lane to the exit area and slowed to the speed of the bottlenecking traffic.

The vibration of the turbine settled, giving rise to the aroma of warm engine oil filling his nostrils. And as they inched their way toward the ramp to go topside, he caught Magnus in the mirror sitting up.

"Looks as though you've gotten us here, Mr. Ryder," said Magnus, scanning the surroundings and stretching the sleep from his arms.

Kaiden nodded as he eased on the thruster.

The Beast lurched forward and ascended the ramp in their fore, lifting past the edge of the path and bringing to view the magnificence of the Empire in all its glory.

Kaiden's piercing eyes took it in. The lines were gracefully foreign. There was a softness to them that was delicate and fluid, as though a woman had had a hand in their creation.

Whereas his city was a harsh bombardment of industrial facilities and pollution-gray drabness, this was a rolling terracotta skyline embellished with splashes of gold and pastel brushstrokes, a scene more aptly found framed on a museum wall than by a web of outer-sphere expressways. And right when he thought he could be no more impressed by the view, the grandeur of the Imperial Opera House presented itself—its size and scope further driving home the reality of the coming evening.

As they approached the entrance a guard emerged from a small shed—body like a globe, holster on his hip, his disheveled shirt straining to remain tucked in his trousers. He lifted a hand and halted them.

Kaiden slowed the Beast to a stop.

"Started over an hour ago," the guard said gruffly. "Might as well go home."

"I'm on tonight's bill," said Kaiden. "In the second half."

The guard looked up to Kaiden, did a double-take as if attempting to place the foreign features.

Kaiden held a vacant stare on the guard. "Has intermission started yet?"

"Yeah," said the guard, "few minutes ago." He slid a digital list from his belt and drew it back from his eyes, squinting as he strained to focus on it. "Name?"

"Kaiden Ryder."

"Hang on." The guard entered the name into the device with resentful stabs as Kaiden's gaze lifted to the entrance before him and to the palatial structure beyond it. "Okay. You're good," said the guard. "Need to scan you first though. Heightened security tonight." He pointed at Magnus. "Who's he?"

"His guest," said Magnus. "Surely Mr. Ryder is allowed one, is he not?"

"Sure. Gotta scan you too though," said the guard, indicating a large overhanging disc with a flick of a finger. He looked to Boomer. "What's with the critter?"

Kaiden kept his gaze on the guard. "He's with us."

The guard rolled his eyes. "Well it'll have to stay in the craft. I got rules ya know."

Kaiden nodded. "Boomer. With me."

Boomer snapped to attention and zipped into the cockpit, settling comfortably at Kaiden's side.

The guard grunted something unintelligible as he backed away and waved them through.

Kaiden eased on the thruster. The turbine rumbled beneath him as he inched the craft forward and came to a stop beneath the disc, the airbrake emitting a snake-like hiss as he engaged it.

The guard shuffled toward a waist-high console outside the shack.

"I'd like to stay, by the way," said Magnus, "for the show."

"Really?" said Kaiden, finding Magnus in the mirror. "Why, yes, of course. I mean, nothing's been arranged. But…"

"Oh, not to worry," said Magnus. "I can take care of myself. You just do whatever you have to do and I'll—"

"Scanning!" shouted the guard, running a fat finger along a panel on the console. The sound of a hum grew as

28

the space beneath the disc was saturated in a stream of soft blue light.

Boomer stiffened, came alert, his ears spiking up in the direction of the disc when...

The bark of a siren jolted the area!

The light went red. The guard's eyes bugged out, practically popping out of their sockets.

Boomer buried his head deep into the Beast's seat in an attempt to damp out the howl.

Magnus and Kaiden found each other in the mirror, each querying the other visually.

The guard scrambled, his hands in a frantic flurry on the console.

The siren continued to churn as a mechanical voice from above thundered a recurring and unsympathetic announcement: "Kaiden Ryder, you are being detained for breach of security. Kaiden Ryder, you are being detained for breach of security. Kaiden Ryder..."

The guard's senior darted from the shed, blaster drawn, military influence in his every move. "What? A *Red* Alert?"

"Yup!" said the guard.

"Holy shit!" snapped the Senior. "Source?"

The guard nodded emphatically. "No idea."

"No idea."

"Locate it!"

"Sir!" The guard crisply saluted the senior and dropped a hand to a panel on the console labeled *hyper-scan*. The light of a secondary stream trickled down and around the Beast.

An area of Kaiden's belt instantly lit up, a golden glow now brightly emanating from the attached device. It was a small rectangular prism, its brushed silver surface dulled by age and marked with faint, shimmering engravings.

The glow began to increase.

Kaiden looked down to his belt, then up to the guard. "No," he said. "It's nothing. Just my—"

"There!" shouted the guard.

"Got it," said the senior. "Contain him! Now!"

The guard swept a hand across the panel.

A translucent field dropped down and around the Beast.

The glow continued to grow until...

Boom!

An array of brilliant beams instantly burst forth from the device and formed into a holographic apparatus inches from Kaiden's chest, its pulsing glow lighting up his taught torso. There were intermingling multi-boards, a tangle of modulation hoses, and rows of frequency oscillators lining its sides.

"Shit," whispered Kaiden. He released the seatbelt from his waist and stood, the apparatus moving with him as he twisted toward the guards.

"Hey!" shouted the senior, his blaster now fixed on Kaiden. "Hands up! Now!"

As Kaiden reluctantly lifted his arms, Boomer squirmed and jolted the steering yoke to the side causing the Beast to buck. Tossed from the cockpit, Kaiden landed like a cat crouched with one hand to the ground and the other in the air for balance.

Magnus, still belted in, clung to the fuselage.

Boomer submerged his head even deeper into the seat as the craft leveled itself on its airlift cushion.

The guards just stood motionless gawking at the contraption.

Kaiden remained alertly poised, his eyes locked on the guards. He broke the stare and was reaching for the device to deactivate it when...

It erupted into song!

It instantly matched the siren's note, duplicating its cadence, then surpassed it in volume as though mocking its capabilities.

Everyone's arms shot to their ears. The tone wavered and surged even louder. The guards writhed, mentally struggling with the scene.

Kaiden dropped a hand long enough to slam the kill-switch. But it continued its howling challenge.

The senior, hands pressed to his head, still maintaining a precarious hold on the blaster, made eye contact with his junior. "Shut it down!"

The guard stared blankly and shook his head. "What?"

"The scanner!" The senior tried again, this time emphatically mouthing the words as he shouted at the top of his lungs. "*Shut! It! Down!*"

"Sir!" The guard deactivated the scanner with a swipe of a hand.

The insanity instantly ceased. The voice went silent. The device powered off and the holograph dissipated. And the siren's wail wound down. A blinking light, however, remained, as did the security field containing the Beast and the offenders.

Everyone's arms carefully came down. Boomer slowly lifted his head. Kaiden stood.

Magnus unbelted himself and stepped down from the craft, tucked his scarf into his collar. Looked to Kaiden. "You okay?"

Kaiden nodded.

The senior again ordered Kaiden's hands to the air and pointed at Magnus. "Remove the weapon and place it in the security circle to your left."

"What?" snapped Magnus.

"I said remove it," the guard repeated.

"Don't be absurd." Magnus steeled his face, lifted his sizable chin, straightened his sleeves. "I'm quite certain there's an explanation for—"

"Now!" snapped the senior.

Magnus shot a displeased glare at the senior, then turned to Kaiden and questioned him with his eyes. Kaiden shrugged an approval. Magnus unclipped the device and placed it in the indicated circle, a smaller laser-field springing up to engulf it as he removed his hand.

The senior, training his blaster on Kaiden with one hand, tossed a pair of plasma-cuffs to Magnus with the other. "Now. His hands—in these."

That was it. Enough was enough. Magnus snapped the scarf from his neck and dabbed his broad brow, staring the senior down as he thrust the scarf into his pocket, then in a solemn, sobering voice said, "Have you *any* inkling as to my station in this realm?"

Deafening silence ensued.

Magnus waited, neatly tucking at the remainder of the scarf's corner as he did. Then: "Well, *have you?*"

"I don't care *who* you are!" said the senior. "Cuff him. Now!"

"Very well, then. Let me enlighten you. I am Magnus Vasudum Rue the Ninth, reigning ruler of Ruechestire Borough in the Greater Amana Empire."

The senior shot him a cynical look. "Yeah, sure. An' I'm the Prime Minister of Vietrus." He pointed to Kaiden. "Cuff him."

Magnus reached to his coat.

The senior swung the blaster to Magnus. "Halt!"

"My good sir," said Magnus, calmly, "I do anticipate an apology from you. But for now, do you really think I have anything that could possibly penetrate your security field?"

The senior sneered. "Of course not. Best there is."

Magnus smirked. "Then where's the harm?"

The senior took a moment, considered it, his arrogance now officially challenged. "All right, let's see whatcha got. Slow though."

Magnus unbuttoned his coat, opened his woolen vest and removed a shiny badge—violet in color with an intricate design adorning its circular edge. And in the middle: the Empire's royal emblem. He stood, unamused, a stern stare locked on the senior's blaster. "Now, I trust you have the means to verify this?"

The senior said nothing, just activated the scanner.

A laser stream swept over the badge. The console blipped. The senior directed a dismissive gaze to the verdict now displaying itself on the screen before him. And as he read the response, the blood drained from his now gaping face.

Insignia and bearer of: AUTHENTIC. Rue, Lord Magnus Vasudum the IXth, Ruechestire Borough, Empire Amana.

"Holy mother of..." the senior whispered to himself. Then: "Sir, I beg your forgiveness. It seems my junior here has made a mistake. A grave one. What can I do to—"

"You can release the item and provide my friend here immediate access along with any additional assistance he may need."

"But... We have strict policy against weapons and—"

"It's not a weapon," said Kaiden, calmly. "It's a synthesizer."

"A synthesizer?" parroted the senior.

"Yes."

"What does that even mean?"

"It synthesizes sound," said Kaiden. He gazed at the senior, saw the uncertainty in his eyes. "It's a musical instrument."

"But that makes no sense. There's no record of anything like that in the system."

"That's because there *are* no others," said Kaiden.

The senior scratched his head, looked to the junior. The junior shrugged. The senior looked back to Kaiden. "Well, that may be the case, but I still can't just let you through without—"

"Without what?" asked Magnus, returning the badge to his vest pocket. "Does your scanner indicate anything dangerous?"

The senior paused, checked some readings, consulted his junior, then double-checked. "Well, actually..." He scratched his head some more. "...no. But it *is* undocumented and so I'm required to—"

"Very well," said Magnus, curtly cutting him off. "Mr. Ryder here is in a hurry. The Empress *is* expecting us. And I shall personally vouch for him and the item. I trust that will suffice?"

The senior stood speechless.

Magnus squared his shoulders, lifted his long nose and stared down it—a towering man with towering influence ever at his disposal. "Or would you rather I—"

"No," blurted the senior. "Nothing dangerous here. Just a misunderstanding." He bowed his head. "Again, I beg your forgiveness."

"Not to worry," said Magnus. "You're just doing your job." He lifted his chin even more. "Now, may we *please* be on our way?"

"Why yes, of course," said the senior as he shot his junior a disapproving look, "*Lord* Magnus."

Kaiden looked to Magnus. "*Lord?*"

"I'll explain later," whispered Magnus, hint of a smile betrayed by his eyes.

The senior released the instrument. Kaiden gathered it and boarded the Beast.

The light shifted to blue and the security field disintegrated.

CHAPTER FIVE

Chakeena sat at her private window in the opera house gazing out into the brilliant crimson space and vast Empire below. It was a place of comfort, one of the smaller chambers in the structure reserved for her and her alone. And know it well she did, from the elaborate pattern of the Vetrusian rug with the sequined coffee table on its center, to the ancient hangings on every wall etched with faces of ancestors past. All of it memorized down to the most minute detail imaginable. And filling the air, the subtle oaky aroma of the antique armoire and hints of licorice tea, not only her preferred daytime drink but a scent she'd come to associate with the comfort of home.

Privacy for some unknown reason had always provided a measure of the peace she so craved, and this was her place for that. Though the symptoms yet remained, they were somehow made more bearable.

Part of Vietrus could be seen poking out from behind the skyline's mountain of structures, and tonight the planet loomed larger than usual and especially serene.

A disturbance at the main entrance had briefly entertained her during her break from the others. There were sirens, lights, and a lot of shouting. It was of course no threat to her. Such things never were. Not with the wealth of protection insulating her from not only harm to her life, but also, ironically, from life itself. She had always been told how fortunate she'd been that things like poverty and chance would never befall her. She'd been reassured count-less times that they led only to disappointment. And while this may be a very sound fact, she'd never had cause to confirm it. On the contrary, the only truth to which she could attest was that an abundance of predictability and protection can and does stale the soul, as it had hers. *This* Chakeena knew. For the only unpredictable aspect of her entire existence was the disease, and even that had some inevitability in it.

Intermission's end was approaching and she would soon need to find her mother's side. So she took in one last look from her window, finished off her tea, then lifted herself to leave, the weight of her voluptuous coat bearing heavily on her ailing body. She checked herself in the mirror, a brush of her hair, a twist of her headdress, then made her way through the marble hall to the awaiting elevator-tube, secu-rity spotting and instantly flanking her. They boarded the tube and entered the coordinates, the tea still freshly warm in her stomach as they descended to the officials' area.

As the doors opened, Chakeena spotted her mother off in a corner. And with her, a partial view of a man. Elderly, sturdy build, bright blue coat, and waves of silver hair resting on his thickset shoulders. He was laughing, deep and resonantly, his face familiar but as yet unplaced. In a sea of uninteresting others, he was indeed an exception. But just who exactly *was* he?

Her mind ravenously went to work on the question as

she advanced toward them, security parting the endless onlookers. And as she neared the man, she was finally handed an answer in the form of a memory. It took a moment to orient to it, still distant and indistinct. But once she did, more memories followed. She gasped, her hands lifting to cup her ivory-white face as it widened in shock. *No! Could it be?*

It had been years since she'd seen him last and he had aged, but upon closer inspection it became unmistakable. Her eyes lit up and a smile burst forth. "Magnus!" She suddenly came to life, prodding security and hurrying herself in his direction, the tap of her heels clicking faster and seizing even more of the room's attention. And as she arrived, shedding every shred of etiquette carefully bred into her, she wrapped herself around his large, consoling body.

"Chakeena?" he said. "My darling! Is that you?"

She could not answer, could only squeeze—trembling as she held him tight, emotions long since repressed gushing forth into an unstoppable sob as her head was flooded with even more memories: The time they'd spent together at the private facility, the pain they'd endured from the disease, the stories he'd told, the secrets she'd revealed, and the bond they'd formed. Her sob grew stronger as the emotions moved in on her even more.

The room wondered at the reunion—some moved by it, others confused, but all absorbed.

Security, alert and eager for orders, searched the Empress for a sign but found only a smile and teary eyes.

Magnus struggled with his own sentiments knowing he should have stayed in touch. But the burden of his work and reluctance to remind her of her health had kept him from it, a reservation that was now instantly rendered a mistake and one he would not make again.

He looked down to her and summoned a whisper. "Chakeena, I barely recognize you. How you've grown."

Chakeena said nothing, merely buried her face even deeper.

Historically the Empress would have announced something to justify such an interruption. But not this time. Not this moment—this monumental moment. For it was far too precious to blemish and far too profound to interrupt.

Once Chakeena did at last let go, she lifted her head and faced her old friend. They caught up, reminisced, laughed. Magnus shared how he'd found himself in her vicinity and thought it a perfect opportunity to visit. He told her of the symptoms that had presented themselves and of the young man he'd befriended. And Chakeena simply smiled and stared at him, riveted on his every word.

Unknown to the others, Magnus had arranged for security to escort Kaiden to the officials' area once he was settled into his dressing room. He'd also explained to Kaiden the reason for not initially revealing his identity. For with Magnus's status came the need of discretion.

His health, in this case, had not been public knowledge and his advisors very much wished to keep it that way. It had been a delightful evening for a drive, and even old Magnus needed some time to himself occasionally without the bother of an entire entourage, which is all he'd initially intended. But with the episode came the need for caution. And although he'd enjoyed the brief bit of anonymity, it was never meant to intentionally deceive. It had merely been a matter of privacy and politics. He'd failed, however, to mention just how well he knew the Empress. For *that* he'd wanted to remain a surprise.

Spotting Kaiden across the room, Magnus excused himself from his conversation with Chakeena. "Mr. Ryder!" he shouted, waving at Kaiden. "Over here!"

Kaiden, head down and engulfed in the crowd, heard nothing as he progressed slowly through the room circled by security, his attention fixed on the coming evening.

Normally the time before a performance would have been reserved for preparation in a more isolated setting—and this was far from that. But Magnus had practically begged him to drop in for a minute, and so he'd agreed to it. The crowd and all the hubbub, however, had him reconsidering, and just as he was about to abort the visit, he stopped dead, frozen in his tracks. *What?* He shook his head. Squinted. Looked again. For there before him, mere meters away, stood the Empress, her hooded cape slung over her head just like he'd seen it. Just like the visions. *Precisely* like them. But it was not only the Empress that was the same; it was the entire scene: Same room. Same crowd. And... Same girl, faceless from afar, her long back cloaked in a deep red from neck to toe.

He stood and stared, attempting to make sense of it. The visions, the room, the pain and the people, and the girl—all of it fiercely familiar as though an unfurling of destiny itself was being presented before his very eyes.

"Mr. Ryder!" shouted Magnus again. "Over here!"

Kaiden did his best to shake it off, attempted to compose himself—an all-but-impossible proposition as the reality of it continued to set in. He gestured to Magnus and continued in his direction, his eyes incapable of looking at anything but the girl, an overwhelmingly unusual sensation growing within as he neared her.

As he arrived, Magnus grasped him by the shoulders, turned him to face the Empress, and patted him on the back, practically knocking him over with the force.

"Empress, I'd like you to meet a friend of mine and one of tonight's performers, Mr. Kaiden Ryder."

Kaiden's eyes ached to look at the girl. But he resisted. Refrained. Quieted his mind and forced his gaze to the Empress. "It's an honor to meet you," he said with a subtle dip of his head.

The Empress reached out her hand, her arm sheathed in a golden evening glove. "Pleasure to make your acquaintance, Mr. Ryder."

Kaiden grasped the glove and lifted his eyes, absorbing her poise and arresting features.

"And this," said Magnus, "is the Empress's daughter and a *very* dear friend of mine, Princess Chakeena."

Kaiden turned to Chakeena as she glanced up at him. It was a formal and forced look at first. But then a second, more significant one. The glance became a gaze followed by the unmistakable look of fascination. She just stood and stared at him, in him, practically through him, her glittering headdress framing her inky eyes.

In a situation that would otherwise be unnerving, Kaiden remained remarkably calm. Time seemed to slow as he took in the moment—the face, the girl, the cloaked mystery finally revealed. There was a flood of images flitting in his head as he stood half expecting to wake from one of his episodes when she suddenly reached out her hand and spoke. "Pleasure to meet you."

Kaiden moved his hand to hers and grasped it. It was frail, soft, and compelling evidence that it was indeed not a dream. Now wholly immersed in the encounter, the room had all but disappeared. It was as if he could see her soul, her life, a deep detachment from others, and... Pain?

The Empress watched on in awe of the exchange. Never

had she seen her daughter is such a state. Never had she witnessed such a thing. Though Chakeena's life required many respectful greetings, they'd always been cursory when it came to strangers. And this was certainly that. But Chakeena yet remained engaged in a way that defied it all. The Empress looked to Magnus, who merely responded with an almost invisible shrug of his eyes.

The silence, awkward and impossible to ignore—now transmitting through the entirety of the hall—was finally broken by a voice from a loudspeaker above: "Ladies and gentlemen. The second half of tonight's performance will commence shortly. Please return to your seats."

The lights dimmed to emphasize the announcement.

"Well, Mr. Ryder," said Magnus, "I suppose you'll need to be leaving us then?"

Kaiden, too engrossed to reply, said nothing.

Magnus smiled, placed a hand on Kaiden's shoulder. "Mr. Ryder?"

Kaiden snapped out of it, broke the gaze and returned to the room. He looked to Magnus, nodded, then back to Chakeena, her captivating stare drawing him in yet again. He'd meant to let go of her hand but had not. Yet neither had she.

Magnus leaned in to Kaiden. "I do look forward to your performance."

"Yes," said the Empress, her emerald eyes maintaining their lock on Kaiden, "as do I."

Kaiden smiled at Chakeena and looked down at their hands. "I'd better go."

"Oh... Yes, of course," said Chakeena. She released his hand but maintained the gaze, the astonishment still radiating from her.

"Ladies and gentlemen. The second half of tonight's

performance will commence shortly," repeated the loud-speaker. "Please return to your seats."

Chakeena dipped her head and lowered her eyes. "It was very nice to have met you."

Kaiden said nothing, took one last glance, then turned and slowly moved away, security moving with him at his side.

Magnus and the Empress again looked to each other, still in shock. Chakeena looked too, but it was at Kaiden. She watched only him, his indelible influence lingering as he distanced himself into the ocean of onlookers.

And then he was gone.

CHAPTER SIX

The network of suspended concert lights dimmed in unison, and with it the mood of the vast audience below. Murmurs ebbed. Fingers pressed to pursed lips shushed the stragglers as a veil of silence slowly cloaked the enormity of the arena.

High above the crowd in the Imperial Balcony sat Chakeena nestled between her mother and Magnus, all of them embraced by the voluptuous velvet of the center sofa. For one whose exciting encounters in life were so very rare, today had indeed proven exceptional. She'd somehow run the entire gamut of emotions in the span of but a few minutes. The lower extremes were of course well charted. The uppers were not. In fact, virtually unexplored, the experience leaving her head swimming and heart gushing in an eddy of foreign sensations along with an undeniable interest in the upcoming performances. Or at least one of them.

As Kaiden emerged from the wings, a single beam from a spotlight above came to life, found him, announcing him to the tens of thousands who watched on eagerly, his black-on-black attire sharply contrasting the white of the light and the brilliance of the moon. He gathered his thoughts and moved across the stage to its center, then paused to allow his mistress—silence herself—some time to fully awaken before proceeding. For the past had taught him that she was most receptive when fully alert, and he did not take for granted the importance of her role in his story. After all, she *was* his canvas and without her he had nothing. He waited patiently for her to beckon. And so she did.

Now in his element, Kaiden too awoke. He activated his synth, its lasers springing forth and instantly projecting the three-dimensional instrument before him. It was a virtual simulation of an artifact he'd altered years ago, an interactive image formed by the interference of light beams from a laser source—an audio generator unlike any other.

He drew the mouthpiece toward him and placed his lean hands near the keys. Not so close as to touch them, however, for how crude were those who applied even an iota of *force* to their art—the one sure way to debase anything of beauty.

He took a moment to search, for what he was about to do required he be elsewhere, not physically but in the mind. And having found his place, and with his mistress at his side, he was set. And so they danced.

He began with a pulse just below auditory range, slow and rhythmic, carefully placed so as to be felt but not heard. Next, a tone with a smooth vibrato at the top of the sonic register—undetectably high to most species. He held it for a moment, letting the audience adapt to what would certainly be a new sensation for all. And after a time, just enough in his estimation, he summoned a fully audible note and boldly *slammed* it straight into the middle of the anchors, precisely between the infrasonic pulse and the ultrasonic pitch.

It pierced the field, perfectly splitting the sound spectrum in half. The result resounded and sent a bell-like ring echoing throughout the arena with overtones oscillating to the outermost reaches of the structure.

Next he fed in a harmonic backdrop. A seven-note chord —minor in nature, soft and silky at first—and allowed it to develop. He wobbled the center note as a test, a hint of a warp in the surrounding space indicating it was established.

And now came the tricky part: adding the melody without bending things too far out of place. For Kaiden had just taken command of the immediate environment and subsequently those therein.

He lifted his gaze and searched the private balcony high above for Chakeena, met her distant glance, the face that had long eluded him in the visions now etched indelibly in his mind.

He closed his eyes and took in a breath, held it a moment, then let it out in the direction of the mouthpiece, mentally implying a melody. And once it had materialized and he was certain he could retain control, he yielded to the inevitable and lifted from the stage, his belt's repulser-field stabilizing him above it.

He vamped on the melody for a time before modifying the mode. Still minor but more emotionally inclined. Deeper, richer, sweeter, the timbre reminiscent of classical instruments of the past—an orchestral palette with underpinnings of an electronic nature.

The space again strained to shift but he caught it and reined it in, keeping it closely in check.

In the balcony above, Chakeena's breathing slowed. A sensation of expansion pervaded her. She struggled to differentiate between herself and the others. Her body buzzed. Her heart fluttered. Her mind drifted as a wash of unfamiliar imagery moved in on her... *Space. A foreign sector. A flotilla of starships. A peculiar planet. And...*

Beside her, the muscles in Magnus's shoulders relaxed. The tension in his temples dissipated. A feeling of weight-lessness overcame his hulk-like frame along with a soothing vibration deep in his bones. His attention dropped to the audience and widened as a wave of emotions descended upon him, their thoughts and fears, hopes and desires—an overwhelming influx of everyone and everything at once. He saw himself as an infant. Saw his mother, his father. The future?

On the stage below, Kaiden's symphony was in full swing as he navigated through the main motif imbuing the entire atmosphere with it. As he maneuvered into the final move-ment, he reshaped the melody, gracefully reducing its interval jumps, before slowing it to a stop and locking back onto the splitter tone. And then, holding it secure like the linchpin of an ancient axel, released the remainder of the notes and summoned them to gradually rearrange them-selves from minor to major.

A warp threatened the space but he anticipated it and retrieved control. And when it had finally finished aligning itself, he held it tight, absorbed it, and relished in it as the sound saturated the theater and those therein. He main-tained it, sustained it, increased the intensity, punching up the pressure bit by bit to its pinnacle, then pushed it even further. He added a narrow vibrato to the chord and widened it ever so slowly, teasing the space to twist without authorizing it to actually do so. And when he'd finally gone as far as he dared, his command on the verge of collapse, his authority about to be overthrown, he let go—unharnessing and propelling the finale directly *at and into* the audience.

It reverberated amongst the crowd—speeding up,

careening faster and deeper throughout. He gave way to it, embraced it, basking in it knowing he'd once again achieved absolute and all-pervading harmony. And realizing it was possibly his best to date, he permitted it to persist longer than usual—much longer—before reeling it in and retracting everything he'd put forth, yanking it back and absorbing it in its entirety causing it to culminate in an explosive subsonic boom!

The space warped.

Kaiden dropped to the stage.

Chakeena gasped.

Part Two

THE ANOMALY

CHAPTER SEVEN

The previous night hadn't granted Dr. Hulaksen much sleep. Recent events had occupied his thoughts along with the anticipation of the morning meeting at the Empress's palace. Over the past week Chakeena's disease had taken a turn and one for the better as it turned out. In fact, her symptoms had disappeared entirely. A first for her. But then they returned. And when they did they returned with a vengeance, stronger than ever, which was even more perplexing than the unprecedented disappearance in the first place.

Magnus and another of Dr. Hulaksen's patients, Vice Minister Bulsara Wu, had also experienced the unique remission and both within hours of Chakeena's. And just like hers, Magnus's condition had now reverted too. The doctor expected Wu's would follow.

Initial investigations hadn't revealed much. The only thing the three had in common for certain was the disease. But now with the relapses, the investigations had quickly turned imperative. A potential cure had presented itself—or at least something unique enough to demand an extensive look into it. So the doctor called the meeting with the three in an attempt to come up with some answers. The others were already waiting for him when he arrived.

He entered abruptly and closed the door, the eyes of his perishing patients following him as he moved across the palatial reception room, the urgency of the day nagging at him and manifesting itself as knots in his neck.

Near a window stood Magnus, imposing as ever, his massive frame backlit by the morning sun. And next to him, Chakeena, her complexion pale and smooth compared to his heavily creviced face, its lines indicating more time spent smiling than not over his fifty-something years of life.

Vice Minister Wu had been admiring the display of Vietrusian art on one of the windowless walls, his vibrant robe of orange and aquamarine blending well with the objects of his admiration. His affinity for the planet and her culture was obviously far greater than Chakeena's, for those same artifacts had been on that same reception room wall for as long as she could remember yet had never stirred even the slightest interest in her. She studied the Vice Minister and his interest in the art, took in his hawkish features and lanky physique, then directed her attention to the doctor.

"I apologize for my belated arrival," said Hulaksen, his age and lack of sleep revealed in his sagging eyes. "Thank you for coming."

Each greeted him then sat in one of the many chairs bordering the room, its opulence evident in every inch of it —furniture finished in a platinum-pearl veneer, meter-wide moldings crowning the arched doorways with glistening hand-glazed tile of an emerald green underlying the artwork on the walls.

"My original queries were private," said the doctor.

"However, having gotten no real answers, and due to the gravity of the situation, I'd hoped that the four of us together might be more successful in bringing something to light. I do realize the sensitive nature of this, so I think anything discussed here should remain amongst only us for the time being."

He stopped, scanned the room, was met with various gestures of agreement.

"Okay then. That said, I'd like to get right to it. I'll start off by informing you of something you may not be aware of, unless there have been some discoveries in speaking amongst yourselves, that is."

No one said a thing, the silence as thick as the hundred-year-old rug beneath their feet.

He nodded. "Well, through my discussions with each of you, I did find a common denominator of sorts—something you all shared just prior to your remissions. I hadn't put it together immediately, but realized it just last night in going over my notes. It seems you all attended an event recently hosted by the Empress. Shortly thereafter you each experienced the unprecedented recoveries."

He paused a moment, raked a hand across his jaw as his attention drew inward. "You see, it puts you all in the same place at the same time the night before this... Anomaly. Truthfully, I'm not sure how one could have anything to do with the other, but given the magnitude of the occurrence I think it's certainly worth looking at. And it was the only commonality I could find besides the disease itself. I would encourage you to take a look and see if anything comes to mind that you feel would be pertinent."

Various puzzled looks presented themselves on the patients' faces. Wu's thick brow tightened in thought. He at once recalled the disagreement he'd had with the Prime Minister, then realized he'd best stay focused.

Magnus grinned at the memories. His unscheduled reunion with Chakeena, the now amusing encounter with the guards, the exquisite entertainment, and his new friend Kaiden.

As for Chakeena, her first thought was how Magnus had surprised her with his visit. And then there was the matter of the boy. Many nights since had revealed him in her dreams. No, she had not forgotten about him. Neither had she forgotten the feelings she'd felt. This was of course unusual, though anything approximating the realm of romance was for her.

His potent performance flicked in her mind but quickly dissolved as her thoughts drifted back to the boy himself. She'd come to regret not having spoken to him after the show. Even in all the excitement of the night she should have made it a point to find him. It was a mistake, and one she now wished she could rectify.

"Would anyone like to start?" asked the doctor.

No one said a thing.

"How about you, Vice Minister?"

Wu slowly shook his head as he considered the question. Then heaved a sigh and spoke. "I'm not sure. Nothing in particular comes to mind."

"I see," said the doctor. "Magnus?"

Magnus's hands rested on his coat, the brass buttons and piped edges of his chosen daywear resembling the military dress of a general. "Well, I did have an interesting encounter with security. I wonder if it could have anything to do with the scanning system?"

But Chakeena promptly disabused him of it since she and the Empress were never scanned. She rolled back her

mind, sifting through the details. "Weren't we all in the officials' area for a time?

"I was not," said Wu. "I was preoccupied with the Prime
Minister." He lifted his hand, rested a finger on his
protruding cheekbone as he thought about it. "What about
the imported drink? It was unique, and very rare."

"Yes, it was," said Magnus. "Chakeena?"

She shook her head. "I didn't have any."

The doctor watched the room, its occupants already
appearing disheartened. "Well, obviously," he said, "the
variables here may be many. But remember, the result was
dramatic. And with an effect like that it would follow that
the cause would have been dramatic as well. I believe we're
looking for something extraordinary—something I would
imagine would stand out in one's mind. Now, did *anything*
out of the ordinary occur that evening, regardless of how
irrelevant it may seem? Anything at all?"

He watched closely for an indication, his glare intent on
getting an answer. And then, a glint in Wu's eyes. "Vice
Minister, a thought?"

"Actually," said Wu. "I do recall something. And it *was*
rather remarkable. But..."

"Go on," prompted the doctor.

"Yes, well... It was during one of the performances.
There was a feeling that came over me. Taking into account
what you've disclosed here, it might be worthy of note. In
fact I took note of it myself at the time. I'm not exactly sure
how it could be related, but... Well, at first I thought it was
simply due to the ambiance of the evening or space-lag from
my travels. But there was something more to it. I dare say I
felt... Well, I suppose intoxicated would be one way to
put it."

"Intoxicated?" said the doctor, the statement causing his forehead to furrow. "In what way?"

"I'm not sure. But in a way I've never experienced. Not what one would experience from drink. Besides, I'd had none until after the concert." He thought for a moment. "It's difficult to describe. It was as if I were floating. Like in a dream. A kind of weightlessness and a distinct sensation in my body. Like an agitation deep within that was yet comforting at the same time. I know that may sound somewhat absurd, but—"

"No!" blurted Chakeena.

Silence gripped the room. All eyes shifted to her.

She surveyed the others and backed down as she suddenly became aware of her reaction. Then, more quietly: "No. It does *not* sound absurd." She looked to the doctor. "I had a similar experience."

"Similar?" asked Dr. Hulaksen. "The same night?"

"Yes," she said. "Same night. Same sensations."

Hulaksen stared at her, now utterly absorbed. "Really? Had you experienced anything like this before?"

Chakeena shook her head. "Never."

Magnus listened, a somber squint forming as he awed at the exchange. "Actually, I did as well," he said. "I felt it too." He sounded like a man who didn't believe his own words. He continued, his attention now inward and fixed on the evening in question. "To be honest I'd wondered if I was not exactly stable. You see, I'd just been through one of my episodes before arriving. And, well, with that and the disease's progress, I guess I'd half forgotten and half wanted to forget." Magnus looked to Wu. "When was it? When did you experience this?"

Wu took a moment and looked it over. "It was after the

intermission, I believe. Yes, immediately afterwards. During a performance. A young man. Brilliant composition."

Magnus nodded, attention still inward. "Yes, me as well. Immediately after the intermission."

Chakeena surfaced from her thoughts, eyes brightening, unwell lips hinting at a smile. She turned to Magnus knowingly. "Me too."

The doctor's jaw dropped. "Are you sure?" he asked. "Same performance?"

"Yes," said Chakeena. "Same performance."

"Actually," said Magnus, "it was one of the most powerful things I've ever felt."

The doctor again examined the room, took in the scene as a whole. It wasn't the statements that had seized him as much as the unwavering certainty in their eyes. He could see that they'd hit on something undeniable. An obvious agreement. But on *what*? He stared silently at nothing, wrestling with his pragmatic ways, then finally broke the silence. "Is there anything else you can think of? Anything besides this? Anything else in the way of an explanation?"

They all sat still. Stared silently at each other.

"Well," he said tentatively. "I suppose I could check the records for any spacial anomalies that evening. It's been known to happen, so that's a possibility. Or maybe even the—"

"It was him," said Chakeena to herself.

The doctor directed his attention to the Princess. "What was that, my dear?"

She looked up. "It was him."

The doctor puzzled at the statement. "Who?"

"Yes," said Wu under his breath. "The music."

"No," said Chakeena. "Not the music. The *musician*."

Magnus nodded, utterly intrigued at this point. "Yes. Or maybe even both."

Chakeena sat up, adjusted herself in the chair. "It was him. Somehow. Someway. Call it a gut feeling. Intuition. Call it what you will. But I *know* it."

The doctor again observed the undeniable agreement. Just how it applied to the field of medicine still escaped him entirely, defying everything he knew or anything he'd experienced in his very long and very illustrious career. But with nothing else to go on, and at the risk of denying his patients a chance at a normal life, a life devoid of disease, he reluctantly detached himself from the lack of logic and surrendered to the idea. "Well, we can of course continue our talks. And I will still check on any spacial anomalies that may have occurred that evening. But meanwhile, I suppose we should look into this mysterious performer. Try to find out just who he is and what else we may be able to discover about him."

Chakeena and Magnus smiled and exchanged a glinting look at each other, for this was an answer they *did* have. He offered her the lead by way of a subtle facial flick, but she politely offered it right back. He nodded and spoke up. "His name is Kaiden Ryder, Doctor," he said, slowly sweeping his gaze back to Chakeena, his grin growing as he did, "and he lives in Suspended City."

CHAPTER EIGHT

The bright red of the day burst into Magnus's office through the vast glass walls where he stood admiring the thousands who scuffled about below, busy doing whatever they did down in his own little borough of Ruechestire.

Memories of him as a young boy swam through his head as he pondered the very real possibility of the rightful heir to all that stood before him prematurely taking his place in the event of an early demise. Yes, these same paths where he'd spent many a day playing blaster with his friends, where his father's father had done the same, and his father too, could soon be under the rule of a tenth generation Rue. For it was a certainty that his only son *would* succeed him. It was only a question of when. And time was ticking.

The last solid week saw numerous steps taken to find Kaiden. Magnus had gotten his staff to check the local tracking channels. He'd assumed that Kaiden would be a cinch to find, but he'd been wrong. No listing at all in the Greater Suspended City area. So he'd searched the entire Conglomerate—all the neighboring areas as well as Vietrus itself. But there was nothing. No trace of Kaiden anywhere. Could he have been from another sector?

The next nearest system was light years away and, though one *could* travel to and from, it was neither easy nor quick, and would also require an authorized sector-pass. But such passes were extremely rare and issued only to persons of chief positions in society or for official and pressing reasons and Kaiden obviously didn't qualify for that. Of course one could always be bought for exorbitant prices on the black market, but again, highly doubtful.

Having exhausted his immediate resources, Magnus had teamed up with the Vice Minister and the Empress to combine their efforts. With all the resources these three had, one would have expected more promising results. Yet still, nothing. Had Kaiden never been entered into the system? Not likely since it was nearly impossible to avoid. And no real reason to avoid it either, except for the serious criminal.

At one point the Empress had suggested they be more overt in their search and inform others, or maybe even put it out on the media feeds. But Wu and Magnus emphatically advised against it knowing all too well how it could draw unnecessary attention from those with baser motives. She of course knew they were right, but her rationality of late had been shaken and understandably so given the stakes. Chakeena had hit an all-new low, adding even more urgency. And so they decided to regroup.

Another plan was needed and fast. Numerous options were proposed and rejected before one was finally agreed to when Magnus suggested hiring a close friend. The friend, Lieutenant Bronson Cannon Decker, had held a high rank in the Secret Service for many years until the assassination of the late Prime Minister of Vietrus, Sir Temgan G. Reochi.

It had occurred on Bronson's watch and the findings from the investigation had proven there was nothing that could have been done to prevent it. But there yet remained the matter of blame. At least *some* of it needed to be placed somewhere, if only to appease the masses. And since it had already begun to render Bronson a stigma to the service, the decision was made to dishonorably discharge him. He'd since gone private.

"Computer," said Magnus, "screen up."

A blip sounded as the screen rose from his polished sterling desk. He strolled over and slumped into a chair of the same material, searched the database for the contact details, and composed a message.

Outgoing I.T.S. Transmission:
To: Bronson C. Decker | From: Magnus V. Rue IX
Priority: High
Hello old friend. No time for pleasantries. Your wife has taken ill. She needs you home—fast. Please respond at your earliest convenience.
End Transmission

Magnus looked it over, hand to jowl as his mind rummaged through a collection of memories past, the exploits of a time long ago filling him with a sense of sentimentality. He smiled, nodded, then stabbed the *send* key.

"Message sent, sir," said the computer.

Though fiercely denied by the accused, a number of government agencies as well as many other less savory syndicates continually and illegally monitored the Interspacial Telecommunication System.

Thus, Magnus had needed a way to alert Bronson without raising suspicion in those who may be surveilling.

So he'd deliberately been cryptic. Bronson had never been married and was well aware that Magnus knew it. And Magnus was certain it would guarantee a response while also avoiding curiosity to the wrong ears.

Magnus leaned back into the chair, its springs straining under his stoutly heft. He settled into it and turned his attention to the steamy waft of coffee lingering above his favorite cup as the morning sunlight streamed through it and danced on the desk. He grasped the cup and took a sip. "Well then, computer, what have we on the agenda for the day?"

"The Regional Civic Council has sent a number of proposed laws on which you are to advise, sir. I've pulled it up for your review. If you prefer, I could read it to you."

"Yes," said Magnus. "Proceed."

The computer began a monotonous delivery of municipal legalese as Magnus swiveled his view to the north and sipped at his steaming cup.

A beep echoed through the room. The computer paused its delivery. "Sir, incoming I.T.S. transmission for you. Do you wish to view it at this time?"

"Sender?"

"Bronson Decker, sir."

Magnus lifted his brow. "That was fast." He swiveled back to the screen. "Yes, I'll view it now."

"Right away, sir."

The message sprang to the screen:

Incoming I.T.S. Transmission:
> *To: Magnus V. Rue IX | From: Bronson C. Decker*
> *Priority: High*
> *Message received. Tell her I'll be there soon.*
> *End Transmission*

The corners of Magnus's mouth rounded as he read the message. A welcome transmission if there ever were one. For if anyone could discover the whereabouts of this Mr. Ryder, it would be Bronson. Yes, Dolph's fate to rule Rueche-stire might just yet be delayed.

Magnus placed his thumb on a section of the screen marked "Outgoing Messages." The screen pulsed a soft purple. As he spoke, his words appeared across the screen. "Begin message. Dear All, good news. My friend is on his way. I'll update you as I know more. We're going to find this fellow and beat this thing yet. I'm certain of it. End message."

"Priority level?" asked the computer.

"Top," said Magnus.

"Recipients?"

"Empress and Princess Amana, Dr. Hulaksen, Vice Minister Wu..." But he stopped, taking a moment to assess his actions. He'd yet to set up a private file, and the nature of the situation certainly called for the added security: The phenomenon itself, the unknown aspects of Ryder, the state and stations of the affected patients—all would better be served by a much more private approach.

He sat back and considered it. He could designate a project name, assign specific recipients to it, and limit the communication systems used for correspondence. By avoiding the I.T.S. altogether, he could bypass the moni-toring eyes and also be less cryptic with his communi-cations.

"Computer. Cancel that."

"Cancelled sir," said the computer.

"Please create a new file."

"Yes, sir. File name?"

"Project..." He thought for a moment, his squinting eyes

betraying their age as he stared blankly at the screen. Then: "Project Vivace."

"Done, sir. Recipients with authorized access to Project Vivace?"

"Empress and Princess Amana, Dr. Hulaksen, Vice Minister Wu, Bronson Decker, and myself."

"Communication systems?"

"Exec-Comm only. Private. No transmissions related to Project Vivace are to be sent over the I.T.S. or any other such system."

"Done sir. Would you like me to send the message now?"

"Yes."

There was a light blip. "Message sent, sir."

"What's Project Vivace, Father?"

Magnus swung around to find his son gliding across the room toward him, the click of his knee-high boots resounding throughout the room as he neared. His crisply cut hair topped a tall frame wrapped in the flawless fit of a snug racing outfit, the royal gait revealing one steeped heavily in a cultured upbringing.

"You startled me, Son," said Magnus. "You trying to give your old man a heart attack?"

Dolph smiled. "Oh you'll manage that easily enough on your own with those midnight blaster workouts."

Magnus laughed. "Ha! Where'd you hear such nonsense?"

"From the Chief of Security himself."

"Oh, the old inebriate, eh? A little too much of Vietrus's finest I should think," said Magnus. "But, then again, we *do* have the most secure vinoh cellar in all of Ruechestire."

"Well, maybe so," said Dolph, "but you should still be careful. You know what your doctor says."

Magnus leaned forward to stand. "What happened to your morning laps?"

"There's no need to get up, Father." But Dolph knew it would not stop him—not the great Lord Magnus Rue. No, he and his emphatic etiquette would ignore the statement just as he always had and likely just as he always would. In all of Dolph's twenty-three standard years he'd never once seen his father fault in that department. Not once. Not even with his own son in private. So why start today?

Dolph shrugged it off mentally and greeted his father with a grasp of the shoulder. "Something's off with the timing. The mechanic's looking at it as we speak."

"I'm sure it'll be fine," said Magnus. "Good mechanic. Good craft."

"So, what is it, Father? Or is it another of your private issues you're *unable* to discuss?"

Withholding such information from Dolph pained Magnus greatly. Yet decades of protocol and policy implored he do just that—divulge nothing, ever, not to anyone. But this was his son, the next to serve the very policy denied him. And even though the conflict continually tore at him, still, deep down, he knew there was only one right answer. "I'm afraid so, Son. You'll soon enough have security clearance to more than you'll care to know. You're just going to have to trust your ol' man."

"Well, I hope that day is a distant one."

Magnus sighed. "As do I, Son. As do I."

Dolph sensed he'd hit on something more than the ordinary business of the day. But what? Political discretion was far from new, in fact almost a daily occurrence. Yet there was a look in his father's eyes on this. Something more personal? Something more substantial?

"Have you had breakfast?" asked Magnus.

"Not yet."

"Well then, shall we?"

Dolph gave a reserved nod, noticeably still stuck on the secret. "Sounds good. Let me change first, though."

"Everything okay?"

"Yes, Father," he said, groping for a believable response. "Just a little tired. Rough sleep last night."

The deception did not get by Magnus, but he quickly discarded it. After all, it could be any of a number of things and likely of little importance—and he certainly was not in the mood to badger his son on such a fine morning as this. "Well, maybe some food will help," he said. "Meet you downstairs?"

"Yes, sir. I'll only be a minute." Dolph turned, moved nonchalantly across the room and into the hall, proceeding down it with an ear glued behind him, conscious of the measured pace he kept. And once he'd rounded the corner and was certain he was out of earshot, he picked up the pace, but not before a final glance over his shoulder—just to be sure.

His boots clicked more quickly as he neared the wing leading to the sleeping/bed chambers, his mind continuing to obsess on the question. Yet another mysterious project. Yet another confidential matter his father would deny him. And as he continued his journey to his quarters, the images of that horrible day resumed their years-long assault on him...

He was just a boy when it happened. And were it not for the day in question forever etched in his mind through the annual commemorations, he would have been too young to remember the precise date. But he remembered the *event*. He remembered *what occurred*. He remembered it all in excruciatingly vivid detail—the sights, the smells, the setting, and the savagery.

It was his mother. She'd been sick. She'd fallen into what the doctors had called a "vegetative state"—an offensive term if ever there were one, and yet *another* crime on top of the already inexcusable atrocity.

For weeks she'd remained in that bed connected to the machines. Weeks of agony. Weeks of hell. And though his father had been granted unlimited access, Dolph had been emphatically forbidden from entering, instead reduced to peering tippy-toed through the imprisoning wall of glass, his face pressed to it for hours on end—torrents of unstoppable sobs flowing for the one he'd loved so dearly and had so ruthlessly lost.

The decision to "pull the plug" was ultimately made by his father, and by his father alone. A selfish act beyond belief. No mention to young Dolph. No warning or preparation of the premeditated offense. And worst of all, no good bye.

It of course had been framed as the "right" thing to do. It was colored and slanted and twisted and presented as something "good," a benevolent act to put her out of her misery—an act of righteousness, compassion, even heroism. But they were lies. Lies from liars. Lies upon lies up on lies! And for Dolph there was only one way to view it. Only one word to describe the vicious and unthinkable act that would so brutally bereave him of his mother. One word to describe the extinguishing of one so full of love and so full of hope. And that word was *murder!*

Dolph's world that day went dark. For not only did he lose his mother, but also a portion of his soul. And not a small part. A sizable part. An irreplaceable part that would forever render him incomplete. And just as it is said that nature abhors a vacuum, so his was filled.

It started with an idea—a simple one festering within. But with every passing day it grew, systematically taking hold of his every thought that eventually formed into a purpose. A purpose that became clear, concise, and wholly crystallized. A purpose so deeply entrenched so as never to be loosed from his grip. A purpose that would ultimately avenge his mother and *exact revenge upon her executioner and everything for which he stood!*

Yes, he would hit his father where it counted most—in the so-called "good" others saw in him: His stellar status. His impeccable reputation. The bullshit benevolence. But it could not be done superficially. No, it must be deep, cutting, sweeping, and substantial.

And so the hatching of the plan began. From that day forth, Dolph would champion hate. It would be what would drive him. To live a life intent on harm. That would be the revenge he'd show *the killer!* That would be how he'd repay him. Be the son that brought shame on the name. Be the son he'd wished he'd never brought into this world. And do it right under his nose without it ever being suspected—slowly and insidiously.

And once the plan was in place and he'd secured his spot in the Network's upper ranks, once that glorious day had finally arrived, he would crush his father to the fullest extent with one unimaginably blindsiding blow. The *final* blow delivered to him while he was still alive and cognizant. This Dolph would do. And this he would do soon. Yes, he *would* have his day of wrath. But with the disease looming larger by the day, time was running out and the pressure to pull it off was quickly mounting.

Arriving to his room, Dolph tugged off his glove and

pressed his hand to the lock. The door slid open. He darted to the desk, briskly took a seat.

"Computer," he said, attempting a whisper," search database for—

"Please verify identity."

"Damn it!" spit Dolph, slamming his hand on the verifier.

"Thank you, sir. How may I be of assistance?"

"Search database for the word 'vivace' and give me anything you find."

"Checking, sir," said the computer. There were some soft clicks, a whir or two, then: "*Vivace. A musical term characterizing a deep and meaningful manner.*"

"What!" He smacked his hand on the sterling desk, shouted in a condescending tone: "More, you useless machine!"

"Yes, sir," said the computer. "It comes from the word *vivify*, which means *to give life to, to animate, to make more vivid or striking. Vivify* derives from the late Vietrusian word *vivifacable*, which itself derives from the ancient Kearthian word *vivilati*, meaning *to make complete or intact, to satisfy the demands of—*"

"Enough!" demanded Dolph.

"Yes, sir," replied the computer.

Dolph's mind went to work. He'd seen the conflict in his father's eyes. There was something he'd wanted to say. And since his father would never be so anxious to give up bad news, then... Could it be something good? But why hold back?

He zipped open his racing suit and searched the closet for some appropriate daywear. Perhaps he could gather more at breakfast. Perhaps there was a way to work some of his magic—the subtle, manipulative stuff he'd carefully groomed his faculties for over the years.

But as it would turn out, nothing came from it. No additional information or progress in the least, rendering Dolph for the remainder of the day haunted by the same irritating thought cycling incessantly in his head: *vivace... to give life to... vivace...*

CHAPTER NINE

Bronson's morning had been a busy one. In the time since
he'd woken he'd already received a curious message from an
old friend, booked an off-planet flight to visit said friend,
argued with a ditzy booking agent about the extravagant
carry-on costs, blasted to smithereens some kinda varmint
that had been helping itself to the *wrong* ex-serviceman's
rations at the *wrong* time, received a verbal beating from his
newest female friend for "*annihilating* such a harmless little
creature," made up with said female friend—twice—for the
"obvious" mistake, and skinned a shin while trying to pack
as an impatient shuttle driver hammered on the door shouting, "You got thirty seconds and I'm outta here. And I mean
it this time, Mr. 'I gotta flight to catch off this godforsaken
planet and I can't be late!'" And all of it in less than an hour.

The rattle of the shuttle as it hovered down the planet-
path compounded by the driver's incessant whining about
having to wait had given Bronson a headache. Of course the
prior night's ungodly amount of vinoh couldn't possibly be
helping. And when the verbal threats leveled at the driver to
"shut his goddamn yap-hole" proved unsuccessful, Bronson,

in a final attempt for some peace, placed the tip of the varmint-annihilating blaster on the back of the driver's head and calmly shushed him.

Silence, finally.

Bronson put in a call to his client to inform her he'd be taking a break from the case due to a serious "family matter." The client's begging and offers of increased pay were not difficult to turn down. Not after being cooped up in a decaying apartment staring from one window to another across an alley for days on end awaiting evidence of some moron's alleged betrayal. No, that was not his idea of a good time. But it did pay, and not too badly at that.

Though the driver's hate-laced glare in the mirror was off-putting, Bronson did his best to ignore it. He could, of course, just vaporize the idiot—the quick-fix. But in the end it would only put him behind schedule. And besides, his many years in the service had conditioned him for so much more than anything this cocky little imbecile could throw his way.

Whipping by were the many neighborhoods of Bronson's youth, flooding his head with a wash of memories. Vietrus was where he'd grown up. It was his planet of birth. And in his fifty-five years of existence he'd managed to see almost everything and every place it had to offer. Yet no matter how seedy it seemed at times, it would always be home for him.

Bronson ran a hand over his unshaven jaw and through his coal-colored hair as he stared at the morning sky and out into the expanse of the Conglomerate's space: A tangled cacophony of cities and expressways sprawling into the deep maroon outer-sphere above, the inevitable overflow of a planet bursting at its seams with nowhere else to evolve to but out. He struggled to distinguish between the distant colonies, each having its own tale to tell. And as he did, his thoughts drifted to a flight he'd taken years ago with Magnus...

They were young, ambitious, and undercover at the time. They'd been following a traitor, a fellow serviceman who'd sold secrets to the Underpath Network—information that put at risk Emperor Ashlam, the then ruler of the Conglomerate.

The evidence had been verified and they'd been assigned the task to capture and contain the man seated mere meters before them to prevent his escape from the sector. A simple enough assignment for someone with Bronson's skillset, but he and Magnus were yet at odds on it.

Magnus had wanted to secure the target immediately upon spotting him. And he'd indeed been spotted. But Bronson had wanted to relax without having a cuffed complainer at his side for the duration of the flight. He was ultimately overruled by Magnus, who was right of course. No point risking an escape. Even on such a flight, a number of things could yet transpire to soil the plan.

The compromise? Bronson stepped up and secretly stuck the traitor with a little something to help him "relax," then cuffed him to his *own damn seat* in his *own damn row*. And just for good measure, planted a tracking device on him in the unlikely event he were to come to and try anything funny. So there "snoozed" the traitor, secured in plain sight, leaving Bronson and Magnus the added legroom to comfortably enjoy a beverage while they...

The wail of a horn sounded, harsh and jarring, jerking Bronson back to the present.

The increase of vessels indicated they were nearing the spaceport. His gaze swept back into the shuttle and was greeted by a resenting glare in the mirror. He swiftly sunk a boot into the back of the seat. The driver jumped, then tried to play it off as nothing. Bronson feigned a mistake and "apologized" before returning his attention to the traffic.

It was a welcome sight indeed—nothing short of sheer mayhem—the chaos leading into the spaceport teeming with an impatient assortment of everything and everyone imaginable all desperately bound for some outlying destination. He grinned as they entered the madness, the perfect remedy for the stakeout and its painstaking pettiness.

A shuttle pulled up beside them. It contained a female. She was long with an unusual shape. Bright blue skin, white hair—her iridescent bodysuit glistening in the bright red daylight.

She glanced at Bronson, a mischievous glint forming in her amber eyes. He smiled, gave a wink. She responded by throwing her head back and revealing a mouthful of daggerlike fangs, her tongue slithering across them before carefully concealing them again behind a devious smile and deep purple lips.

"She's nice, huh?" sneered the driver. "The Quadladrite, I mean."

Bronson looked at him silently, then back to the female.

"You *do* know about her species, don't you?"

Bronson attempted to ignore the question—a practically impossible feat given his profession.

"Well, let me fill ya in, mister. They're new to the sector. But where they're from they feed mainly on humans—or at least their ancestors did. Yeah, it's forbidden in the Conglomerate. But I still wouldn't get too friendly with her if ya know what I mean." There was a moment of silence before the driver burst into a cynical laugh.

Bronson didn't flinch. He'd of course heard of the species but had yet to witness one. He peered back at her, took her in. And in her piercing glare he could see it: a hint of the unsettling urge—a desire to devour him, literally. Maybe not at first. And maybe she possessed the willpower to resist. But it was there—the savage truth of her struggle to keep the compulsions at bay, something Bronson was certainly no stranger to, for he was not without his own demons that required repressing. Most were harmless in the bigger picture. But there was one that was more prominent —a daily struggle from a time when he was captured back in his military days. A potent drug manufactured illegally known as "k-mite" had been introduced to him while in enemy hands.

It was physical manipulation to be sure, but in hindsight it was the mental side that had done the real damage. For sixty straight days he'd been confined—each day less suste-nance, each day a higher dose. To that was eventually added appealing companionship and endless intoxicating stimu-lants. It was indeed mental manipulation at its best. No pain, no torture or fear—the epitome of psychological warfare. Any anxiety or hint of being in the hands of the enemy was obliterated by the "k." To this day he yearned for the peace it had provided. The drug was still in circulation, and merely knowing so was a source of agony. Yes, from that day forth it had constituted "control by the enemy" and a portion of his life that would never be returned to him.

Following his release he'd required rehab for the better part of a year to alleviate the aftermath. But in truth he'd never fully recovered, and likely never would.

As he watched the Quadladrite's transport disappear into the traffic, he adjusted his stocky frame and looked to the driver's scowl in the mirror. "How much longer?"

"Depends. Where ya goin'?"

"Ruechestire Borough, Empire Amana."

"Just ahead," snarled the driver. "Space-dock 4."

Bronson peered ahead, spotted his salvation beyond the droves of drivers, a sign for space-dock 4 displayed prominently above the path.

The driver nudged his way over lane by lane as they neared the dock, the traffic countering his every attempt. Seeing an opening, and before any of the barbarians had a chance to block him again, he gunned the shuttle and seized the targeted lane. "Hah!"

Bronson rolled his ice-gray eyes and gathered his effects. "This'll do. I'll walk the rest."

"But what about—"

"I'll walk."

The driver shrugged and slid to a stop, instantly bombarded by a flurry of protests. He checked the credit counter. "Forty-six."

"Forty-six? Absolutely criminal. I oughta vaporize you right here and—"

"Criminal?" said the driver. "You know damn well how long I waited for you!"

Bronson shook his head as he leaned over and grudgingly swept a hand across the machine. Its screen lit up, blinked a florescent green. He okayed the transfer. "Now let me outta this stinkin' rattle-trap." He grabbed his travel case and slid out of the shuttle, slamming the door behind him as the driver screeched off into the traffic.

As Bronson stomped in the direction of the terminal, an electronic voice bellowing from above bled into his world, "...Space-dock 4. Suspended City. Ruechestire Borough. Empire Amana. Space-dock 4..."

The terminal door swished open, inviting Bronson in. And as he entered, his instincts instantly lit up. But it was not soon enough. Before he had a chance to react, a giant

paw seized his neck. He went for his blaster. No good—
another paw had beat him to it.

"You lookin' for this?" asked a gruff voice from behind as
it sunk the muzzle deep into Bronson's belly.

Bronson writhed in an attempt to free himself but the
grip only tightened. A creak of his vertebrae indicated it was
on the verge of snapping. He locked onto the paw, heaved at
it. It did not budge. He heaved again and gasped for a
breath. But the vice-like grip persisted.

"Decker," said the owner of the paw. "Bronson *damn*
Decker. What a nice surprise. Been lookin' for you. I knew
you'd turn up sooner or later."

The voice gave it away. It was Grivel Gromme, an old
rival. An evil creature and godawful ugly too, its apish
physique shrouded in a matted coat of flea-bitten fur. Just
how he was still alive escaped Bronson entirely, but *evidently*
he still was.

Bronson quickly calculated options. No time to waste.
Grivel would think nothing of ending him even in a place as
public as this. His hands lifted into the air to signal a surren-
der. He didn't have a choice; if he didn't break free soon it
would be over.

"What's the matter, nothin' to say to your ol' friend?"
slurped Grivel as he let up on the grip.

Bronson wheezed in some air, which came with it the
putrid stench of the monster. A compulsive cough immediately attempted to expel it. He gasp for air, coughed again,
then: "Grivel. How ya been? Long time old friend."

"Yer damn right long time. Thought I was dead, did ya?"

"Well..." Bronson strained to speak, swallowed hard, "...
one can always hope."

"Yeah, real funny," said Grivel as he proceeded to drag
Bronson across the floor of the concourse. "If I didn't think

you were more valuable alive, I'd crush your skinny little neck right now. You should consider yourself lucky."

The animal's voice dimmed in Bronson's world along with his vision. Next would be a full-blown blackout if he didn't take charge soon.

His mind raced for an answer as needles of numbness trickled into his legs. What did he know of the monster? What could he use against it? A weakness? A flaw? And then, with the blackness on the brink of engulfing him entirely, it came to him in a burst of brilliance: "Hey, Gromme. How's your leg?"

"Ha!" barked Grivel. "Don't worry, I haven't forgot. Still hurts like hell."

In a prior encounter, Bronson had sunk a severed electrical cable into Grivel's thigh. Searing flesh and a flash of fire followed. The roar had been deafening, and gratifying.

Bronson quickly consulted the incident from his oxygen-deprived memory. Left leg? Right? Had to be sure—he'd likely have only one chance. He strained for a view of Grivel's gait, the blurry limp revealing a favored *left*. Jackpot! He drew back and—with all the strength he could muster—heaved his lead-lined case down!

A wash of spattering blood spewed from the area of impact. The blaster hit the floor and discharged. Grivel roared. Screams echoed through the spaceport as the crowd scattered.

Grivel grasped his leg with one paw but maintained his lock on Bronson's neck with the other as his giant body gave way and thudded to the floor. The constriction grew even tighter.

Bronson wrenched his body in an attempt to free himself, fought in vain for a breath, quickly lifted the case and delivered two more precisely placed blows. The first crushed Grivel's paw, the second his knee. There was more blood, more roars, and finally... The release of the death-grip.

Bronson gulped at the air—gasp after gasp as he kneaded at his neck—then quickly gathered himself and sprung up, skidding across the floor as he scooped up his blaster. He scanned for authorities, retrieved his bloodied case, then tromped back to the thrashing animal. "Okay, Gromme, gotta go now. Got a flight to catch. You take care of that leg now," he said as he heaved the case down for a final blow.

Grivel went unconscious.

CHAPTER TEN

The shuttle pulled up to Magnus's estate and slowed to a stop, the silver spikes of the main gate extending into space like a giant hand warding off would-be intruders.

Beyond the gate stood the mansion—the largest of many structures, its theme consistent throughout: polished-metal framework with the surface areas dressed in flawless sheets of glass all seated atop an acre-sized terraplate, its grounds immaculately landscaped and its perimeter neatly wrapped in a steel-covered wall a meter thick and the height of many men.

The daylight, now diminishing as evening approached, drenched the surrounding space and the entire borough in a blanket of rich maroon.

Bronson had not known Magnus as a reigning ruler. He'd known him as any other serviceman—thriving and young, prepared to rid the Conglomerate of every criminal and parasitic element that sought to feed off her political power. *That* was the Magnus he'd known. And yet there had always been an air of nobility with him. Not something asserted. In fact, quite the opposite. Magnus had always remained humble, never drawing unneeded attention to the fact that through his veins coursed the blood of his royal ancestors.

But even though Bronson was well aware of Magnus's lineage, as well as his status in this quarter of the Conglomerate, he yet found himself unprepared for what stood before him. It was a sight to behold and further evidence that his ex-colleague of many a covert mission was indeed part of that same royal stratum they'd both served to protect so many years ago.

"This it?" asked Bronson.

"Oh yes," said the driver. "If you're looking for Ruechestire Manor, this is definitely the place."

"Hell of a home," said Bronson, gathering his things.

"Yes indeed. You can see it glittering from anywhere in the borough. From bordering ones too."

Bronson nodded. "What'd I owe ya?"

"Twenty-nine," said the driver.

Bronson authorized the transaction and slid out of the shuttle. Still adjusting to the effects of the gravity pods, he wavered, grasped the door to stabilize himself. He looked up at the monstrous gate before him, shielding his eyes from the slivers of reflecting glare.

"You want me to wait?" asked the driver.

Bronson shook his head, grabbed his case. "No. I'm good. Thanks."

"All right. Have a good one then." The driver gave a wave.

Bronson closed the door with a swipe of his hand and watched the shuttle hover off, the sound of the electric drive like a bug buzzing off into the dusk. He took in the moment, relieved to have escaped the dismal view of the prior job, then widened his gaze to the surrounding space and an impressive view of the planet he'd just come from.

He straightened the sleeves of his jacket, a dark green bomber made of leather-lined neoprene, and stepped up to the gate, inspecting the intercom. There was a glassy panel covering a camera and a single call-button. He pushed it.

"Yes?" asked a voice.

"Magnus?" said Bronson.

"Who's this?"

"Bronson."

"Aye, Mr. Decker. Lord Magnus is expecting you. One moment, sir." The lens behind the panel looked up, looked him over. Then: "Mr. Decker, protocol requires that I scan you. I'm sure you understand."

"I have a weapon," said Bronson. "Actually, a couple."

"Yes of course. Only confirming your identity, sir. This'll just take a moment." A stream of lights sprung from the panel, encircled Bronson, held for a moment, then withdrew with a swish. "You're cleared. Please come in. I'll inform Lord Magnus of your arrival."

A laser-wall appeared behind Bronson as the giant hand drew open and invited him in, the intercom's eye following him as he stepped through. The gate closed with a clank and the laser-wall disintegrated.

Bronson surveyed the area with the eye of an expert. Six TX9 thermal-optic sensors, all placed for optimum visibility. Two infra-blue motion detectors before him with another two behind. Saturating the estate's space were particle waves from the phase-shifter relay disc, probably the SDR-VII—latest edition. And below the soles of his whale-hide boots murmured the discernible drone of a finely tuned pressure-path. No, make that exceptionally tuned. Bronson was impressed—Magnus was indeed a well-guarded man.

"Over here, sir," said a voice from the mansion's main entrance.

Bronson looked up to find a uniformed man. Graying hair. Bit of a belly. Weathered skin. Rosy nose.

"Come on in," said the man. "I'll take you to the study."

"Thanks," said Bronson as he strolled through the palatial entrance.

They made their way along the sheer hallways to a waiting area where the man stopped and faced Bronson. "Please, have a seat," he said. "Lord Magnus will be down in a moment."

Bronson offered his hand. "Name's Bronson."

The man smiled, grasped it and gave it a hearty shake. "Aye, of course you are. How rude of me. Drusher. Montgomery Drusher—Chief of Security." He let go. "Honored to meet you. You're somewhat of a legend around here. You should hear the stories Lord Magnus tells about you. The mighty Bronson Decker."

"Oh, I'm sure that's all they are. Stories. Time has a way of exaggerating stuff like that."

"Not according to Lord Magnus."

Bronson smiled, the creases in his leathered brow deepening. "All due respect, but I'm sure what he really meant was—"

"Like hell I did!" snapped a cavernous voice from behind. "You gonna tell me you *didn't* put out of their misery five frothing convicts with your bare hands in the cell of a Cileyian incarceration block?"

Bronson spun to find Magnus advancing toward him. Older, portlier, impeccably posh.

Magnus grasped Bronson's shoulders and held him at

arm's length, stared him down, his deep hazel eyes betraying the wisdom inherited from the decades of rule over his realm since his honorable discharge from the service. "Bronson my old friend."

"Magnus," said Bronson, returning the grasp. "Or should I call you Lord?"

Magnus lifted his hand, pointed a formidable finger. "You do and I'll have you vaporized on the spot!"

Bronson laughed. "Good luck with that."

They released each other and chuckled like a couple of fresh cadets.

"How long's it been?" asked Bronson.

"Twenty years? Maybe more. Too long, that's for sure. You look good."

"You too," said Bronson.

"You're a liar, my friend. And a good one at that. Nothing new there." Magnus slung Bronson under an arm and tugged him along. "Come on, let me show you around. You've of course met Chief Drusher."

"Yes," said Bronson, turning to the Chief. "Top-notch security out there."

"Aye, Mr. Decker," he said, moving with them. "I do try."

"The Chief's been with me forever," said Magnus. "Best there is."

"Thank you, sir," said the Chief. "Is there anything else?"

"No," said Magnus. "I'll take it from here."

"Very well." The Chief bowed his head, turned and departed.

Magnus gave Bronson a tour of the estate and brought him up to speed on the situation with Kaiden and the anomaly. It was the first Bronson had heard of Magnus's bout with the disease—a subject he was not unfamiliar with having lost his own mother to it.

As they moved through the mansion's sectioned structures, the remaining slice of the sun tucking itself behind Vietrus could be seen through the vast glass walls of the walkways.

Magnus stopped at a doorway and placed his hand on a verifier. It unlocked and opened. "And this is where I spend most of my time," said Magnus, entering his office.

Bronson inspected the room. There was the sterling desk in the center, its mirrored reflection visible in the polished floor beneath it, and scores of humanitarian accolades and congressional commendations draping the walls. And on a pedestal in the corner furthest the door, a digital photoprint of Magnus's late wife displayed under a heedfully aimed light-rod. Bronson averted his gaze from the print, returning it back to the accolades. "Impressive."

"Yes, well, it serves its purpose." He took in the room for a moment, then back to Bronson. "Well, I suppose we should discuss next steps. Please, have a seat."

"Incoming transmission, sir," said a voice from the console. "It's marked 'urgent.'"

"I'd better get this," said Magnus.

"I'll wait in the hall," said Bronson.

"Hang on." Magnus turned to the console. "Nature of the message?"

"It's secured," said the computer, "regarding Project Vivace."

Magnus lifted a hand and gestured to Bronson. "Stay," he said. "This concerns you." He tapped the screen. A message materialized on it:

Exec-Comm Transmission—URGENT:
   Re: Project Vivace, PRIVATE
   Magnus; The Vice Minister's health has worsened. A drastic

decline. Please meet me at his residence as soon as possible. He's asked to see you. I'm there now. I've informed the others to do the same. I'm afraid we haven't much time. Dr. Hulaksen.

Magnus sighed and shook his head as the weight of it sunk in. He tapped the screen, closing out the transmission, and turned to Bronson. "Bad news, old friend. Come on. I'll fill you in on the way."

CHAPTER ELEVEN

Vice Minister Wu lay weary in his bed, the room surrounding him strewn with legions of artifacts assembled from his many years of travels to countless far-off sectors.

His arid eyes, dull and squinting, failed to detect the mounds of communications covering the dust-ridden nightstand at his side, much less the persistent bits of starlight streaming through the tightly fastened shutters despite all efforts to prevent them.

Dr. Hulaksen hadn't the means to bring Wu back this time. The final stage of the disease was upon him and ravenously devouring his body. Yet no matter how unpalatable, it was not unexpected. After all, this *was* its usual course: to lie latent, awaiting its time to attack, teasing the patient periodically with a taste of its power. And then, within hours and without warning, to unleash the full brunt on the host delivering with it a swift and certain death.

The recourse to this ruthless fate? Whatever means available to ease the effects, usually in the form of drugs. Not as a solution, but an alleviation of the inevitable. This Hulaksen knew. This Hulaksen loathed.

Wu, soon to depart this stratum of existence, would do so spouseless, spawnless, and practically friendless. For this was his lot in life. This was what his political passion had secured for him.

He'd always supposed that after his term in office he would embark on the voyage of family. He'd supposed the same during each of the last six terms. Yet it seems his loyalty, though admirable in the extreme, had penalized him in the gravest of ways and his secret dream of offspring would now never transpire. His worst nightmare, however, had.

But still the day had taught him something. He'd learned the importance of compromises if one truly wanted to live, and he'd also realized he'd made none. Those who were aware of this fact were indeed a fortunate few, while the many who were not were yet destined for this same regrettable day. Oh how he yearned to forward that very point to all who would listen. It was the reason he'd asked for the others. But sadly, the strength to do so was now gone, and with it, his time.

"Our friends are in the hall, sir. Here to see you, as you requested," said Hulaksen. "May I bring them in?"

Wu struggled to focus. Managed a hoarse groan.

Certain that this was the best he would get, Hulaksen took it as a yes and left to gather the others.

In the hall sat Magnus, Bronson, and Empress Amana, all in a neat line on an ottoman-style sofa of golden embroidered upholstery. And beside them—body frail, face pale—Chakeena, her swollen eyes drenched in desperation as they glanced to the approaching doctor.

"Please, follow me," he said.

They stood and proceeded into the bedroom.

Chakeena entered and was instantly assaulted by the

stench of death. She gulped back a gag and froze in her tracks. And although she'd just been dealt an unwelcome dose of reality, it seemed more like some kind of vile hallucination.

She clutched her wits and reluctantly inched her way closer—Wu's eyes twitching in response as he strained to part his lids. And as she hovered over him, her guts churning at the sight now before her, she wondered how it could even be the same man. He'd reduced to almost nothing. His face gaunt and gray, his emaciated physique nothing but a withered bag of sinew and bones, a scene no amount of warning could have prepared her for, not with the intimate relationship she had with the same merciless disease.

She knelt beside him, touched his hand. It was clammy and stiff—the bulging veins on his wrist blending into bruises and festering lesions marking his arms. "Sir..." she whispered. It was then that she realized she'd come to know and even care about the man before her without ever knowing his given name. "Vice Minister," she said. "It's me. Chakeena."

The Empress stood and looked on in awe of her daughter and the remarkable strength she demonstrated.

Magnus clasped the Empress's trembling hand, consoling her as best he could.

Bronson took in the scene, unable to ignore the fact that the life of his friend could very well hinge on the mission he was charged with executing, and that failure thereof could result in this same fate.

The Empress began to break. Magnus took her in his arms. She sunk her face into his shoulder and wept.

The doctor knelt and checked Wu's pulse. Still alive but barely.

"Sir?" Chakeena whispered again. Then a little louder: "Sir?"

She dropped her head to Wu's chest. Her throat tightened. A surge of sorrow crept up and spilled from her eyes, her head reeling with a thousand thoughts. Aside from her father, whom she'd lost when she was very young, this was her first real exposure to death and she hadn't a clue as to propriety.

Wu struggled to draw in a breath. He managed a small one, then began to shake. Was he trying to speak?

She lifted her head. "Sir? What is it?"

He drew in another one, still shaking, and exhaled a faint but indecipherable sound. Then another attempt, this time a partial delivery by way of a parched throat: "Go..." But it was all he had.

"No!" pleaded Chakeena, her face now soaked in tears. She waited for more. But there was nothing. "Vice Minister! What is it? I'm here. I'm listening."

The room watched on as the life drained from not only the body of Wu, but also from the eyes of Chakeena.

The silence was finally broken by the labored sound of his lungs filling themselves with one last gasp. Chakeena looked on in shock as he slowly let it out, a gargled groan delivering with it his final message to her: "*Go... Live!*"

Chakeena gripped his nightshirt as her head fell to his empty chest. "No!"

Part Three

THE TRAITOR

CHAPTER TWELVE

Chakeena had been unable to repress the upsurge of fury and had consequently unleashed it on anyone and anything she'd encountered since Wu's ill-timed and unsettling death.

Life for her had become even more confusing as it bludgeoned her with questions of such an irrational nature that she was *certain* she'd seen the last of her sanity. And as a result, she'd locked herself in her bedroom and had remained there for the last two days with all attempts by the Empress to reach her emotionally or otherwise failing entirely.

She'd drawn the curtains to her once favorite window and entered an even worse state of recluse, her latest outburst leaving an aftermath of shattered trinkets and shredded clothing sprawled across the bedroom floor.

Sleep had been impossible. She'd tried once but was instantly besieged by the horrifying images of Wu's last gasp, each pound in her chest subsequently drawing taut the muscles in her throat and bringing to bear on her a very real and suffocating sense of death. Time eventually calmed her enough to breathe, but not enough to rid her of the disturbing images. And certainly not enough to provide her even a moment's rest since.

So there she sat, slouched in exhaustion and resenting the irony that she now faced. For Wu, though very much dead, yet lived *in her*, haunting her in the most morbid ways imaginable.

The sound of his death-day rang in her ears and she'd been pleading for it to stop when suddenly it did—only to be replaced by a thought not yet considered since that horrible day: Who was next? For it *would* be one of them. It was only a matter of which and when.

She cried out at the thought of it, clawing at her arms and legs, craving to be out of her now-crawling skin. And with no escape in sight, she'd begun a back-and-forth pace across her room—hyperventilating, shaking—a crazed look now residing in her usually calm, if somber, eyes. The room whirled. Weakness invaded her knees, forcing them to finally give way. She tumbled to the floor, connecting her skull to the corner of the nightstand on the way down and sending her into a not-unwelcome state of unconsciousness.

Black.

When she came to, she was met by a blurry silhouette of her mother. "Chakeena. Can you..." But the darkness, eager to return, again consumed her, submerging her again into the whirling blackness...

A vague image of Wu's dying eyes appeared, imploring for her assistance, begging her to help release the constriction death's hand had on him. She attempted to reach out but was unable, arms locked to her sides as if straight-jacketed to her torso. And then *Magnus's* eyes appeared, also dying. The darkness finally let loose and ebbed enough to again reveal the Empress's silhouette...

"...can you hear me? Chakeena?" The Empress ran her fingers through her daughter's matted mane, searching for the source of blood. "What's happened? Are you okay?" She turned to an attendant: "Get the doctor!" Chakeena's eyelids dipped, again growing heavy. "No!" shouted the Empress. "Chakeena! Stay with me!" But she was unable as the darkness drew her back into its cavernous void...

Chakeena found herself floating. No, flying. And below her a blanket of buildings lighting the night's space like stars in the distant galaxies.

Kaiden's music resounded in the distance, echoing throughout the Empire and lullabying it to sleep. She relished in it as the song she'd once applauded again filled her within, its power and peaceful sensation drenching her thirsty soul. And as the sound grew nearer, a body emerged from the haze of the bloody black space, a female figure clad in a sheer robe dancing about, hair whisking in the wind. And beside the woman, Kaiden—and now *he* was dying!

Chakeena attempted a scream but was unable as the mysterious woman turned and revealed herself. It was her mother—skin rotting, shards of teeth dangling from her bloody gums. She locked eyes with Chakeena, threw her arms spaceward and let out a screech too loud to bear...

Chakeena shot up out of the nightmare, body jolting forward, instantly awake and agitated.

"It's okay!" snapped Hulaksen. "Chakeena, calm down! It's okay." He forced her sopping body back down to the bed.

Her eyes batted about attempting to orient herself. She was no longer in her own bedroom. She was now in her mother's. But was it even real? She half expected Hulaksen to throttle her.

The Empress rushed up and cradled her daughter's

head in her hands. "No. My darling," said the Empress. "It's me. You've been in a coma and…"

But another wave of blackness washed over her and drew her yet again down into the bottomless abyss…

CHAPTER THIRTEEN

"I'm sorry, that is an invalid code," said the computer's tinny voice emitting from an audio portal in Dolph's desk. "Please enter the correct access code or place your hand on the verifier to—"

"You useless hunk of junk!" barked Dolph, dropping a fist to the console.

"I fail to understand your comment, sir," it said indifferently. "If I were a 'useless hunk of junk' then—"

"Sound off!" commanded Dolph, instantly overriding its voice system.

Too many attempts to access his father's private files would automatically trigger alarms and warn of the security threat. This Dolph knew. Maybe it already had. It was certainly possible. And maybe his father had even added measures of which Dolph was unaware, or had altered the default settings. No, two attempts in one week were plenty and another would only be asking for trouble. His hope was that the computer would view them as simple oversights.

Bronson's arrival and the hushed meetings with Magnus had driven Dolph's curiosity to the point of obsession. His suspicion that Bronson had been involved was confirmed when he'd "accidentally" walked in on a recent meeting. His father and Bronson had been discussing the project in question when Dolph made an unannounced entrance. Dolph had pretended not to notice what his father had said. His father had pretended not to care what Dolph had heard. And Bronson had pretended not to be in the middle of such an obviously awkward situation. None was successful.

But even though Dolph *had* managed to worm his way in, he yet came away empty handed. And worse yet, with more questions. Like what the hell was a "kaigen"? It was what his father had said, he was certain of it.

Further searches, however, were just as unsuccessful as his initial one: no contemporary definitions, all obscure and archaic significances, and certainly nothing that made any sense. Evidently in one ancient language—one so ancient that Dolph, though extremely well studied in galaxian history, hadn't even heard of—the word meant "to open, unfold or unseal."

Okay. So what? It was also a food source in the Hironi Sector over fourteen thousand years ago. But both the word and food perished alongside its people in their annihilation at the infamous "Attack of the Changan Order," the Hironian's then warmongering and victorious enemy.

Dolph again slammed a fist on the console, more forcefully this time, its impact resounding throughout the room. How could he have been so stupid? He should've leaked *nothing* until he'd had more. For once in his life he should've kept his big mouth shut. Yet just as it had so very many times in the past, greed had gotten the best of him prompting him to inform his Network contact of the "extraordinary findings" he had to share at their next meeting.

But in truth, he had nothing. Oh sure, circumstantial evidence of something that *must* be big—big enough to bring into the picture one Bronson Cannon Decker. But beyond that, nothing. And he was going to need a lot more than that if he was ever going to enter the upper ranks of the Conglomerate's Underworld.

At this rate it would not only remain an unattainable dream, but also quite possibly render him an imbecile in the eyes of his malicious peers. And that was unacceptable! Yes, he needed something of substance—something that made sense. And he needed it now.

The incessant blink of an amber light on the console arrested his attention. The computer had been attempting to notify him.

"What is it?" he snapped as he ran a hand over his head, wiping at the beading sweat that lay beneath the tight layer of his fiery bronze hair.

Silence.

"Yes? What is it you *stupid*… Damn it! Sound on!"

"Sir, I've been attempting to—"

"To the point!" demanded Dolph.

"Yes, sir. The Chief of Security has inquired as to your whereabouts."

"Tell him I'm very busy and not to be disturbed."

"Are you certain, sir? The inflections in the Chief's voice seemed to convey an element of urgency. And your schedule appears to be rather light at the moment since—"

"I gave you my answer!" asserted Dolph. "Just send it."

"Very well, sir," it said, followed by the blip of an internal transmission being delivered.

Dolph stared blankly at the computer. Any remaining respect he'd held for the Chief was merely remnants from the days when he truly *was* the best there was. Back when he'd exercised utter control and ingenuity. Back when nothing had gotten by his impeccable intuition, ever—intuition long since diluted by age and other less favorable factors.

Admittedly, a nice man, sure. Admittedly, too, a drunk. So much so that Dolph for some time now had viewed the Security *Chief* as more of a security *risk*.

Of course, Dolph's concern for his father's safety was negligible, except to keep him around long enough to witness the retribution in store for him. Yet he still thought it too dense to fathom that Lord Magnus Vasudum Rue the IXth, the reigning ruler of Ruechestire Borough, would keep the old drunk appointed in arguably one of the most essential positions in the Empire. It was downright embarrassing. Unacceptable, in fact, even if...

And then it hit him! And when it did, he himself felt dense. It'd been staring him straight in the face the whole time yet had been obscured by his contempt. This was his way in! The answer to his sordid ends. Who better to manipulate than one with faculties so dulled? Whose station and circumstances had more to offer than his? *Security risk indeed!* And to think all this time he'd been viewing the old inebriate as completely worthless when in fact he might be one of the most valuable resources at his disposal.

Yes, this was it! This was the answer he was waiting for! What better way to undermine security than by infiltrating it directly? And when better to start than now?

"Computer!"

"Sir?"

"I've changed my mind," he said cheerfully. "Please put Chief Drusher through to me immediately."

"Yes sir. One moment, please..."

Dolph's mind went straight to work. The old fool would

be putty in his hands. But still he must remain alert. After all, he'd already pushed his luck far further than he should have with the file.

And so he calmed himself, reminded himself of the Montgomery Drusher of yesteryear, sharp and shrewd. Yes, he'd treat the Chief as though his faculties were as formidable as ever. That would be the best approach. That would be the appropriate posture to assume. *Over*estimate him on everything. For now, just observe. Watch for weakness and opportunity. For his time was limited and he could afford no mistakes. And neither could he afford to be discovered. And then, as opportunities arise…

Drusher's raspy voice crackled through the computer. "Sir Dolph, are you there?"

"Yes," said Dolph, careful to maintain the cordial facade he'd fostered over the years. "How are you today, Chief?"

"Fine, sir. And you?"

"Fine also. Thank you. How might I assist?"

"I'd like to discuss something with you," said Drusher. "Do you have a few minutes?"

"Of course," said Dolph. "Shall I come to you?"

There was a pause. An oddly long one. And then: "Oh, that's not necessary, sir. I don't mind coming up to—"

"Nonsense," said Dolph. "I'm on my way down. I need to stretch my legs anyway."

"I see, sir," said the Chief, his response carrying with it a detectible measure of apprehension. "So… I'll see you soon then?"

"Yes," said Dolph. "I'll be right down."

There was more static. More silence. And then: "Aye, sir. I'll see you soon."

CHAPTER FOURTEEN

Chief Drusher scurried about the security area straightening up and disposing of potential evidence as quickly as possible.

He swung his chair so as to face the many rows of screens he was supposed to have been monitoring, one of which displayed an unfinished game of *Path Patterns* on it. As he raked his arm across the computer's console, sweeping a pile of paraphernalia into a drawer below, a forgotten vinoh bottle rolled out from underneath and snuck under his boot, then waited patiently until...

His foot came down and caught the bottle's edge, launching it across the floor and straight at the adjacent wall, the impact shattering the bottle and soaking the Vietrusian marble floor beneath it.

"Crap," he whispered on his way to the floor. "Crap!" again as he hit with a thud. The odor of the bottle's contents made its way to his nostrils. He shook his head, pushed up to his elbows, then grunted his way to his feet.

As he attempted to sort himself out—tidy his coat, tighten his belt—his peripheral caught Dolph on one of the screens. Bottom row, second from the left: maid's quarters. He was close. And if the area was not in order then...

The unfinished game on the screen seized his attention. He smiled. Contemplated a move. Placed a chubby finger on his chin and had just begun to weigh some strategic options when...

"What the hell am I thinking!" He snapped himself out of it, placed his focus back on the task at hand. "Computer!"

"Yes, sir."

"Screen D2, resume image!"

"Yes, sir."

The game disappeared and a still overview of the rear entrance took its rightful place. He wobbled across the floor, flung his coat off and dropped it over the bits of broken bottle. He wiped the console, straightened the scattered checklists and inspection reports on his desk, and dimmed the lights—just in case he'd missed something—then plunked himself down on his favorite chair and let out a sigh of relief, filling the area with vinoh-and-afternoon-snack stench. "Crap!"

He yanked at the desk's drawers, a cursory look at first, then fumbled through the top one. No good. The next one —nothing. "Where is that *damned*...?" Ah! Under the protocol manual, exactly where he'd put it so he *wouldn't forget where he'd put it!*

He popped off the cap and took a sizable swig of neutral-izer then coughed a stream of it down his chin. "Damn that Dolph!" he said. "What the hell is he thinking? No one *ever* comes down here. No one ever wants to!"

His reddened eyes darted about the area in a final check, weighing the scene in his mind against the seconds that remained. Far from perfect, but it would have to do. An approving nod followed as he dabbed his chin on his jacket sleeve and searched the screens for Dolph. Security corridor —right around the corner. Okay.

He shuffled across the room, fighting the lurching sways, and placed a hand on the verifier. The door swished open, exposing his lair to the hall. He stepped out and waited to greet the approaching Lord-to-Be, unable to rid his forced smile of its awkwardness. He wavered, caught himself— guilt thudding in his chest.

Dolph's boots clicked closer as he rounded the corner, schemes still grinding away in his skull when...

"Ah! Chief!" he snapped. "You startled me."

"Sorry, sir. Didn't mean to," replied Drusher. "Thank you for being so prompt."

"Not at all," said Dolph. "It's my pleasure."

Drusher stepped back and motioned Dolph in. "Please, come in."

Dolph swept through the doorway hyper-alert to the scene, a cave-like environment save the lighted wall of screens. He squinted as his eyes adjusted, sensing an unease in the silent air. He shifted his stare to the Chief. "You know, I can't remember the last time I was down here. Must be years."

"Yes, must be," said the Chief with a slight slur. The door swished shut. "Please, have a seat. Make yourself at home."

Dolph nodded, scanning the area as he seated himself. It was the odor that hit him first. A mixture of many things. The heat of electrical equipment, the aroma of the leather chairs, the not-so-subtle lingering of lunch and vinoh, and the somewhat fresh scent of neutralizer in an otherwise stuffy environment. But there was something else—something impervious to the power of the neutralizer. He couldn't put his finger on it at first, but when he did, it became impossible to ignore: The place utterly *reeked* of boredom. An alarmingly uneventful atmosphere. And even with the dwindling of Dolph's respect over the years, the thought was still a tough one to swallow. That the great Montgomery Drusher—once revered by all who knew of him, the choice sentry for many a monarch over the course of his long life, and director of countless security details assigned to top heads of state—had sunk to such dismal depths was indeed an unfathomable idea to him.

"So, this is where you spend your time is it?" said Dolph, settling into the seat.

"Aye," said the Chief. "That it is. And a lot of time at that."

"Well," Dolph shook off the gloom, "your years of commitment to my father and me have not gone unnoticed. You're very much appreciated around here."

"Thank you, sir. That's kind of you to say," said Drusher. "Truth is, I'm honored. Always have been."

Dolph smiled. "So, what's on your mind, Chief?"

"Right." Drusher sat up and cleared the neutralizer from his throat, buying time to recall just why he'd contacted Dolph in the first place. "Ah, yes. There's been some activity in the computer system that concerns me, and…"

Dolph's stomach sunk. *He knew! Shit!* So much for over-estimating. His mind went straight to work scrambling for a solution, clawing for a scrap of anything that could possibly help explain the…

"…and I wanted to check with you before I investigated further because—"

"Because the activity occurred from my chambers," said Dolph, matter-of-factly.

"Oh. Why, yes… That's right," said Drusher, thrown off by the admission. "You know about this?"

He did indeed. And coming right out with it would

reduce suspicion and *increase trust*. "Yes, I do. It was twice, I believe. Accidentally pulled up the wrong file, so it seems, and when I tried to access it, I couldn't. Apparently it was one of my father's and..." *Quick! Why?* "...and I haven't really been myself lately with Bronson here and all—you know he wouldn't be here unless Father were in some sort of a predicament. And something serious at that."

He looked down at his hands and wrung them in a way to convey concern. He was proud of himself. He was doing well. "Frankly," he continued, "I'm worried about him. I suppose I should've told you but I—"

"Not at all," said Drusher as he leaned forward and delivered to Dolph a firm pat on the shoulder. "It's okay, Dolph. I understand. To be honest, I'm glad it was you. Better you than someone else. You just made my job a lot easier."

"Yes, I suppose. But—"

"But nothing. Forget it. I suspected it might be something as simple as this. Normally I'd have gone straight to your father, but I didn't want to bother him either. Like you said, he seems to have his hands full with Mr. Decker. I've had some attention on it too. But you know your father. He knows what he's doing."

"Yes, you're right." It was working. He'd hooked and had begun to reel the old guy in, slowly but ever so surely. And now for the pièce de résistance: "And then there's his health. You know? The damned disease. He's all I have and—"

"Aye," said Drusher, "the damned disease." He shook his head, a note of despair in his basso voice. "The *damned disease*."

Dolph let it sit, let the idea sink in and simmer. After all it was a powerful tool. Powerful in the sympathy it placed in the caring hearts of others. But also powerful in ways that were closer to Dolph's long-since-hardened heart. For he knew of things unknown to the general public. Confidential details direct from his detestable sources. Privileged information of the calculated manipulation and even alleged propagation of the disease. Information to which he'd sworn secrecy and had kept to himself ever since. Information that—compromised—would all but guarantee him certain death. Information that—

"Wu's passing was a shock," murmured the Chief.

"I know," said Dolph. "Such a great man."

"Aye, he was. A tragedy. Far too soon." The Chief looked inward, the sentimentality of it sinking in, Dolph's intent taking hold. "You know I first met him many years ago, back before he was a vice minister. Back when..."

And there they sat for the next two hours: commiserating, reminiscing, laughing, and—on the part of Dolph—scheming. He would refrain from pushing too hard. He would ask only the right question at the right time and let the old guy spill his unguarded guts. He would gather what he could, bit by bit, and file it in the appropriate portion of his mind. Anything that could be of use. Anything that could help him achieve his ends. And when the day was finally done, he'd indeed gathered a sizable amount—certainly enough to get started.

And now that he had the Chief to all intents and purposes at his disposal, even more was undoubtedly within reach. Yes, it was the dawn of a new day in Dolph's world. He would of course have to remain cautious. And he would have to continually overestimate. But it was all well worth the risk. For today Security Chief Montgomery Drusher and his nightmare of a life had already begun to move Dolph one significant step closer to his dreams.

CHAPTER FIFTEEN

"Yes!" barked Bronson. He clapped his hands and flopped back onto an awaiting seat, letting out an uncharacteristic giggle. "I got him!"

"Got him," mumbled Magnus, stirring from a nap on a couch at the east side of the office. "Go get 'im."

Bronson swung his chair around to face his friend. "Magnus!"

Magnus didn't budge—just lay there blissfully oblivious to it all.

Bronson tried again. "Magnus!"

Magnus twitched, then fought his way out of a snore. "Huh?" He rolled to his side, rubbed the sleep from his eyes. "What?"

"I got him."

"Who?"

"Ryder."

Magnus's lids widened. "You got him?"

"Yup. Right here." He pointed at the computer screen rife with days of data. "Kaiden Ryder, jailed in DeWinton Borough."

Magnus sat up, gathered himself. "DeWinton? Why that's only a couple of boroughs over. He's right here in the —wait... Jailed?"

"Yup."

"When?" asked Magnus.

"Early this morning. They booked him. Entered him into the system—a first for our friend it seems, and a lucky break for us," said Bronson. "But here's the thing, they released him after only a couple of hours."

"What?"

"Yup."

"Place of residence?"

Bronson read some more of the report. "Just says, 'Inner Rim, Suspended City.'"

Magnus flopped back onto the couch. "Not a lot of help there."

"Yes, but this is good. He's now in the system. We caught a break. It's what we've needed. And you know as well as I do we've tracked people down on a lot less than this."

Magnus heaved himself up again. He stood and stretched. "No, you're right. It *is* good. It's more than we had an hour ago."

He approached the glass wall that faced DeWinton Borough and peered out into the panorama bordered by the vast scarlet space. "Just where are you my little friend? And what the hell are you up to?" He turned to Bronson. "What was he arrested for?"

"Hang on." Bronson scanned the screen. "Looks like trespassing. But the charges were dropped. A Chancellor Chung's office filed a formal report." He scanned some more. "Apparently he was a guest of the Chancellor's. Looks like this guy's got more than one friend in high places."

A grin formed on Magnus's face, highlighting the scar

that ran from his chin to the corner of his lower lip, a souvenir from an encounter with a rival's blade during a retrieval mission on Pritheous IV. "I don't doubt that. But what now?"

"Not sure. Maybe a trip to DeWinton." Bronson peered in the direction of the borough in question, thought for a while. Then: "You know this Chancellor?"

"I know *of* him. Never met him though."

Bronson lifted himself and strutted across the floor. "Well, I betcha a thousand credits he knows *of you* too, which could prove helpful." He stopped beside Magnus, took in the view of the borough with him. "One of the perks of being in the good graces of a lord I guess."

"Good graces? That's a bit of a stretch."

"A bit? Probably a lot."

They both had a laugh. They needed it. Magnus had all but given up hope. And even Bronson, typically unshakable, had been feeling the pressure of late having spent every day since his arrival combing the Conglomerate's systems. But now this, a solid clue. And not being one to waste time, Bronson was back. Like a Vietrusian bloodhound, he'd caught a whiff and was itching to get on with the hunt. "Could you put in a personal transmission to him? Worth a try. Could save us a lot of time and trouble."

"Hell of an idea."

"What about a live one?"

Magnus nodded. "Even better. Computer?"

"Sir?" said the computer.

"Put in a request to speak with Chancellor Chung of DeWinton Borough—a live transmission, please."

"Yes, sir."

"And mark it 'Urgent.'"

"Of course, sir. One moment."

The computer whirred away, its lights flickering as Bronson made his way over to the map of Greater Amana Empire that hung on a nearby wall. DeWinton Borough lay midway between Ruechestire and Amana Proper where the Empress resided. This was good. Kaiden was close. Bronson studied the map even closer, gears in his head now awhirl.

The computer's pitch changed to one Magnus knew well. It was the sound of an incoming transmission—a live one. "Ah," said Magnus. "Sounds like we're in luck!"

"Sir, your request has been granted," said the computer. "Chancellor Chung stands ready to receive."

Magnus smiled at Bronson. "Please transmit."

"Certainly, sir."

An image of the Chancellor faded onto the screen. His hairless face and head surrounded a pair of squinty chartreuse eyes. An auburn robe stretching from the fitted neckline clear to the floor draped his round body. He stood respectfully erect, dipping his head toward Magnus. "Lord Magnus of Ruechestire, I'm pleased to finally meet you. Albeit by transmission."

"And I you, Chancellor," said Magnus, too dipping his head. "Thank you for responding, and for your promptness."

"The pleasure is mine. You caught me at a good time. Occasionally I have one."

Magnus smiled. "I'm afraid I know just what you mean."

"Yes, I'm certain you do." Gauging the pleasantries had served their purpose, the Chancellor got right to it. "To what do I owe the pleasure on this fine day, Lord Magnus?"

Magnus was unprepared. He cleared his throat. "Yes, of course. Well, frankly, I'm searching for someone. A friend of mine, actually, whose whereabouts has become of vital importance. And we have reason to believe that you've recently been visited by him."

"I see," said the Chancellor. "And what does this person call himself?"

"His name is Kaiden Ryder," said Magnus. "He was rumored to have—"

An involuntary chuckle burst from deep within Chung's belly, followed immediately by the realization of the offense and an effort to quickly right the wrong. He adjusted his collar and composed himself.

Magnus took note, then brushed it off as best he could and continued. "Well, you see, this Mr. Ryder was rumored to have attended an—"

Another involuntary interruption. But this time the Chancellor suppressed it much more quickly. "Oh my," he said, the uneasiness in his eyes impossible to disguise. "A thousand apologies. Please, do continue."

Magnus did, but much more cautiously this time. "Well, as I was saying, we have reason to believe he attended a gathering of yours and—"

Again with the chuckle.

Magnus looked to Bronson. Bronson shrugged his shoulders, standing off screen and out of Chung's view. They looked back and watched as the reaction grew in intensity, building to its final culmination of an outright snorting fit. It was off-putting to say the least, but Magnus and his flawless decorum stood as politely as possible and merely waited for it to subside.

Chung raised a chubby hand in the direction of Magnus while the other steadied his bouncing belly. And when he'd finally calmed himself enough to speak, he removed a matching handkerchief from his robe's sleeve and dabbed the perspiration from his forehead. "Oh, I do beg your pardon," he said. "How horribly rude of me. Mortifying. I mean you no disrespect. You see, it's just that... Well, how shall I put it?"

But Magnus had already begun to put it together. For he was well aware of the effect Kaiden had on others and this was likely what he'd left in his wake, the aftermath of his extraordinary influence. So how could he be offended?

Magnus smiled—a huge, disarming smile—and did what he could to reduce the discomfort. "Not to worry, Chancellor. No need for apologies. So, I take it you *have* met him then?"

Chung heaved a sigh and dropped his shoulders, observably relieved by the sentiment. "Indeed I have. And what a delight it was, I must say. At one point he had me in utter stitches. A truly unique young man. And his music— breathtaking."

Magnus nodded. "It is indeed."

Bronson, having grown tired of the exchange, shook his head and impatiently shifted his stance. After all, he had a mission to complete and this was all far too formal for him. So now that the facts had been confirmed, he stepped forward into the Chancellor's view and cleared his throat.

"Ah. Yes, of course," realized Magnus. "Chancellor Chung, may I introduce to you an associate of mine? This is—"

"Oh my," said Chung, again erecting his body. "Bronson Decker. Reputed as one of the Conglomerate's very best in intelligence." He wiped some more freshly sprouted sweat from his face and again returned the handkerchief to the sleeve. "Well, I can see you've certainly brought in the big guns on this fine day, Lord Magnus."

Magnus smiled and was about to respond when...

"Honored to meet you, Chancellor," said Bronson, eager to get on with things.

Chung tilted his head. "The honor is mine."

Bronson caught Magnus's attention. "Lord Magnus," he said, gesturing to the Chancellor. "May I?"

Magnus moved aside, a smirk betraying his amusement at the formal address from his friend. "Please."

Bronson moved in closer to the screen. "Chancellor, did this Ryder give any indication of where he was headed?"

"He did."

Bronson's eyebrows rose. "Oh? And where was that?"

"He said he was going home. But if you're going to ask me where home is for our friend, I'm afraid I haven't an answer for you." His face tensed. "Is he in some sort of trouble?"

Magnus chimed in. "Quite the contrary, Chancellor. I can assure you he's done nothing wrong. And although I'm unable to elaborate, I *can* tell you that finding him could possibly save lives."

Chung stood silent for a moment, his attention reaching back to the evening in question. "You know, I'm not surprised. There's something remarkable about him. I noticed it right off. Please, how may I help?"

Magnus looked searchingly at Bronson.

Bronson immediately shifted to interrogator. "How do you know him?"

"He performed at a social function of mine."

"And before that? Did you know of him?"

"No, only just met him that evening."

"I see. Was his performance pre-scheduled?"

"It was."

"Who scheduled it?"

"My assistant. He was in charge of the event. You see,

he'd attended a recent concert hosted by Empress Amana. He was in search of talent for hire. The concert showcased several artists from the Conglomerate. That's how he came to know of our Mr. Ryder."

"Go on," prompted Bronson.

"Well, after the concert, he'd hunted Mr. Ryder down and offered him the job. Ryder accepted. It's really as simple as that."

"And the charge?"

"Oh, merely an oversight. You see, we had extra security for the event and someone mistook him for a trespasser. But once I became aware of the arrest, I took care of it myself."

"I see," said Bronson. "And your assistant? Maybe he has more?"

"Perhaps. His name is Yuly. He's here. Would you like to speak with him?"

"Yes, if you don't mind," said Bronson.

Chung summoned Yuly. Bronson questioned him as well, but Yuly hadn't much more to offer. Only a few details that didn't amount to much. So Bronson wrapped it up—though all too abruptly for Magnus's liking. Magnus made some smalltalk to restore the rapport, then thanked them for their time. They all said their goodbyes and terminated the transmission.

Magnus thought for a moment as the computer whirred down. Then: "Well, home is Suspended City. We knew that. And we now have reason to believe he's there or on his way. But it's still not a lot to go on. Big city."

"Yes," said Bronson. "But the Inner Rim narrows it down quite a bit." He considered options. Considered the digging they'd done. Scratched his head. "I think it's time we go old school, my friend. Feet on the ground. That's what I say."

Magnus looked at him. "Yeah?"

"Yeah," said Bronson. "And the sooner the better."

CHAPTER SIXTEEN

When Dolph had seen his father going over the intricacies of his Spitfire with Bronson and had overheard the reason for the briefing, he feared that Bronson would be gone before day's end. And he was right—afternoon had arrived and Bronson was long gone.

Dolph had watched Bronson from a concealed vantage as he'd loaded it up with supplies and filled it with fuel before shooting off into the mid-morning space. Not, however, before Dolph had planted a tracking device deep within the innermost layer of its door panel. As long as Bronson didn't travel too far, Dolph could monitor his every movement. But what of those movements? What would he do with the details? Or what if he *did* travel beyond the device's range? These and many more were the questions gnawing incessantly at his brain. And the meeting with his Underpath contact scheduled for the next day was weighing on him heavily as well, though less so now with the recent progress he'd made.

He was tracking the renowned Bronson Decker. He'd made inroads with his father's Chief of Security. And he was aware of a secret file for a project very likely of interest to those he was trying to impress. Straining to work out just how to access said file without raising more suspicion, however, had taken its toll in the form of a pounding headache.

One possibility was to access it by way of the bio-verifier itself directly with Drusher's palm print. But that would be tough to pull off undetected. And even if he could, who knew if his father had even granted the Chief access at that level—just one of many challenges yet to face. But for now he would focus on the task at hand and take it one painfully slow step at a time.

Dolph sat perched atop his bed dusting off the remote receiver, the mate to the Spitfire's transmitter. It was running low and in need of a new power source.

He removed the old one and rummaged through a drawer for a cell that fit. Finding one, he inserted it, then secured the cover and powered up the device. The lights on the panel flickered as it re-awoke. It ran a self-diagnostic then lit up recalibrated and ready to go.

Dolph entered the tracking code and waited as the receiver searched. The signal locked. A light blinked and a tone sounded. "Yes!"

"Son?" said Magnus from the other side of the bedroom door.

Dolph jumped. The receiver sprung from his grip. He leapt to catch it but missed. It dropped to the floor causing the case to split and the components to scatter. "Shit!"

"Son?" said Magnus. "Everything okay? May I come in?"

"Of course," said Dolph knowing full well the door was locked.

"It's locked."

"I'll be right there," he said, scrambling to quietly sweep

the remnants under the bed. He scanned the scene, ensuring no evidence remained, then stood and slowly made his way to the door. He unlocked it and it swished open.

"Hello, Son."

"Hello," said Dolph, feigning outward composure with flawless expertise.

"Bronson's gone."

"Oh... Yes I saw you with him earlier."

Magnus smiled and playfully shoved his son. "I realize I've been distant the last few days. Thought I'd come and see how you were doing. You okay?"

"Yes. I'm fine. It's just that..."

"It's just that your father has a habit of blocking you out of his life?"

"No..." said Dolph, unable to unfix his attention from the receiver. He'd plotted, schemed, scrambled for a workable plan, hatched one, and then messed it up. So now what? What the hell was he going to do?

He attempted to center himself within, calm his thoughts. After all there was always a way and this was far from a first for him when it came to predicaments. He took a breath, a deep one, then tabled the problem for the time being.

The tension dispersed allowing him to actually see his father for the first time since he'd entered the room. "...no, I understand, Father. It's nothing."

"Well, how about now? You have some time for your ol' man?"

He didn't really, unless it could serve his plan in some way. He quickly considered options. Anything to help advance things? Any advantage to be gained?

He'd been waiting for an opportunity to plant doubt in

his father's mind as to the Chief's faculties of late—potentially helpful stuff were Dolph to find himself in a tight spot. So why not now? Yes, it was perfect and instantly became the goal of the day.

"Yes of course, Father. That would be great." He gathered himself and gestured them toward the door. "I've actually been meaning to talk to you about something. You see, I have concerns."

"Concerns?" said Magnus. "You always have concerns, Son."

"Yes, I know. But this is different. I really think you should hear what I have to say. It's about the Chief..."

CHAPTER SEVENTEEN

Dr. Hulaksen rested his hand on Chakeena's damp forehead and checked her temperature again. It was still high. And even though she'd technically come out of the coma, becoming at least *partially* conscious at times since the incident, her recovery was taking much longer than he would have expected.

That along with an array of other symptoms left him no choice but to conclude that there was more than just a bump on the head at work. Indeed, the disease must have surfaced from its dormant state and be compounding the effects. It was the only explanation no matter how hard to face.

Her breathing had shallowed, her vitals had slowed to a near stop. In fact when he'd come to check on her the prior day, he could have sworn they'd ceased completely. Luckily it had been a false alarm.

The Empress was a wreck. Her ability to compose herself in even the least trying of social situations had finally and utterly failed. And despite Hulaksen's suggestions to take a break or get some rest, she'd refused, remaining instead day and night at her daughter's side. It had forced her to all but relinquish her duties to her second-in-command, Adviser Jebdine Sherkawa, who would disturb the Empress only when absolutely necessary. Yes, the Empire and its affairs had become the least of her concerns. It would survive this. But would her daughter? Her guts churned at the very thought of it.

A knock on the door snapped the Empress out of the nightmare. Her dull stare swung to the doctor.

He nodded, "Let me get that." He removed his hand from Chakeena's forehead and headed for the door.

The Empress's heart drummed so loud that the words exchanged across the room were but a distant echo of mumbles. She returned her stare to her daughter's gaunt face, her glazed eyes struggling to focus through wells of tears.

The door clicked closed and Hulaksen made his way back to her unnoticed. "Empress," he said. "You have a message. It's from Lord Magnus."

She looked up, wisps of untidy hair escaping the gold encrusted headpiece that wrapped her elegantly aging face. "What?"

"Magnus," he said. "He's sent you a message."

The look in her eyes told him in no uncertain terms that her exhaustion had surpassed itself again and was now bordering on incoherency.

"Shall I read it for you?"

"Yes," she said. "Yes, of course. Please."

He popped the communication open and looked it over. "It says, 'Empress Amana. We've acquired some promising information as to the whereabouts of Mr. Ryder. Bronson left my estate this morning to follow up on the findings. I'm confident we'll have made contact soon. The doctor has kept me up to date on Chakeena's condition. Please give her my love. She's as tough as they come. She'll recover. I know it. Meanwhile, stay strong and I shall visit as soon as I can. All my best, Magnus.'"

Hulaksen looked to the Empress.

"Well," she said, tucking the stray strands of hair back into their rightful place, "encouraging news for a change."

"It would seem so." Hulaksen closed the transmission and handed it to the Empress. But her innate sense of security emerged, along with a measure of coherency. She motioned that he keep it.

"Erase it," she said. "We needn't any evidence floating about. It's already traveled through more hands than it should have."

She sighed and tried to stand. The doctor grasped her arm to assist. "I think I'll take your advice, Doctor. Some rest and then my duties. I've neglected them far too long already and my remaining here is not helping anything. That has become obvious."

"Of course," said the doctor. "I'll inform you of any change immediately."

The Empress bent over and kissed her daughter's colorless cheek.

There was a flinch.

The Empress shot up in shock. "Chakeena?"

Chakeena twisted. Her parched lips trembled. A raspy groan followed.

"Chakeena," said the Empress. "We're here. We're right here with you."

Hulaksen checked Chakeena's pulse. It had risen. "She should rest," he said.

"No!" snapped the Empress.

Hulaksen's stare shot up to the Empress, then dropped. He eased off, backed away and gave her some room.

"What is it, my dear?" asked the Empress. "Can you hear me? What can we do?"

Chakeena scrunched her face. Her eyelids flickered as she slowly parted them, spasms of involuntary squints fighting off the gleaming daylight. "Mother?" she finally managed.

The Empress grasped her daughter's hand, tears again welling in her eyes. "Yes, my dear. I'm here. I'm right here. What is it?"

Chakeena struggled to speak. Was unable. There was a long swallow, more groans. Then, under her breath: "Where is he?"

"He's right here," said the Empress, gesturing to the doctor. "We're both right here."

Chakeena strained to see, saw the doctor, looked back to her mother. "No," she said in a barely discernible whisper. "Where is...?"

"Who?" queried the Empress. "Where is who?"

She swallowed again, dry and labored. Then managed an answer: "Kaiden," she whispered before again drifting off into the darkness.

CHAPTER EIGHTEEN

Kaiden pushed through the well-worn door of his favorite hometown hangout, The Bar Brisk—a dingy hole-in-the-wall adjacent to the 40-story housing complex where he'd kept a planet-view unit for the last many years.

It was the scent of the place that hit him first, and with it a wash of memories followed by the murmur of a dozen drunken dialects and the ringing of *Path Patterns* being played in the back.

Gleaming golden lights flickered from the ceiling. Glasses tinkled behind the bar. A couple of locals slithered on the smokey dance floor to the hypnotic grind droning from the rows of halogen speakers suspended above them. And beyond the dancers: an empty stage. Kaiden's stage. The stage he'd occupied more times than he could count.

At the bar sat Jegge and Gehad, the Yetney brothers, having the same argument over the same stupid bet they'd made the night an entire herd of female Gumladites had come in for a good time. Both sufficiently inebriated, Jegge had bet Gehad that he could offend more of them than Gehad could. Gehad had foolishly accepted. They both wound up in the slammer, but not before an "escorted trip" to the local emergency room to patch up the incurred wounds. Thereafter the argument would be a nightly occurrence. Kaiden had grown tired of the dispute ages ago, yet tonight he welcomed even it.

"Kaiden!" shouted someone from across the room. It was the owner, Hunker, who also served as bartender and consoler to those who frequented his little Inner Rim vin joint. "Kaiden, you son of a bitch! You're back!"

A smirk sprang onto Kaiden's sleek face, pasty and featureless when weighed against the assortment of species surrounding him. He waved back and worked his way in Hunker's direction, the racket of the room bringing with it a sense of reception. He glided up to the bar and seized the nearest stool, straightening the sleeves of his black jetter-jacket as he sat. "Good to see you."

"Good to see you too, old buddy." Hunker bent over the tattered bar top and gave Kaiden a healthy handshake.

"Drink?"

"Sure. The usual."

"Yeah right, the *usual*. I don't think so. This calls for something special." Hunker reached behind the bar and pulled out a sparkly bottle filled with glowing contents—the good stuff, the top-shelf stuff. He filled a glass to the brim for Kaiden and slid it across the bar top to him.

Kaiden smiled and took a long swig of the bubbly liquid, swallowed and set it down. "Pretty good."

"Pretty good? Best vinoh in the Inner Rim!"

Kaiden took another swig and nodded in agreement as he inspected the room with a piercing sapphire stare. "Boy, nothing ever changes around here, does it?"

"Don't *I* know it," said Hunker, his slate-gray skin blending well with his baggy muslin shirt.

He had a tall frame and glistening jewelry hanging from every limb. Bright white eyes, bearded face, and a single braid trailing from the top of his otherwise hairless head.

He was a Ruthinoid whose kind customarily ran such establishments. They were the purveyors of a good time and a number of other legal activities. They also had an inherent knack for calming most species in the Conglomerate— helpful in his line of work when customers got out of hand. And they *always* got out of hand.

"So," said Hunker, directing his indelible grin at Kaiden. "How was it? Everything go as planned?"

Kaiden swallowed a sip and returned a deliberate glance. "Yes. *Everything*."

"No! The Opera House? The Empress?"

Kaiden said nothing, just nodded.

Hunker managed a whispered "Whoa."

"Even met her," said Kaiden. He paused. Looked inward. "It all happened. Just like I saw it."

"Holy shit." Hunker shook his head. He snapped up a towel and wiped down the bar, slung it over his shoulder and looked back to Kaiden. "What about the girl? Did you figure out who she was?"

"It was the Empress's daughter. The Princess."

"*She* was the mystery girl?"

Kaiden took another sip. Nodded. "Met her too. It was odd, like I already knew her." He replayed the encounter in his head, the look in her eyes and the deep, engrossing stare, then returned to the room and gulped back the remainder of his drink.

Hunker poured him another, intentionally ignoring the complaints of slow service from the surrounding patrons.

Sporadic "Hi Kaidens" and "Welcome backs" interrupted the chatter of the room.

Many approached and shook Kaiden's hand or patted him on the back. Others merely nodded in his direction as they walked by. After all, anyone who'd spent any time at The Brisk certainly knew of Kaiden, who simply smiled and accepted it all with ease. And when it finally died down, Hunker continued. "So, what's she like?"

Kaiden glanced up. "The Empress?"

"No. The *Princess*."

"I was only with her for a few minutes." He again considered the encounter. "She was powerful. Pretty. But there was something else. Something harder to describe."

"So you gonna…" Hunker stopped mid-sentence, turned to Tuny, a regular who was still scorning the service, and shot him a dagger-like glare, "…gimme a second here, would ya? I'm talkin' to Kaiden."

Tuny slurred a reply. "Yeah? Well, I spend a lot of credits in here, and…" He turned to Kaiden. "Hi Kaiden…"

Kaiden tilted his glass at Tuny.

Tuny swung back to Hunker and continue. "…so I shouldn' hafta wait for nuthin'."

Kaiden looked to Hunker. "Let me get that for him. Put it on my tab?"

Hunker nodded and went to work on the order.

Tuny tilted his empty glass back at Kaiden. "Many thanks, my friend."

Kaiden sat back, searched the room for Boomer. He'd been racing around greeting everyone in sight with a squeak and a spin and was now over at ol' Reade Rappy's table. Reade was pretending Boomer was invisible again, "searching the area" and calling out his name. It was a simple and very old game, but Boomer never seemed to tire of it. And evidently, neither did ol' Reade Rappy.

Hunker slid Tuny his drink and turned back to Kaiden. "So, you gonna see her again?"

Kaiden looked up, visibly thrown by the question. "What do you mean?"

"What do you mean what do I mean? The *Princess*. Are you gonna see her again?"

There was a brush-off of the question physically, a shrug and tightening of Kaiden's face, though mentally it had undeniably taken hold. But he soon rejected it and reached again for his drink.

Hunker stared him down and pressed on. "Wait a sec. You tellin' me you finally meet the girl of your dreams and you haven't thought about it?" He let out a playful snicker, then picked up a glass and began to polish it. "Oh, this oughta be good." He paused, prepared himself for the answer, then asked the question: "And why not?"

"First of all, she's not the girl of my dreams," said Kaiden, calmly. "She was the girl *in* my dreams. Big difference."

"Mm-hmm." Hunker stood and patiently polished. "And secondly?"

Kaiden considered the question. Dug for something. Mentally dismissed it. Then quietly said, "It's absurd. That's all."

Hunker swept his braid over a shoulder with a twist of his neck and continued. "What's so absurd about it?"

"What's absurd? She's a princess."

Hunker inspected the glass, seemed satisfied with it, picked up another one and went to work on it. Then, nonchalantly: "She married?"

"Of course not. *You* know that. Everyone knows it." Kaiden saw only Hunker now, heard only Hunker's words, the conversation having damped out the drone of the room.

Hunker continued to needlessly polish another glass, fogging it with an invisible plume of his breath from time to time as he proceeded with the line of questioning. "But you said there was a connection."

Kaiden shrugged. "Maybe there was. Maybe there wasn't."

"Nah, there's no maybe with that stuff. What did her eyes say?"

Kaiden smirked, awakening to Hunker's mischievous ways. Yes, he'd met her. And sure, there might have been something in her eyes. But she was a world away and out of his league by light years. And that was just the way it was.

He swiveled his stool, spotted the dart board in the back, looked to Hunker and did his best to deflect. "Anyone beat my score?"

Hunker flashed Kaiden a grin and let him off the hook. "Nope. You're still the reigning champ. But a couple of guys are gettin' close." He topped off Kaiden's drink and capped the bottle.

Kaiden glared at the board, took a sip and swallowed. "*How* close?"

Hunker tapped the tally board on the wall to his right and checked the list. "Grinden Haddock threw a four eighty-seven last night. And Gilly Balm's not far behind him."

Kaiden's almond-shaped eyes narrowed. "Gilly?"

"Yeah. He's been in here every night for the last week. Both have official challenges locked in. There's a wager pool too. Payout's twenty thousand and growing."

"And I'm what? Four ninety-four?"

Hunker nodded.

Kaiden swept a gaze across the sea of faces and buzzing ambience, then slowly focused back on Hunker. "Where's my tab stand?"

Hunker tapped the register's screen. Found Kaiden's account. Scrolled to the bottom. "Couple hundred." He tapped out of the register and looked up, was met with a puckish grin from Kaiden. "Why? You thinking what I'm thinking?"

Kaiden's grin widened. "I think it's time to settle the score for once and for all, don't you? And my tab too?"

"Yeah?" said Hunker.

Kaiden nodded. "Yeah. What to you wanna bet I beat it?"

Hunker guffawed. "Me? Not a chance." He lifted an arm and, with a flourish of his bejeweled limb, swept it across the room as if presenting Kaiden with a room full of treasure. "But I think you'll have your fair share of takers."

Kaiden smiled, downed his drink. "It's settled then. Do it."

Hunker shot him a wink and reached behind the bar, killing the music with a swift twist of a dial. And as the murmur slowly quieted and the attention of the patrons turned to him, he straightened his body even taller than it already was and shouted: "Kaiden's challenging his own score. His toe-tap closes the pool. Bets placed beforehand will be accepted. I'll need an official bid to initiate. The House backs Kaiden." He smiled, let it sink in. Then: "Anyone care to officially counter it?"

Glances darted through the room as the sea of eager eyes awaited an answer. There was a second of silence, then another, broken finally by the clearing of a phlegmy throat far off in the back instantly seizing the attention of the onlookers. It was Kelso Kreed, imposing as ever seated comfortably at his nightly chair of choice, his belly occupying a sizable portion of the vinoh-stained table before him. He flopped a heavy hand down and heaved himself up, his jelly-like jowls swaying as he filled the room with a cavernous and arresting response, "Thousand credits says he can't," before promptly dropping back down to his seat.

A roar of cheer immediately erupted and waned to a wave of odds being discussed and bets being anxiously submitted to the system.

On a screen above the bar appeared the ticking results endeavoring to tally the influx of information. Kaiden glanced at it, nodded, then spun his stool and stood as the crush of patrons parted and a trail of faces led him toward the awaiting board in the back. There were factory workers and freighters, businesswomen and bondsmen, a band of Gadonian cadets freshly back from basic, and an assortment of Imperial trackers circled by credit-thirsty geishas poised to extort the trackers' earnings.

Kaiden stepped up to the case housing the projectiles and pressed a hand to its lock. A glassy panel slid aside inviting him to make his selection as it simultaneously bio-marked his identity. He turned to face the lane, its bound-aries now lined with eager observers. And as he moved toward it, he considered the stakes, adjusted his mind to the appropriate frame, then stepped into the fluorescently lit gaming square.

There would be three attempts only—no warm ups or exceptions. The clock would determine the time. The computer would interpret the results. And there would be no disputing the ruling. He tapped a foot on the toe-line, lighting it up and officially activating the challenge.

A sign above the lane announced with a glowing flash that the *betting booth was now closed*.

As he gauged the dart's balance with a bobbing of his arm, holding it pinched in his fingers and poised for launch, a roaring chant formed around him in his honor: "Kai-den,

Kai-den, Kai-den..." He activated the dart and centered it in his sights, its tip emanating a pulsing glow.

He drew back and took aim, then fired off the first shot.

Watching on from his station at the bar, Hunker's glance was suddenly drawn to the door as a man entered. Large and rugged, imposing demeanor, head shrouded in a hood. And poking from its shadows, the shape of an unfamiliar face.

The man strolled across the room and up to the bar, said nothing, his gaze firmly fixed on the crowd as they maintained their chant. He turned to Hunker and gestured for a drink.

Hunker nodded. Poured a fresh one and slid it to him.

The man took a swig and swallowed. Set the drink back on the bar and returned his gaze to the back. "That the Kaiden Ryder I've been hearing about?"

Hunker, sensing a degree of deception, remained cautious. "Who?"

The man did not buy it but showed no sign, merely smirked and said, "I heard he's good."

A thunderous cheer from the back seized their attention. Hunker looked to the board as the odds adjusted to the real-time results, then returned to the man who greeted him with a steely stare. Hunker looked deeper into the shadowy hood to get a proper read. And when his gut had finally given him the green light, he extended a hand and welcomed the mysterious visitor. "I'm Hunker. The owner."

The man's unshaven jaw tightened, cracking a hint of a smile at the curiosity in Hunker's eyes. "How well you know him?" asked the man.

"He's a friend," said Hunker, hand still extended. "A very *close* friend."

The man raised his arms and pulled down his hood, then tugged off a tattered glove and grasped the awaiting hand with a firm grip. "Name's Decker. Bronson Decker."

CHAPTER NINETEEN

The view was vast and wonderful. The cool artificial wind fluttering against Kaiden's face was working wonders on his hangover. He and Bronson, belted into the Beast and escorted by Boomer, left the limits of the city and soared in the direction of the day's destination, glistening lights flickering from the oncoming traffic as the early morning commuters whizzed by.

Navigating his way through the network of expressways, Bronson maneuvered the Beast like the pilots Kaiden had known at the track as Boomer glided alongside flawlessly anticipating their every move. Spotting their off-ramp, Bronson rolled the craft hard-left and descended to the lane below, then slowed to a stop amid the congestion...

Kaiden's trail had been a somewhat simple one to follow once Bronson had reached the Inner Rim subsection of town. Some routine investigating and a few questions to a few locals had narrowed things quickly. And a few more to a few others led him eventually to The Brisk. Secretly, the detective in him had wished for more of a challenge, but with lives at stake—and the life of a close friend at that—he was ultimately glad it had not been.

When he'd introduced himself to Kaiden, he'd avoided getting into specifics, emphasizing only that it was crucial they get back to Magnus as soon as possible. But Kaiden had insisted on a couple of drinks in celebration of his winnings before departing.

Bronson, accustomed to getting what he wants, always, was shocked at Kaiden's resolve. For no matter what means of persuasion he'd employed, Kaiden had remained unyielding in a way that was inflexible yet somehow not upsetting.

Of course Bronson always had brute force to fall back on, something he had no problem employing if needed. But his background in psychological tactics begged for an alternate approach and ultimately found one. After all, Kaiden's interest in Chakeena had become increasingly obvious as the night had progressed. And even though the mission did require discretion, time was ticking and Bronson had needed something a little more compelling. It was then that he brought the Princess into play, mentioning that the trip concerned her. And when Kaiden queried it further, Bronson simply raised an imposing brow and pointed at the door, then calmly and with sufficient conviction *told* Kaiden it was time to go. Kaiden agreed.

They threw back their drinks and headed for the Beast, but not before Bronson sent off a transmission to Magnus alerting him that they were on their way...

As Bronson was taking in the soothing rumble of the Beast's idle, his attention was gripped by a gravelly voice from above bellowing down at him. "Good lookin' machine. What isss it? A Mustang?"

Bronson swept his glare upward and to the left as his hand crept to his blaster's grip, his hawkish eyes obscured by the tinted eyewear he was wearing. He assessed the traveler, said nothing, wrapped his hand around the weapon and flicked the safety with a thumb in a stealth-like movement.

The traveler continued his inspection of the Beast. His lime-green eyes and vertical lid-blinks indicated reptilian roots, as did his skin and snout. There was a partially concealed Phantom hurling-dagger strapped to his side suggesting he was not one to be toyed with. And etched into his bony hand in radiantly glowing ink was the insignia of the Cardo militia, an offshoot of a special forces unit trained in advanced weaponry and counterterrorism. He returned his stare to Bronson and repeated the question, an inherent hiss in his snake-like diction. "The craft. It'sss a Mustang?"

Kaiden looked up. "It's a Spitfire."

Bronson slowly slid the weapon from its holster, tilting its muzzle inconspicuously up at the traveler.

The traveler gave a grunt followed by a flurry of blinks. Then nodded, still eying the Beast. "Ah yesss. A Spitfire. I see it now. Mine's a Hellcat. A '49. Had it restored."

"Nice ride," said Kaiden, studying the craft, its bone line and rocker panels confirming the suggested circa.

The traveler shrugged it off and patted the pearl-white fuselage with a clawed hand. "I guess. Getsss me to where I gotta go."

Bronson remained locked on the traveler, anticipating the conversation's course.

"Ssso..." hissed the traveler, "where you headed?"

Bronson twisted around and snapped a cold glare at Kaiden. Shook his head.

Spotting the blaster, the traveler instinctively went for his dagger.

"That would be a mistake," said Bronson as he lifted his arm and placed the beam of his laser-sights on the traveler's large snout. "Claws where I can see 'em."

The traveler cautiously complied, raised his scaly limbs as he bared his knife-like fangs at Bronson. "Listen friend, I don't know what your problem is, but you got that thing pointed at the wrong reptilian. I suggest you holster your weapon before you find yourself in a world of hurt."

"Yeah? Well, I got another idea," said Bronson. "You quit asking questions and be on your way or *you'll* find yourself in a world of *dead*? How 'bout that... *Friend?*"

The traveler growled, subdued the urge to go for the dagger, irrepressible hate now seething from its dilated eyes. It defiantly revved the Hellcat's engine and dropped it into gear, roaring it into an adjacent lane and widening its distance from the Beast.

Bronson kept the sights on the traveler and quickly scanned the area, prompting the surrounding witnesses to instantly mind their own business, then lowered the blaster and pressed the craft forward into the crush of traffic.

As Kaiden contemplated the incident, Bronson turned to him and lowered his voice. "Listen, I should've been more clear. I'm here to deliver you safely. And to do that you need to do exactly what I tell you, which means no talking to anyone. Got it?"

Kaiden nodded, but his deep-blue eyes dismissed it as nonsense.

Bronson shot a stinging glare at him to emphasize the order, "I *mean* it, kid," then swung frontward and checked his communicator for transmissions, cursing its spotty service as he vigilantly inched the Beast forward.

The traveler, maintaining his distance, glanced back at Bronson and delivered a resentful scowl. Those ahead pushed their way through the intersection and, once through, sped off into the dawning space. And Kaiden just sat back and took it all in, still internally scorning the silly overreaction.

CHAPTER TWENTY

Dolph would have preferred more evidence before presenting anything to his Underpath contact, but time had run out. The rendezvous day had arrived and there was no putting it off.

The price for prematurely opening his mouth would soon be realized in one of two ways: by rendering him a buffoon in the eyes of the entire Network or by securing him, for once and for all, the long-awaited respect of his malicious peers along with a lofty position in their upper ranks. The latter had been a dream for as long as he could remember and was the only acceptable outcome. For the Network *would* forget success, habitually in fact, but never would they forget failure. No, there would be no second chance for a first impression on the assignment entrusted him. Today would be, for better or for worse, his day of reckoning.

He'd traveled to the tenements near Old Ruechestire Square where he kept a room under a fictitious name. It was a private workplace for his most devious activities—ones so devious that engaging in them at his father's estate would be completely out of the question. He could put himself in only so much risk there and he'd already pushed it way too far, not only with his attempts to access the private file but also with the recent accusations against Drusher.

Dolph had always been vocal about the Chief's weakness with the bottle, and it was certainly not lost on his father either. But now it had been taken to an entirely new level by implying that the Chief might be more than just an inept drunk.

The idea was to plant a seed, to place a kernel of doubt in his father's mind as to the Chief's *loyalty*. A measure of recourse, an allotment of ammunition in the unlikely event that Dolph and his underhanded activities were ever compromised.

Magnus had listened to his son's concerns. But with nothing more than a "bad feeling" and no real evidence of anything malicious, he'd promptly thanked his son and brushed it off. But all seeds begin buried and unseen. It's their nature. And all seeds as well, if nurtured, if tended to, eventually sprout and surface. And Dolph would certainly tend to this seed.

From the outside, the room blended in with all the other crap-holes in the building. From the inside, however, it did not.

The vault-grade security door Dolph had installed came equipped with biometric and voice verification as well as a separate key panel requiring a ten-digit code within seconds after the activation of the first two authenticators.

Tacked to the soundproofed wall was a map of the Conglomerate highlighting an array of various establishments, meeting sites, manufacturing plants, and other top-secret locations.

Below the map stood a comm-station strewn with

surreptitiously captured transmissions from well-known and highly sought criminals, Underpath contacts, and even heads of state.

And in the center of the room a desk with the remnants of what evidence he'd assembled on the matter at hand scattered chaotically across it.

When Dolph had first dropped the receiver, he'd panicked. But fate would soon after play to his advantage when he'd acquired a newer version with capabilities far beyond the former.

The new one had allowed him to track Bronson's transmitter much more accurately—in and of itself an improvement. But in addition to that, it also allowed Dolph to lock on and highjack the signal from Bronson's communicator enabling him to not only intercept transmissions directly from it, but even to listen in "live" within a reasonable distance.

In essence, Dolph had a full-blown bug on Bronson. Sure, its signal was spotty, rendering it unreliable at times. But a triumph nonetheless and one that had already reaped a reward when he'd been testing it and happened upon a conversation Bronson was having with someone. That someone, as it turned out, was one *Kaiden Ryder*, finally solving the matter of the mysterious word.

The conversation had lasted only a few minutes before he'd lost the signal, and had revealed very little else besides a bunch of indiscernible background noise. But connecting the dots between Kaiden and Project Vivace put Dolph one giant step closer to the goal and would provide additional evidence for his peers.

Dolph had regained the signal and had continued to monitor into the night, though it was ultimately uneventful. Morning, however, had been the bearer of yet another gift: A transmission to his father stating "the 'package' had been acquired and would be delivered before the day's end."

It had been crackly and hard to distinguish at first, but the computer had cleaned it up for him. It was significant in that it offered an option completely unlooked for. It not only told him where Bronson *was*, but where he *was going*, which was no small thing. An advantage to be sure, though just how exactly he could profit from it did not immediately present itself.

He'd racked his brains for hours before it finally hit him: What if he could deliver this Kaiden character straight into the hands of his associates? What if they could intercept and obtain the coveted "package" before it even reached his father? And on top of that, what if he could throw in Bronson Decker for good measure? It might be just enough to finally seal the deal and secure his status, so was certainly worth proposing.

Dolph worked quickly to assemble a summary of his findings. And as he did, he became more delighted with himself. For the list, when viewed as a whole, had shaped up to be more impressive than he'd previously realized:

INTELLIGENCE REPORT:

1. Lord Magnus Rue, ex-Secret Service, sets up secured file (contents unknown); name: "Project Vivace"; assigns "TOP SECRET" status;
2. Rue corresponds with (at least) two other prominent government figures regarding Project. (Transmissions encrypted and therefore content unknown; mere fact of correspondence indicates significance and scope of operation);

3. Rue engages private investigator Bronson Decker, ex-Secret Service, highly decorated, to work Project;

4. Decker fired off into field; purpose of mission undetermined;

5. Network Operative plants tracking device prior to Decker's departure; successfully captures signal, monitors movements; surveils exchanges; records transmissions;

6. Decker accomplishes mission; identity of objective revealed to be one "Kaiden Ryder" (reason for acquisition as yet unknown);

7. Intel: discussions digitally captured and secured;

8. Intel: transmissions intercepted; route and destination of targets revealed;

9. Intel: transmitter undetected; targets CURRENTLY en route, *remain trackable*;

10. Operative proposes: Immediate interception and acquisition of targets based on intel herein.

Dolph snickered. He might just pull this thing off yet!

The door buzzer squealed. He froze mid-breath, heart skipping a beat at the thought of the visitor. He slowly swept his stare to the security screen. Yup, ready or not, it was time.

He reached over and stabbed the intercom button—"One moment"—then darted over to the door. He took a breath, calmed himself as he disarmed the system. The pneumatic door unlatched with a clank. "Come in," he whispered.

The contact grunted as it ducked its head and stumped into the room, the accompanying stench following close behind.

Dolph gestured for it to sit, rearming the door behind him. "How are you?"

It said nothing, merely limped into the room and sat. Creaks from the chair broke the silence as it strained under the weight of the enormous occupant slumping into it.

Though tempted, Dolph refrained from bringing up the injury again. At their last meeting he'd noticed the limp had gotten worse. He'd been curious. He'd asked about it. It was a mistake.

Neither was addressed by name. They'd been assigned aliases and used only those in correspondence and in-person encounters. But each was well aware of the other.

Dolph was known because of his father and the creature because of its crimes. And although it was one of the most-wanted criminals in the Conglomerate, it yet remained at large—undoubtedly due to its unscrupulous contacts in the Imperial Council.

The creature bore scars of all shapes and sizes on its oversized body parts, its matted coat housing a whole host of filthy and parasitic insects.

The patina of the copper breastplate strapped to its chest boasted of victorious battles with blaster scorching from fruitless though undoubtedly valiant attempts at its life. And the weapon hanging on its hip, a sawed-off plasma pulse rifle smeared in blood and seared by lasers strikes, somehow surpassed the odor of the animal with the pungent scent of rancid gun oil exuding from it.

Everything about it screamed quintessential Klanu, an abomination of a species and one of the most loathed in the parsec. Its name was Grivel Gromme, and it was an evil, evil creature.

Part Four

THE AMBUSH

CHAPTER TWENTY-ONE

Grivel let out a room-shaking roar! The stench of his breath permeated the room as the guttural sounds that followed dissipated. He shifted in the chair, again testing its limits with his overwhelming burden. Then, even louder: "*Damn it!*"

Dolph froze, speechless, gulped back a gag from the odor. Beads of sweat sprung from his finely defined brow. A twitch in his arm grew to a tremble. He instantly decided he liked the silent Grivel better.

Dolph had given Grivel the list of findings. Grivel had begun to look it over when all of a sudden, this. What the hell was wrong? This was good news. Good intel. What could possibly be so upsetting?

The creature's eyes went red. It looked up, knifelike glare thrusting at the heir apparent's very being. "How accurate is this?"

Dolph scrambled mentally. "Is something wrong?"

It snorted a couple of times.

Dolph instinctively stepped back.

It snorted some more. Or was that its *laugh*?

"You tellin' me you have Bronson Decker's location?"

Still wary of the reaction, Dolph replied with a tentative, "Yes."

"Right now? You have him bugged?"

"Yes, that's right," said Dolph.

"And you know where he's headed?"

Dolph nodded, "I have the transmission to support it."

"Right now," the monster confirmed. "You have his *current location*?"

"Yes," said Dolph.

"And he's involved in all of this?"

"Why yes, intimately, actually. Listen, if I've done something to upset you I—"

"Upset me?" A flood of snorts followed. Grivel heaved back a paw and swung it at Dolph, a playful slap on the back that sent him straight to the floor and smashing into the comm-station. "That's funny," said Grivel, promptly returning to the list, a trace of drool now verging from his smacking chops. "Sonny, you just made my day."

Dolph sat up, eyes locked on Grivel, slowly stood and brushed himself off—careful to remain a safer distance this time.

It appeared as though he'd pleased the beast, which was a relief. But then, another mistake. "Why? Was there something that—"

"Why!" Another roar shook the room. "Because that *son of a bitch* gave me half these scars, that's *why*! And my leg." It bashed a fist down on the table, sending a stack of Dolph's papers fluttering to the floor. "Shoulda taken care of that son of a bitch when I had his skinny little neck in my paw."

A smirk materialized at the edge of Dolph's tightly drawn mouth. The information was good. He'd not only given the monster something of value, but something that was intensely *personal* to it. Ingenious! He took a moment to marvel at himself—a fine feeling compared to the less impressive ones he'd experienced of late. But what now? What next? What else could he do to please the beast? "So, what do you think?" asked Dolph. "You could have him by day's end."

The creature stared at the list, claw scratching at its weather-beaten beard. "Yes, you're right. I could."

"And you could do whatever you want with him. Even torture."

Grivel smiled. His breathing deepened, filling the air again with the sickening odor. He studied the list some more, pulsing amber eyes intently focused, still taking in the findings and all the potential ramifications. "Yes, I could. I could indeed. *But...*"

Grivel suddenly leapt up and plunged straight at Dolph, seizing his neck with an enormous paw, locking Dolph in a vice-like death-grip. "...I warn you right now you puny little imbecile! If this is some sort of twisted plot to impress the Network and you don't *actually* have what you say you have here, *you're dead!* You hear me? I will personally shred you to bits. Flay you like a fish. Slowly. And I'll enjoy it! You understand what I'm saying?"

The question was easy enough to answer. In fact, in Dolph's mind, he'd already answered it. But out loud was another story. He strained, fought in vain for a breath, finally opted for a nod.

Grivel let go.

Dolph collapsed to the floor, gasping for air. "Holy hell," he snapped, followed by a flock of barking coughs. "What the—?"

Grivel turned and delivered another roar! Swung a paw.

"Silence!" A claw connected with Dolph's face taking with it a sizable slice.

Dolph recoiled—obeying the order—and checked his cheek for blood. He struggled to think clearly, tough with the animal snorting down his neck. He looked to his blaster, considered vaporizing the damn thing right here and now. But even in such an enraged and irrational state he knew it would solve nothing. Not in the long run. Not if he wanted to protect the progress he'd worked so hard for. Not if he wanted out of his stagnant life of hell.

He quickly considered options. Report the monster to the Network? Something false and compromising? But to what end? Ultimately it would be his word against its, and the godawful thing outranked him by light years. Besides, it would think nothing of hunting him down when it eventually found out. And it *would* find out, of that there was no doubt. No, better to just wait. Remain alert. See what it did next and let an idea present itself. He slowed his breathing and did his best to again calm himself, keeping a close eye on the monster's every action.

Grivel again returned to the list, utterly unmoved by the inflicted injury. He sat down. Scratched at his head. Nodded. Then finally looked up. "What'd you have in mind?"

Dolph gawped at the question. It was astonishingly calm —even polite—like nothing at all had happened much less the violence. What kind of psychotic creature *was* this?

"Well?" pressed Grivel. "You have a plan?"

He didn't but had to say something, though he would be *much* more careful with his words this time. "You mean about intercepting them?"

"Yes."

"Well…" He paused, held his bloody face as he plotted, then, "…I do have some ideas but was hoping to hear what *you* thought. After all, you're far more experienced at such things than I am."

"True. Finally something smart from you," said Grivel, a brief snort accompanying the statement. "I'll of course need to act fast. If the information is accurate then there's certainly something significant here. And I may not have another opportunity like this. Bronson's no dummy. I'm surprised he hasn't already discovered the bug. Of course, maybe he has and *you're* the one being deceived."

"Good point," said Dolph. "Never thought of that."

"Figures," mumbled Grivel. "And as for my personal business with him, there'll be time enough for that *after* he's no longer of use to me or the Network. You know the old saying, 'Deity, Network, self.' Or whatever the hell it is."

Dolph said nothing, just listened and agreed. He also noted the animal's failure to include him in anything it said. Everything was "I," never "we." Somehow he had to change that. Somehow he had to work his way into its favor. Cater to its inflated ego. Let it believe *it* was in control. Stop trying to "prove" himself.

Oh, he'd of course have to gain *some* respect eventually, but that could be done by throwing in an ingenious comment from time to time—just enough to prove his worth. But only after he'd gained the acceptance. Yes, once again, Dolph would have to swallow his precious pride and put on the pretense of a moron. Excruciating. Humiliating. But a worthwhile sacrifice to achieve his ultimate goal of power. Not the revered kind. Not the respected kind. The dark kind. The kind society at large can't even imagine exists. The kind scoffed at and brushed off as nothing more than myth. The kind that...

"Yes, an ambush. That could work," said Grivel, slurping at the drool again issuing from his immense maw. He twisted at his paws, cracked his enormous knuckles. "But I'll need someone to take care of it. Better for me to remain out of the picture for the time being. And not you either. Even if you *could* pull it off, *which you can't*, if Bronson found out you were involved your cover would be blown and that would be the end of that."

"Yes," said Dolph. "You're right." Obvious, but let the animal take credit. "What if you hired someone. You know, no trail back to you or me."

"Yes," said Grivel, reluctantly. "Pretty good."

"Do you know anyone? Someone who could be trusted?"

"Bah! No one can be trusted. Not in my business." He lifted himself and paced the room. Snorted some more. "But there *is* someone. A team. The Network has used their services in the past. Idiots of course, though they've done surprisingly well. And they're as close to trustworthy as we're gonna get."

Dolph grinned. It said, "we." Oh *yes* it did! He was making progress already. And now that he had, he would do everything in his power to foster it.

They went straight to work and sent an emergency transmission to the Network proposing the plan. It was approved almost immediately. They hunted down Grivel's guys, routing all communications through the Network's encrypted system. They plotted Bronson's course, worked out the ideal interception point, and ascertained the time of impact—all while Dolph continued to cater, scheme, gulp down bellyfuls of pride, throw in an ingenious comment from time to time, and do everything possible to avoid getting himself killed.

They had the means, the time, the place, the plan, and the targets. Yes, Dolph Vaviliun Rue, heir to Ruechestire Borough, son of the great Lord Magnus Rue, apprentice to some of the darkest hearts in the Conglomerate, would deliver to the Underpath Network the legendary Bronson Decker and this mysterious Kaiden Ryder. And he would do it today.

Dolph could barely contain himself.

CHAPTER TWENTY-TWO

Chakeena's eyelids parted. Her pupils instantly constricted pulling in on them the surrounding irises so dark in color as to leave little distinction between the two.

The tightly drawn window coverings kept the bulk of the light back, but what little crept through was still far too much for her. She squinted, squeezed her face, twisted her sickly frame, tried to roll away but was unable.

Magnus placed himself between her and the window, his body acting as a giant awning obstructing the persistent bits of sun from her.

It helped. She settled.

"Chakeena, it's Magnus. Can you hear me?"

She moaned—a strong response, or at least the strongest yet. She swallowed. Cleared her throat. Then, hoarsely, managed, "It's so bright."

She spoke!

Magnus's first instinct was to shoot off and let the others know, but he instead stayed, allowing her to adjust first. "Try to relax, my dear. It'll be better in a minute."

"He's coming," groaned Chakeena. "I can feel it."

Magnus looked questioningly at her. She knew. But how could it be? Then again, how could any of it be?

Logically, the entire notion that a man or his music could in some way heal the sick was absurd. And yet, when he ignored his head and listened to only his heart, it all somehow seemed to make sense. "Yes, my dear. You're right. He is."

Her eyes, though still swollen, began to relax. She looked up at him and tried to focus. "How long?"

"A few days. You fell and hit your head."

"No," she whispered. "How long until he's here?"

He smiled. "Oh, of course. Soon enough I should think. He's with Bronson. I just sent word for them to come straight to the palace."

Chakeena heaved a sigh, dropped her head back to her silken pillow.

"Chakeena, I'm going to get your mother," he said. "I'll be right back."

She nodded, closed her eyes, was greeted by an image of Kaiden. His funny hands, the way he walked, the feeling she felt as he approached, and the draining sensation she felt as he left. *I should have gone to him afterwards*, she thought. *I should've found him. I should've—*

"Chakeena!" said the Empress as she rushed to the bedside.

Chakeena opened her eyes. "Mother."

"My dear, I'm here. And so is the doctor." She knelt and wrapped her arms around her daughter. "How are you feeling?"

Chakeena considered the question. Then: "Hungry."

The Empress took her daughter's hand. "I bet you are. I had some broth made for you. How does that sound?"

She struggled to swallow. Stretched at her neck. "Really good, actually."

The Empress looked to the doctor. "Would you mind?"

He let out a slight sigh. He of course wanted to examine his patient, but it could wait. After all, she was obviously doing better. She was awake and coherent—and even better: hungry. He returned an ungrudging glance and took off in search of soup.

Chakeena tried to sit, strained her emaciated arms. Groaned and gave way to the bed.

"What is it?" asked the Empress, her regal features displaying the toll the episode had taken on her. "What can I do?"

"I'm sore."

"Where?"

"Everywhere."

Magnus handed the Empress a pillow and slid his hands under the Princess. He lifted her. It was easy. She'd lost even more weight and was now little more than bones. "Let me know if I'm hurting you."

"I will," said Chakeena. But it was a lie. It hurt like hell, though it was not in her nature to complain about such things. And besides, this was a different kind of pain. It came with it the touch of a friend and the relief of her atrophied muscles finally getting some necessary attention. And so she welcomed it.

The Empress slid the embroidered pillow under her daughter's back as Magnus lowered her onto the bed.

"It's on its way," said Hulaksen, returning to Chakeena's side. He moved in closer. "How do you feel?"

"Honestly?" There was a thoughtful pause, a crinkle in her porcelain brow. Then: "Like I've been trampled by a Vietrusian rhino…"—the sentiment interrupted by a light chuckle and a subdued cough—"...then chewed up and spit out because it didn't like my taste."

Hulaksen and Magnus laughed. Her sense of humor, though rarely expressed, was intact—another positive sign.

A young servant in a hooded robe arrived at the door. "Some broth for the Princess?"

"Yes," said the Empress. "Come in."

"M'lady." The servant glided across the room pushing a wheeled tray, a crisp tablecloth draping down its sides with a steamy bowl perched above.

The scent trailed behind and caught up, worked its way to Chakeena, filling her nostrils and moistening her mouth. Her eyes brightened. "Mia. It smells delicious."

Mia smiled and knelt beside Chakeena, her crystalline eyes of blue held downward, then scooped up a spoonful and allowed it to cool before pouring it through Chakeena's lips.

Chakeena's face cringed as she swallowed, suppressing the pain as best she could.

The servant fed her another, then another—allowing each spoonful to cool before carefully placing it in the Princess's mouth—slowly filling the void in Chakeena's shrunken stomach, her pangs easing up with each swallow. She nodded to keep it coming but the doctor stepped in and cautioned her against too much too fast.

Chakeena took heed, looked up at the servant. "Thank you, Mia. That'll be all."

"M'lady," said Mia. She bowed her head and started to stand, a golden lock of hair escaping her hood. She quickly tucked it back and turned to leave.

Chakeena reached for the servant's robe, attempted to clasp its rich wine fabric, but was unable. Her hand fell to the bed. She coughed. Then: "Mia."

Mia stopped. Turned back. Straightened her stance. "Yes, m'lady?"

"Your niece. Whatever became of...?" There was more coughing. She stifled some of it. Gathered herself, continued. "...What name was she given?"

Mia's demeanor softened, head dipping even further. "Oh, m'lady," she said, reluctance in her tone, "her name is Keena Rose."

"Keena?" said Chakeena. Her head tilted curiously.

The servant smiled. "M'lady, she was named after *you*. In your honor."

Chakeena looked inward, the corners of her mouth lifting as she settled into the idea. "Why that's... That's beautiful." She closed her eyes, tears pressing out from beneath her lids as the notion of a child of her own someday now seemed even more out of reach.

"Oh, m'lady, I do hope I haven't... I mean... I meant no offense. I humbly beg your—"

"On the contrary, Mia." Chakeena opened her glossy eyes, a glint of pride now residing in them. "I'm truly honored by it."

Mia again dropped her head. "Thank you, m'lady. Grace to Ijo." She glanced up briefly, a moment of eye contact, then turned and left.

Chakeena watched the servant walk away and in a whispered tone to herself, said, "Grace to Ijo." She looked to her mother. "May we send a gift?"

The Empress gave a single nod, her own eyes also betraying the welling of a tear.

Magnus moved in to comfort the Empress as the doctor stepped up and began his examination. He poked and prodded, closely surveying her condition as the liquid gurgled its way through her famished body. "What do you remember?"

Chakeena tensed. "Nightmares."

The doctor nodded. "And before that?"

She strained, considered the question. "I don't know. I can't really recall much of..." But then she did. And when she did, she wished she hadn't—the memory forcing on her a swift and stern reminder of the atrocity. "The Vice Minister." She fought back a gag. "I remember the Vice Minister and... His death."

The doctor frowned. That she remembered was of course good. *What* she remembered, however, was not. "Yes, Chakeena. A terrible loss." He gently took her wrist, gauged her pulse. "Do you remember anything else?"

"I was upset. I must have fallen."

Though the doctor had been reluctant to get into it, he did need to know how much memory she'd retained. But she seemed okay. Better than okay, actually—given what she'd just been through. And based on the other initial evidence, it appeared this bout with the disease had eased off too, probably returning to Chakeena the strength to overcome the coma.

Two times of late her affliction had raised its head and roared. And two times it had retreated. About as medically out of the ordinary as he could imagine. He was again understandably in awe. "Well, it looks like you're doing quite well, everything considered. Are you tired?"

"I feel weak. I slept enough though, don't you think?"

"Yes, I suppose," he said. "But even still, it would be good to get as much rest as you can."

"I understand." She looked up to the doctor. "Promise you'll wake me the minute Kaiden arrives?"

The Empress's attention swung to Magnus.

Chakeena saw it and cleared her throat. "Mother, he

only confirmed what I already knew. Will you please wake me?"

The Empress lowered herself and placed a kiss on Chakeena's forehead. "Yes, of course, my dear. I promise. For now we'll let you rest."

Hulaksen worked his way to the hall. The others followed. The Empress had just closed the door behind her when she heard the shriek. They all rushed back in. "What is it? What's the matter?" asked the Empress.

Chakeena lifted herself. Glared at her mother, terror now residing in her ink-black eyes. "Mother! He's in danger!"

The Empress dropped to her daughter. Grasped her hand. Squeezed it. "No, my dear. There's nothing to worry about. It's okay. You just need to rest. I promise I'll let you know the moment he arrives."

Chakeena locked onto Magnus—a knowing, impassioned look. "Magnus, he's in danger. I know it. He's—"

"No, he's on his way," said the Empress. "I can assure you."

Magnus remained engaged with Chakeena. Saw her certainty. Felt the conviction.

The Empress observed the exchange and visually queried Magnus. He returned a somber glance, urging the Empress to refrain from challenging her daughter on the point.

The Empress nodded and backed down, stroked her daughters hand.

Chakeena shifted her glare back to her mother. "Yes, Mother. He *is* on his way. But he's also in danger."

CHAPTER TWENTY-THREE

The larger of the two Quadladrites sat fiddling with his X-5000 War-Forged Phase Rifle. He'd run its self-diagnostic sequence too many times to count. He'd loaded charge after charge into its blasting chamber only to then power it down and charge it up again at a different setting: warn, stun, maim, kill, and now, vaporize—a completely unnecessary act with no purpose beyond the desire to hear the whine of the weapon as it primed itself to fire.

He'd field stripped it, reassembled it, then field stripped it again many times over, each time inspecting its guts for even the slightest flaw. He'd drooled over and polished its surface until it shined brighter than any star in the brilliant space above, and then polished it even more, stopping only to admire his reflection in the glaring muzzle, slick his heavy mane to perfection, and confirm just how well the years had indeed treated him—if he did say so himself.

He was a vain, stocky-turned-somewhat-plump beast who, though undoubtedly wanting in the brains department, nevertheless possessed the exacting patience necessary for his profession of choice. He was a killer for hire. A

hitman. More accurately, a sniper. And at that he was exceptional. His name was Gluke. And he sure did love his rifle.

Gluke and his partner Thyrro had arrived at the border
area with plenty of time to spare. They'd parked their van in
the perfect spot to view those entering the Empire. They'd
set up a path-block just beyond the border which stood
ready to remotely activate in the *extremely* unlikely event
that Gluke were to miss his mark. They had the frequency to
the bug, had bribed the border guards to "not see nuthin',"
and had been closely tracking with malice aforethought the
targets for the last hour. More accurately, Thyrro had been
tracking. Gluke had been driving Thyrro nuts with *that
godforsaken rifle!*

"Gluke!" barked Thyrro, at wits end. "*Please!*"

Gluke flinched and let out an instinctual hiss sending
down the flap of his saggy jowls a stream of pungent slob-
ber. Then, *yet again*, played dumb. "What!"

Thyrro sighed, rolled his amber eyes in his ape-like
skull. "Just knock it off for a while, would ya?"

Gluke glared back as the rage flowed into his chest. It
was what he felt to any challenge from foe *or* friend. But
Thyrro just strengthened his stare and, with a haughty lift of
an eyebrow, firmly repeated himself: "I said *knock it off*. And
put that damn thing back in stun. Don't want you screwin'
this up."

It wasn't the words that so sobered Gluke. It was that
eyebrow. For it alone conveyed more threat than any rifle
he'd ever fired. And he'd fired them all. He of course denied
ever having taken the precious weapon *out of* stun. But the
eyebrow rejected the lie and once more commanded
compliance. Gluke reminded himself of the task at hand,
reined in the rage as best he could, and powered down the
rifle.

The van had been altered to resemble an ambulance. They'd parked it in the perfect spot for an ideal vantage. They'd squeezed themselves into some appropriate uniforms. They looked like utter idiots. The idea was to incapacitate the targets and then—being the "right medical personnel in the right place at the right time"—swoop in to save the day, rushing the targets off to the nearest "medical facility."

They had detection devices dialed in and scanning the vicinity for any local law enforcement. They had orders and a plan to deliver the targets to a predetermined location. And they had a provision on the order demanding they deliver the targets "alive or not at all," which did not mean if they killed them to then not deliver them. It meant—and it was very clear on this point—that *under no circumstances do they kill them!* And moreover, if for any reason they felt they could not accomplish the mission as ordered, they were to immediately abort without the targets ever having caught a whiff of them.

A blip from the receiver rang out. Its pitch heightened. The targets were close. "Okay," said Thyrro. "Any minute now."

Gluke dropped his hulking figure to a small opening that faced the border area. He squirmed to find a comfortable position then powered up his rifle and scanned the area through the laser scope, adjusting the sights to various travelers as they entered the realm until he was certain it was dialed in. He double and triple checked the other settings and confirmed again that it was indeed in stun.

He loaded four marker-charged cartridges into the chamber and slammed the forestock forward. The whine's pitch indicated the correct mode as the primer powered up. It also sent chills down his gargantuan spine.

"You good to go?" asked Thyrro.

"Yessir!" snapped Gluke. It was ingrained conditioning —his military discipline long since branded into his very being.

"And you're gonna mark 'em first, right?"

There was no response, just the dull hum of defiant tension.

Thyrro sighed and upped the emphasis: "*Right?*"

The silence hung heavy, clinging to the moment. Then, in a disappointed and droning tone: "Yeah, I'm gonna mark 'em first."

This Gluke was less than enthusiastic about, and for good reason. For as one of its many functions, the X-5000 had the ability to mark its target with a silent and virtually undetectable subsonic wave that would for a short period of time emit a signal.

The advantages were twofold. If you were to miss with a wave-marker you could get off another one without raising much suspicion; whereas a traditional blast at *any* setting, in the event of a miss, would surely get the intended recipient's attention.

The other advantage was that once marked one could lock on and then fire a guided blast. If the guided blast were to initially miss, a search-and-destroy feature could be activated by the shooter causing it to then pursue and deliver to that which was marked its predetermined charge level.

Attempts to evade such guided blasts were almost always futile. Sure, it was a fail-safe of sorts, which reduced the challenge considerably and thus a good portion of the fun for Gluke. But while a traditional shot alone would be so much more satisfying, the mission was vital enough to warrant the precaution.

And so Gluke complied. But there was an upside to it in

that whatever challenge may be lost with the precaution was more than made up for by the target's significance. For Gluke would not be marking just any old target. No, he would not be marking some run-of-the-mill halfwit. He would be marking and then firing upon one of the most formidable targets of his entire career: The great and renowned Bronson Cannon Decker—any sniper's dream come true. Yes, for Gluke this was far more than mere proto-col. It was personal. A quiet, lifelong goal about to finally enter his eagerly awaiting sights.

His focus sharpened, the urge to act surging deep within his massive bones.

CHAPTER TWENTY-FOUR

Kaiden watched the wide border light turn green and invite them to enter the region that possessed both the name and person of the one on his mind.

His thoughts drifted to the first time he'd laid eyes on her Empire and how foreign it had looked to him. Yet with Chakeena it was just the opposite. It was as though he'd always known her, like meeting with a fast friend after only a short time apart. And as he and Bronson drifted across the border snuggly strapped into the Beast's rumbling cockpit, he tried to rationalize just why this might be, but succeeded only in straining his hungover head without even an inkling of an answer.

Bronson had gotten a message from Magnus warning him of danger. But no specifics. Only that Chakeena had expressed a bad feeling and so thought it worth mentioning. Silly as it seemed on the surface, Bronson still took heed and acknowledged him promising added care and attention. After all, who was he to ignore a client's request. And so he'd assumed an even more alert posture and continued on with the day.

Ever attentive to his newest friend, Boomer stuck close to the Beast as she advanced in traffic. *She* moved with grace. He, however, did not. His lack of patience had him spinning and squeaking up a storm, raring to shoot off down the expressway at speeds he was so rarely able to entertain yet for some reason unknown to him was *encouraged* to on this day. And so that's what he'd done. That along with taking in the sights offered by the Conglomerate's tangled interchanges and swarms of captivating travelers. Yes, indeed, for one of his kind, life didn't get much better. And just when it seemed like nothing could go wrong on this gloriously perfect day, it did...

Boom!

Something collided with Boomer. Something powerful! The blow sent him sideways, sent a paralyzing shock through his entire structure, a bolt out of the blue followed by instant internal chaos. A muffled squeak barely made it out before he was slammed into the side of the Beast's fuselage, the ringing in his ears like rasps of screeching land-birds wholly overloading his sensory system.

His equilibrium now off, he struggled to stay afloat, to stay conscious, but was dunked immediately into a swirling blackness relentlessly seeking to hold him down. He reeled, warred against the whirling vortex, resurfaced briefly only to be drawn back in as though in the throws of a violent seastorm. He groped in vain for even the smallest scrap of an answer, his bearings now impossible to retrieve. And then, in the midst of it all, even in such a compromised state, his most innate instincts kicked in and took charge: the irrepressible urge to protect his master. He heaved with every erg of energy available to lift himself from the darkness, pulling himself from the imminent unconsciousness enough to trumpet as loudly as he possibly could a bombardment of shrieking squeals!

Kaiden's arms launched straight to his ears. That was a warning! He'd heard it before, though never as intense.

Bronson went instantly for his blaster and ordered Kaiden to the floorboards as he visually swept the area for any obvious threat. Nothing on initial inspection. He zeroed in on an emergency vehicle a couple hundred meters from the path—a van parked in a rest-stop area. There was plenty of cover and medical personnel to boot. A blessing? An omen? Who knew? But with nothing more to go on it would have to do. He swung the Beast in its direction and shot off.

Movement was key now in case they really *were* in danger. Of course he still wasn't entirely convinced. All he had was a flimsy warning from Magnus and a crazed critter, and who knew what was really going on with the creature anyway. Could easily be a false alarm. After all, the damn thing had been a squeaking nightmare for the entire trip. A logistical pain in the ass and distracting as hell when it came to...

The first flicker from the van merely caught his eye. The second sealed the deal. This was indeed *no* false alarm. For if there was one thing Bronson knew, it was weapons. And before him, protruding from the vehicle directly in his line of sight and closing fast, danced the sun's radiating beams playing against the chrome of a well-polished rifle. And from the look of it, an X-5000. No doubt he was squarely in the sights of a laser scope—a perilous position at best and far from a first for *this* ex-serviceman.

He banked the Beast to the right, the groan of iron from the maneuver's crushing force permeating the cockpit. Then a jarring left, evasive instincts instilled deep in him from back in his service days. And just as he was about to drop it into hyperdrive and leave the scene long behind, three distinct pulses from the muzzle caught his eye.

"Shit!" Those were *no* blasts. They were markers. Silent, but from his distinct vantage point, unmistakably wave discharges. He'd bet his life on it. Then again if he didn't get his ass in gear he might not have the means to make such a wager. Question was: Was he already marked? Had the gunman been successful? Impossible to know until it was too late and to spend another moment on it would be a reckless waste of time. All that mattered now was his next move.

An X-5000 was a serious weapon and indicated a serious shooter. Certainly an assassin or sniper of comparable skills. Yes, he would assume he was indeed already marked. And if that were the case an escape would be pointless since the guided blast would certainly follow, and even more certain would be its success in finding its target. An alternate option was needed and fast. A nanosecond of fluttering thoughts, then... Eliminate the sniper! Don't let him get off another shot. And then pray there's only one of them up there. That was the answer. The *only* answer.

He yanked at the steering column and put the Beast on a course directly *at* the van as he raised his blaster and cocked it with a swipe of a thumb. No time for mistakes or many shots. If he didn't take this son of a bitch out soon, he'd be dead or caught—and who knew what sordid ends were behind all of this.

His arm swayed. The van bobbed in and out of the sights, the glints of gleaming chrome like a beacon lighting his way. His mind raced with a barrage of ballistics calculations as he steadied the blaster, the craft maintaining its collision course with the van. More flickers from the barrel, more evasive maneuvers.

"Damn it!" he shouted, his legs riveted to the cockpit's side-panels as he corrected his course and braced himself for the coming recoil. He stabilized the sights and waited as they swung by the glistening rifle, then took a chance by way of one lone, hopeful, deafeningly loud shot!

CHAPTER TWENTY-FIVE

[A Few Minutes Earlier]

"You see him?" asked Thyrro.

Gluke gulped. "Holy crap." He pulled back from the scope to inspect his paw. At first he thought he was imagining it, but he wasn't. His trigger-claw was actually trembling, clicking away at random intervals on the rifle's glaring chrome—a first for him in his long and menacing career. He shook his mane and pushed back to the scope, watched as the target-of-a-lifetime came into focus in the crosshairs. "Bronson Cannon Decker. You sorry son of a bitch."

"Unless you miss!" snapped Thyrro. "Then *you'll* be the sorry one."

"Ain't gonna happen," spit Gluke, his eye remaining glued to the lens. "Not this one."

"Yeah, well you just make damn sure. We need a hit. A sure thing." Thyrro slurped at the thought of it. "And if you can pull that off, you'll be one *rich* son of a bitch!"

Gluke grunted something about the money not mattering this time. Then: "Only problem is…"

A scowl formed on Thyrro's face. "What?"

"...they're in a turbocraft."

"Huh?"

"Yup. Old school. A Spitfire, from the looks of it. Sweet ride, actually. But... Well... You know."

"Yeah," scoffed Thyrro. "Looks like you got your work cut out for you then."

Gluke heard him but was far too absorbed to respond. The craft presented a problem all right. Its sheer speed alone was a formidable deterrent, much less the maneuverability. But the real issue was its propulsion system. While your everyday e-pod could be immobilized with a simple electromagnetic pulse placed pretty much anywhere in its vicinity—a no-brainer for someone with Gluke's skill set and rifle features—the Spitfire's turbine was powered by an internal combustion engine and old-school analog components. And although its ancient design did employ *some* minor digital modules to run, they were not its weakness. So to shut it down would require something much more strategically placed and much more powerful than a mere muzzle-pulse in its general direction. And it *would* need to be stopped. For if it weren't there was an excellent chance it could shoot off with the "neutralized" prize in its cockpit, and that was unacceptable.

Gluke zoomed in, scouting for soft spots—anything to remove unnecessary improvisation or uninformed judgement calls. He studied the craft closely, inspecting its turbine—now larger than life in his lens. The fan blades were probably the answer: Slow it down quick with minimal risk of an explosion. But it would require a shot straight down the snout and that was not a viable angle at present. The guide vanes could work too if they were exposed. He zeroed in on the side of the hull and was delighted to find them peeking out from the Beast's underbelly—slivers of static metal catching just enough light to give them away, all unguarded and ready for the taking. That was it. That would work.

His plan B now in place, he swept the scope back to the primary target and was readying himself for the main event when…

He squinted and backed away from the scope. Blinked a couple of times, wiped it, then went tightly back onto it. "What the…?"

At first he thought there was a bug on the lens or that he was seeing things. But he was not. There was something else out there, something buzzing around Bronson. He zoomed in even closer to reveal yet another problem: Some freaked-out rodent was freakin' out right in his line of fire.

"So, how's it look?" asked Thyrro.

"Not great."

"What's not great?"

"Don't worry about it."

"Whatd'ya mean don't worry about it?"

Gluke grimaced, twisted the scope's elevation dial one click clockwise. "There's some kind rodent in the way."

"Pfft! Waste it! Who cares about—"

"Shut it!" barked Gluke. "I'm tryin' to concentrate here."

Thyrro glared at Gluke, a low, rumbling growl accompanying it—considered grabbing him by the mane and slamming his skull into the side of the van for such a contemptuous response, but then reminded himself it was neither the time nor the place, and so resisted.

Gluke blocked out the surroundings and put his attention on the contents of the scope, his trigger-claw now as erratic as the obstructing rodent. His synthetic heart, installed necessarily when he'd taken a direct hit to the chest some years back, was getting a workout too, the blood now thumping in his ears like a pounding war drum. He steadied his paw, fixed the X-5000 on Bronson, then waited for the rodent to flop out of the way, which it would *have* to do eventually the way it was dancing about. And then he'd have his shot.

He calmed himself, slowed his thoughts, and focused in on the task at hand as a soothing sense of purpose crept over him. And finally, after what seemed like an eternity, the rodent zipped out of the line of fire leaving the target cleanly exposed.

It was Gluke's chance and he took it. "Yes," he whispered as he squeezed the trigger and launched the first marker. But no sooner had he done so than the rodent flipped back and Gluke could do nothing but watch it take the full brunt of the wave. The whispered curses that followed were many, and more vulgar than usual for Gluke.

Thyrro leapt up. "What!"

Gluke ignored the question and remained still, keeping an amber eye pressed tightly to the scope. The rodent— again blocking the target—continued to freak out but much more so now. Gluke kept his cool and checked the status of the shot. Yup, it was marked all right—and *obviously* not liking it. "It's gonna give us away," he said under his breath.

Thyrro remained locked on his partner. "What the *hell's* happening?"

"Just wait."

What followed would determine the next course of action. If Bronson failed to put two and two together, Gluke would just wait for another chance to mark him. If, however, Bronson were to catch on, Gluke would have no choice but to secure the hit at whatever cost—orders from the higher-ups be damned. He suspected he knew the answer but would await confirmation. Deafening silence ensued, until...

The rodent at last let out a cascade of ear-piercing squeals that could be heard clear to the van and beyond!

Bronson went straight for his blaster, confirming the jig was indeed up. It was now time to take this ex-serviceman out!

Gluke remained trained on his target and the now darting craft. He fired off the remaining markers as quickly as possible, then backed off the scope and, in a flurry of motion, loaded a succession of live rounds into the chamber.

He squished his eye back up to the scope to check the status of the markers, only to be met with the business end of Bronson's blaster leveled straight at him. "Shit."

The flare of a single shot lit up Gluke's eye through the scope's lens. He jumped back. "Incoming!" The blast exploded through the side of the van and tore into Gluke's shoulder, a wash of cobalt blood spattering the walls in a symmetrically spiraled motif. "Damn him!" shouted Gluke. "I'm hit!"

Thyrro's response came in a stream of emphatic obsceni-ties as he was thrown to the floor.

Gluke shot up, darted across the van to a window, then pressed his back against the wall as his shoulder began to go numb. He paused a moment, mumbling some sort of Quad-ladritic prayer, then spun around and searched out Bronson in the scope: Tough target. Evasive maneuvers. No time. He let loose a rapid volley of shots as another of Bronson's blasts rocked the van.

"Shit!" Gluke had to get it together and quick. He pulled back and took cover, held his fire for a moment and summoned the extent of his skills. All he needed was one hit. The *right* hit. This was his world; this is what he knew. And now it was time to deliver. He lurched back to the window, steadied himself, and lowered his eye to the scope.

The target, clear in his sights and still charging straight at him, appeared to be reloading. That was good. That would help—a momentary reprieve from the chaos. He calmed himself. Slowed his breathing. Took a moment. Purposefully placed his now-steady finger over the awaiting trigger and squeezed the take-up slack till it rested on its firing wall. He centered the crosshairs on Bronson's chest, gauged the tactical factors, and exactingly monitored the movements as time yet again creaked still. He was ready. Everything was in place. It was now or never. One last scan of the scene; one more second to be sure, then: "Take this you slippery son of a—"

Boom!

The muzzle flash lit up the van, the shot's compression wave rippling through the vehicle as the audible fallout eventually diminished to silence.

Gluke waited—unmoving, unbreathing—then slowly backed away from the scope and exhaled.

Thyrro, who hadn't stopped cursing the entire time, finally did. "What! What is it?"

"Holy mother of—"

"*What!*"

Gluke dropped the rifle and shrunk to the floor, a stream of blood issuing from his shoulder. He flopped a paw on it, applying pressure to the wound, then looked up to Thyrro with eyes already glazing over from the loss of blood. "I got him."

Part Five

THE SCIENCE

CHAPTER TWENTY-SIX

"Damn," said a young and dashing doctor as he peered down the barrel of a glistening bio-scope in a very large and immaculately sterile laboratory. A bone-white lab coat hugged his fit frame as his sharp facial features focused intently on the newfound discovery. He had shards of yellow hair sprouting from his closely shorn head. There was a lengthy scar on the back of his hand in the shape of a snake, the result of a flesh-eating-virus containment gone awry years back, his skin so pasty as to suggest little time spent outside the confines of the structure.

Dr. Joble Fedder was not a medical doctor; he was a doctor of biological sciences, a DSc, meaning he knew just about everything there was to know about living organisms —from the most micro of all bacteria to the highest evolved species in the sector and everything in between. He was one of the top scientists in the Conglomerate as well as a colleague and dear friend of Dr. Hulaksen.

Before Wu's untimely death, Hulaksen had engaged in a heart-to-heart with the departing Vice Minister. He'd asked if Wu would consider authorizing the release of his body for an autopsy and more research once he had deceased. It was not a comfortable conversation, but in the eyes of both, a necessary one. Wu of course agreed to whatever would help the cause knowing all too well the importance of it.

After Wu's passing, Hulaksen himself had performed the autopsy and had also done a battery of tests on Chakeena and Magnus, including collecting tissue samples and blood-work. With his knowledge limited to the field of medicine, Hulaksen had wanted to enlist more help, particularly someone with a background in science. Just whom he would trust with such a project were but a few. Joble, given his extensive expertise in the area, his tactful application of discretion on past projects, and the personal relationship he had with Hulaksen, was at the very top of that list.

Joble had purposely been given very little. No patient names. No context or reason for the research. No clue as to what he was even looking for or why—just the samples themselves, and the authorization to use whatever means necessary to isolate and identify what, if anything, he could that was out of the ordinary. And he'd just found a doozy.

Common to virtually everything that exists in the known universe with regard to living organisms is the hereditary material known as "DNA." Every cell in the body of every species contains it. Any individual from any given species has genetic similarities to each of the others in the group, and even particular commonalities from species to species.

It's a complex and complicated subject, but the long and short of it is that what now lay before Joble's astounded eyes was the missing piece of all missing pieces—a portion of a gene strand that until now had not existed in any test or sample or specimen or species in this or any sector known of. Yet it *should have*.

It had long been known that a genetic flaw resided in the

DNA of all organisms—a flaw that rendered them susceptible to many undesirable things, particularly disease. Yet it
had never been discovered just what the key to that flaw
was. But here it lay on this glorious morning—somehow,
someway—beneath his lens.

Joble went in for another look in case his eyes had been
playing tricks on him. But they had not been. And now that
he knew what to look for, it would undoubtedly be a cinch
to find in the other samples if it were present there as well.

CHAPTER TWENTY-SEVEN

Joble had pored over the discovery for hours before bringing it up to Hulaksen. Though it had been difficult to contain himself, he'd needed to be sure he'd done his due diligence and could provide, if possible, more than just the fact of having found it—some contextual details, some additional results, anything that may be of use. And of course, if he was really lucky, maybe even an explanation. But as it turned out, luck had not been on his side. For his "perfect" little beauty—the genetic element with the exact makeup of what had been missing on a cellular level in all biological research to date—turned out to be not so perfect after all. In fact, not by any means.

"Computer," said Joble. "New log entry."

"Of course," said the computer. "One moment."

A mechanical voice labeled the entry:

[Log entry #TX501-24, J. Fedder, DSc]

"Recording," said the computer. "Please proceed."

The doctor considered his findings, cleared his throat,

then began: "There exists at the cellular level an imperfection in all evolved humanoid species that renders the organism susceptible to a number of diseases, all of which are incurable at the time of this entry, but none as deadly or more rampant than the disease known as *Mortiferum*.

"Until now, historically, this imperfection has remained a mystery. But a partial advance has been made by this scientist with the discovery of the genetic element hereafter referred to as *JF1Kx*.

"An analogy to help illustrate could follow as such. Take a puzzle—a simple jigsaw puzzle. And let us say this puzzle is the fundamental DNA makeup of all organisms in the known universe.

"Let us further say, as an arbitrary number, that the completed puzzle is composed of one thousand pieces in total. Yet in our case, evolution has provided only nine hundred and ninety-nine. The majority to be sure, and to all intents and purposes DNA that has made for well-functioning organisms on the whole, but organisms that yet lacked something. The DNA had a missing piece. *One* missing piece.

"The discovery of *JF1Kx* is significant in that it appears to be this very missing piece—the piece the organism has lacked in its every cell all along. A perfect fit for the puzzle in every respect with only one problem. *JF1Kx*, in and of itself, is incomplete. One might say it is 'perfectly imperfect.' Perfect in that it appears to fit the genetic puzzle exactly. Yet imperfect in that it also appears to have, for the sake of this analogy, a broken corner. It's a broken piece.

"That it is the missing piece makes it likely helpful in ways not yet imagined—a virtual scientific triumph. That it is broken, however, makes it at the same time extremely unstable and, very likely, dangerous."

CHAPTER TWENTY-EIGHT

"But sir," said the computer, calmly, "I've already checked several times. I can assure you there have been no communications from Bronson Decker since—"

"Check again!" bellowed Magnus.

"Yes, sir."

Magnus had returned home. It was the best place for him. Here he had his office and its resources. Here was his headquarters. If Bronson's communicator had been down, this is where he'd come. Of course it was still possible that all was well and there'd merely been a delay or some other explanation, but the likelihood of that was slim—and that was being generous. For deep down Magnus knew Bronson would never be so careless. No, he was now convinced that Chakeena had been right. Something was indeed off. Way off.

He plunked himself down on a chair and removed his boot, the snugness of the leather resisting as he cautiously wriggled it off. He'd kicked a wall and his foot was throbbing. Worse than that he'd done it in front of Chakeena—a mistake he would not soon forget but prayed she somehow could.

Until today he'd considered himself a source of stability for her. But in light of his inappropriate fit, his fear was that now just the opposite would be true. For Magnus was not one to lose his cool. To the contrary, no political predicament in the entirety of his lengthy career had ever broken him. No conflict, campaign, or battle had shaken him in the least. Not even the loss of his own wife had succeeded in impairing him.

But this was another matter entirely: He'd found *and then lost* what may be the only known cure to the most insidious disease in the history of the Conglomerate. It was a blunder above all blunders and impossible to confront. And on top of that, he was dying. There was no denying it. The most recent relapse was the strongest yet. He would of course hide it from Chakeena for as long as he could. But it was not *his* health that worried him as much as hers. That was the real concern. It had taken Wu out. It was now in the process of taking *him* out. And next would inevitably be Chakeena.

"Sir," said the computer.

Magnus was too immersed in the regret to hear it.

The computer increased its volume. "Lord Magnus. I have an answer to your request."

He shifted his weight forward, set the problem aside for a moment, and glanced at the screen. "What is it?"

"No new transmissions have been received from Bronson Decker."

Magnus sighed and returned to the land of remorse.

The computer waited a moment, then calmly repeated the update: "Sir, no new transmissions have been received from—"

"I heard you!" snapped Magnus, hanging his head as he continued to process the situation. Bronson was the best. And if Bronson hadn't made it then...

"Sir, I have an incoming transmission from Princess Chakeena. A live one. Shall I put it through?"

The shame swelled in him as the reality of it set in. He lifted his head, did his best to shake it off, then gathered his wits and slid on his boot, his winces emphasized by the furrows on his forehead. "Yes of course. On screen."

"Yes, sir," said the computer.

Chakeena's soft voice faded into his hell. "...Magnus? Are you okay?"

Her fresh face appeared on the screen. The food had done her good. She had some color. Her cheeks were flush, her lips a blushing pink. The circles under her eyes were all but gone. Mia had given her a massage. The Empress had given her a bath. And the doctor had given her a clean bill of health, at least for the time being.

But she too had a secret. And she too would hide it for as long as she could from not only Magnus and the doctor, but also *and especially* from her mother. For even though all appeared okay on the surface, it was not. She could quite literally feel it in her bones. Yes, deep within, taunting at her very core, mocking anything and everything that even approached the realm of optimism, lurked the incessant and ever-increasing whisper of death.

"Magnus, *are* you okay?"

He summoned a smile—a suitable one from his considerable store of them, all practiced and perfected over the years for any number of occasions. "Yes of course, my dear."

"Any word?" she asked.

"I'm afraid not. I suppose I can assume the same on your end?"

She nodded, her dark eyes dropping regrettably. "Nothing here either."

They went quiet. It was awkward. "You look good," he said, breaking the silence. "I knew you'd pull through. You're a tough one."

"Yes, I guess so." She adjusted herself in her chair, her failing frame concealed by a golden robe wrapped in a wide cashmere belt. "How's your foot?"

"Oh, it's nothing. It was silly. You know, I remember back when you were a little girl how you would always—"

"Magnus, what's going on?"

The question was unnerving. And with it came even more discomfort. But Magnus evaded still. "Well, this thing with Bronson is obviously just—"

"I mean *you*. What's going on *with you*?"

This time the silence was far beyond awkward. And since he was not about to lie to her, he relented. "Yes, my dear. I know what you mean."

A soft blip emitted from the computer.

Magnus looked up. "Pardon me, my dear. Let me check that. Just in case."

Chakeena gave an understanding nod, her silken hair dancing on the elaborate neckline of her robe.

"Yes, computer?"

"Incoming transmission."

"On screen." The transmission popped up in the corner of the display, a soft glowing pulse below Chakeena's transmitted image. It was labeled: *Project Vivace, Scientific Findings. URGENT*.

Magnus hit the view button. The transmission opened. There was another blip from the computer. "Computer," said Magnus. "I have it. Looking at it now. No need for—"

"Sir, I have another live transmission. The Chief of Security. He said it's important."

"Chief Drusher?" He again looked at Chakeena. "Very well, put it through."

"Yes, sir." The hum of the computer was followed by a subtle click indicating the connection.

Drusher's voice filled the room, boomy and distressed. "Lord Magnus."

"Yes, Chief."

"I'm sorry to interrupt, but there's been a development."

"Not at all," said Magnus. "What is it?"

"It's your turbocraft, sir. The Spitfire. It's just arrived at the main gate and—"

"What? Thank goodness!" Magnus stood. "I'll be right down!"

"Well, sir, there's more," said the Chief, a despondent note in the tentative statement.

Magnus stopped dead, the relief in his stance waning as a sense of dread came in on him. He sighed. Shook his head. "Go on."

There was a moment of silence. Then: "You see... Well, it's been delivered."

"What?"

"It's been towed, sir."

Magnus dropped to the chair. Sat back and sighed. "Bronson?"

"It's just the craft," said Drusher. "There's some damage to it as well... And... There's an animal in the cockpit."

Magnus stared blankly at the screen, the significance sinking in even further.

"Sir? The driver needs you to formally sign for it."

"I got it," said Magnus. He looked to Chakeena.

"It's okay," she said. "Go."

Magnus nodded. "Yes, of course. Let me get back to you." He sat up, snapped up his coat and hobbled off in the direction of the door. "I'm on my way, Chief."

"Yes, sir."

Chakeena's image faded as the transmission was terminated.

Dolph kept his back pressed hard against the closet's wall and listened intently to the click of his father's boots limping away, the voice and the disturbed utterances dimming to a soft echo until at last the distant swish of a door silenced it all.

He poked his head out and peered down the hall, checking to see if the coast was indeed clear. It was. And so he went to work.

He first ensured the jammer was active. It was a device used to prevent detection by transmitting a frequency synchronized to the security system. He'd been using it a lot of late, having retrieved the signal while the Chief was out cold one night. With it engaged, neither the computer nor security would be any the wiser.

He'd been listening in on the conversation between his father and Chakeena. He'd heard the transmission come in. And he'd heard his father open it and then the distraction. He rushed into the office hoping this might be his chance. Was it possible it was something significant? Was it possible his father would have let his guard down just enough? If ever there were a time that would be worthy of such, this might just be it.

He stepped up to the computer, attention instantly arrested by what now lay before his eyes. It was a private transmission—wide open for the world to see. And even better, one labeled *Project Vivace*. Jackpot!

He dug in his pocket for the transfer stick, an old relic

used back in the day to manually download information. He'd gotten it from Grivel. It had been modified to duplicate the targeted data and wipe any memory from the time it was inserted until it was removed. In other words, it could copy a file, provided it was unsecured and open, and do it completely undetected.

He blew off the dust and jammed it in the port, then typed the file name and hit "copy." The transmission had attachments so it took longer than usual to download. He waited patiently, or as patiently as possible. And when it finally clicked and the blinking light went green, he removed it from the computer and deposited it back into his pocket, half anticipating the alarm to go off. But it didn't. "Yes!" he whispered. He'd done it. It was what he'd been waiting for. He mentally patted himself on the back, acknowledged the moment as one worthy of note, then quickly slunk out of the room like a stalked wildcat, an internal round of applause ringing in his head.

CHAPTER TWENTY-NINE

"...it also appears to have, for the sake of this analogy, a broken corner. It's a broken piece. That it is the missing piece makes it likely helpful in ways not yet imagined—a virtual scientific triumph. That it is broken, however, makes it at the same time extremely unstable and, very likely, dangerous."

"Dangerous," slurped Dolph.

"Sir?" queried the computer, pausing the log playback.

"Nothing!" said Dolph, reprimanding the computer for the interruption with a swipe of his anxious hand in the air. "Continue playback!"

"Yes sir."

[Continue playback: Log Entry #TX501-24, J. Fedder, DSc]

"It is the theory of this scientist that *JF1Kx* could either destroy *Mortiferum* or accelerate it, depending on many factors. Since it is the missing piece, it could potentially prevent the onset of the disease entirely, or cure it in the case of a subject who's already been afflicted. However, the fact that it is itself 'broken' could—and there is some preliminary evidence to support this—render it instead life-*threatening*.

"Therefore, the element has been named accordingly until further advance is made. 'JF' for the discovering scientist. '1K' for the analogy of a thousand-piece puzzle. And, most importantly, 'x' for the broken and potentially lethal nature of the element as it exists in its current form.

"It is the hope of this scientist that the element be restored to its complete and 'unbroken' state, in which case the 'x' could be removed from its title. Though the unadulterated element *JF1K* does remain theoretical at this juncture, it is not implausible.

"Just from where element *JF1Kx* originated in the first place has yet to be discovered, though aggressive efforts in that direction should be undertaken immediately. It is also the opinion of this scientist, which would certainly be in accordance with the hippocratic oath of the scientific communities, that extensive testing be continued in order to further substantiate these findings as well as efforts to achieve the element's theoretically perfect form.

"It is strongly advised, however, that these or any efforts be taken with the following proviso strictly adhered to: That *no* testing on live subjects be attempted until such time as sufficient advance has been made and proven out, since doing so prematurely could result in unnecessary fatalities due to the volatility of the element in its current form. Testing should be restricted to sample specimens *only*, and in isolated environments. End log entry."

[End playback: Log Entry #TX501-24, J. Fedder, DSc]

"Playback next entry," ordered Dolph. "Now!"

"Yes, sir," obeyed the computer.

[Playback: Log Entry #TX501-25, J. Fedder, DSc]

"Since my last entry, I have continued extensive testing on element *JF1Kx*. All attempts to fix the 'broken corner' by simulating synthetic repairs or biological mutations have not only failed but have brought to light the severity of the risk initially theorized. Each alteration thus far has resulted in almost immediate death of the exposed cells, as well as any adjoining ones, which in turn caused chain reactions as new cells were exposed.

"Factually, it was shocking to even this scientist the speed at which the cells were eliminated. A cellular 'massacre' you might say—an overwhelming and systematic response. Further tests will of course be conducted due to the significance of the discovery but with even more stringent precautions put in place. Much more stringent."

[End playback: Log Entry #TX501-25, J. Fedder, DSc]

"Next entry!" snapped Dolph, impatiently.
"Yes, sir," obeyed the computer—again.

[Playback: Log Entry #TX501-26, J. Fedder, DSc]

"There's been a disaster! The lab has been pressure sealed until further notice. Nothing in or out. No exceptions. All remaining *JF1Kx* specimens and variants that were not destroyed have been secured in bio-storage bins at negative 450 degrees. My person has been manually decontaminated and laser-sterilized and currently remains in isolation until the lab's lockdown has officially been lifted.

"Early testing of the element resulted in the loss of all organic material involved but did not show signs of potential contagion from one specimen to the next. Subsequent tests, however, found that synthetically produced mutations resulted in at least one *highly contagious* strain. More accurately, the last sample took out nearly all genetic specimens in the lab, and fast. Were it not for my pressurized biosuit and the additional precautions, I'm certain I would have been eliminated as well.

"Initial concerns of *JF1Kx* and any of its derivatives have now not only been substantiated but have been *surpassed*. In its existing form it *is* unstable and ultimately deadly, though only to the host. But manipulation rendering it contagious is not only not difficult but almost impossible to avoid. The above-mentioned strain, were it released into a population, could potentially take out that entire population and thus the capability of an 'Extinction Level Event' cannot be ruled out.

"Therefore, as a recognized officer of the Inter-Conglomerate Science and Security Committee, I am legally and otherwise obligated to officially designate *JF1Kx*—and any subsequent mutations thereof—a 'T-Con 3' level threat, effective immediately.

"Additionally, I hereby order as further precaution that any known living hosts, should any exist, be isolated from the general population and remain monitored by medical personnel. I further order that the nature of the element's research herein remain top secret since the potential consequences, were it to find its way into the hands of those with less-than-favorable intentions, cannot be ignored."

[End playback: Log Entry #TX501-26, J. Fedder, DSc]

This time Dolph was speechless. The illumination of the computer screen glowed on his shiny forehead, behind which had begun the conceiving of destructive notions, unsavory ideas, and the seed of a dreadful plan already taking root.

CHAPTER THIRTY

Dr. Joble Fedder strained to see past the layer of condensation that had formed on the inside of his hazmat shield. He adjusted the angle of his view and watched as the indicator gauge of the last remaining biohazard container finally pinned itself hard-left and the "live biological matter" light flickered and went black. "And that *is that*," he said, the statement muffled by the mask.

He heaved at the lever and cracked the container's seal, forcing it open. He peered inside, inspected the lone specimen sample, then removed it and exited the isolation room.

Over the past several hours Joble had monitored the remaining samples. But one by one they had each expired. And now it appeared this one had too. He would of course verify it visually and do more extensive tests, but he had no reason to doubt the equipment. It had never failed him before and he was certain it would not now.

He held the specimen dish in a gloved hand and stared despairingly at the bare wall before him, the neon-yellow glow of the bio-containment light filling the room with its hypnotic pulse. His attention drifted to the rhythm of his breathing. It was the only sound he'd heard in hours, amplified exponentially by the pressurized helmet and the respirator fastened to his face. There was a soothing nature to it as though an accompanying companion in the otherwise lifeless lab. He broke the rhythm with a sigh and lifted a glove, punched the alarm panel. The strobing instantly ceased leaving only the stark-white glare of the florescent lights overhead.

As he entered the confines of the meter-wide sterilization chamber, he felt the claustrophobic nature of the biosuit amplified. But there was an anticipation as well that had begun to build knowing he would soon be free of it. The lasers swept through the area and drenched him in a sterilizing hue. The beams withdrew with a swish and the door slid open inviting him to officially end the quarantine.

He stepped out and removed the helmet, slid the stone-gray fabric covering from his face, detached the respirator clamps—his cheeks reluctant to give up the shape of the face-piece. He unlatched the gloves and tossed them to a nearby counter and set off for his station.

His pace was unhurried as he traveled the hall leading to the microbiology wing. Everything would be as he left it, he knew. And anything that had once lived would now undoubtedly be dead.

As he arrived and settled at his station, a hopeful thought flicked in his mind—that maybe there was yet a chance. But when he slid the sample under the scope's lens and zoomed in, he was instantly disabused. He fidgeted with the focus, then shook his head as the reality further took hold. It was indeed dead.

Truthfully, part of him was relieved because of the obvious threat. But there was the other part that was not—the part innately inclined to force forward at any cost the advance of science in the knowable universe. A lofty senti-ment? Sure. Over the top? Perhaps. But whether Joble liked it or not was far from the point. For deep within him lived an irrepressible urge that churned at him day in and day out —an unscratchable itch that would never fully be satisfied. And the truth was, he loved it. So even if he could help himself, he didn't really want to.

Therefore, the question then became: Was it worth the risk? On the one hand, he could leave it alone—isolate any remaining hosts, if any indeed even remained, until, likely very soon, they would die too taking with them the $JF1Kx$ that resided in their every cell. Or, stay the course with the accompanying stakes. It was an impossible decision and hurt his head just thinking about it. But it was certainly time for a change.

He decided the time had come for a meeting. He'd sent the logs to Hulaksen and swapped some transmissions but had not had a proper discussion since taking on the project. He'd provided invaluable information, adhered to the promised discretion, and done it all with nothing recipro-cated except the physical samples themselves and the joy that came with the job. But now it was time for some answers. And given the stakes, he felt it was long overdue and the very least he could ask for. Yes, it was definitely time for a meeting—and the sooner the better.

CHAPTER THIRTY-ONE

Hulaksen sat in Joble's lab before a large monitor. He inserted a disc into the computer and tapped on the illuminated keyboard. Images of Chakeena and Magnus, labeled "Patient 1" and "Patient 2" respectively, appeared on the screen. He sat back, crossed one leg over the other. Removed his reading glasses and looked to Joble. "These are the only two I know of," he said, "besides Patient 3, that is, who as you know passed. It's possible there are more but none that I'm aware of."

Joble leaned in and took a closer look, his deep-green eyes remained reserved, somehow not surprised. "I recognize them. Both of them."

"I'm sure you do, which was the reason for the discretion."

Joble studied the images, his attention already at work factoring in this new information. "They're patients of yours, I presume?"

"Yes. Have been for years. And close acquaintances of each other as well."

"I have no evidence of it being communicable," said Joble. "At least not in its current form."

"Neither do I," said Hulaksen. "I don't think one gave it to the other, which only adds to the mystery of the coincidental timing." He paused, considered how to approach the next bit. Then: "I met with them, as well as Patient 3 before we lost him. We went over many factors to see if we could find something that may be of help in all of this. And we did find something. A common denominator, if you will."

Joble said nothing, just waited.

"You see, it seems all three attended the same gathering."

Joble squinted, twisted his narrow face.

"It was at the Empress's opera house," said Hulaksen.

"A concert?"

"Yes. A concert."

Joble stared at Hulaksen, considered the idea, then slid out a stool and took a seat in front of his favorite microscope. For this, he was all ears.

Hulaksen continued: "And at this gathering there was also a common experience." He stopped and sighed. "Now, this is going to sound a little strange, but just hear me out. During one of the performances that night, all three patients experienced similar phenomena. Tough to describe, and not exactly in the realm of medicine. Possibly not even science. It was physical to some degree, but also mental, or—well, maybe metaphysical or spiritual would be a better way to put it. The stories differ a little but the experiences were all extreme and equally inexplicable. Then shortly thereafter they all began to notice a substantial improvement in their health."

"Let me guess," said Joble. "*Mortiferum*?"

"Yes, exactly. They had all been suffering from it, in and

out of remission, but all noted an improvement after the night in question. An extreme and unprecedented improvement. And it was verified by me medically as well. Truthfully, I've never seen anything like it in all my years of medicine. But then the decline."

"And what do you think?" queried Joble. "Something they ate? Or...?"

"Well as you can imagine, that became the question. And after much discussion, comparing notes and such, it really came down to one thing—and they all felt very strongly about it." Hulaksen paused, looked at the images on the screen, then back to Joble. "They felt it was the music."

A look of shock sprang onto Joble's face. "The *music*?"

Hulaksen gave an understanding nod. "Yes."

Joble sat and took it in. Tried to wrap his head around it. Attempted to instantly process it as though the scientist in him could somehow work it all out in its entirety right then and there with one sweeping solution. But he of course could not.

Hulaksen stood, removed a bio container from the synthetic bag on the workstation and placed it before Joble, then again took a seat. "These are the new blood samples you asked for."

Joble shook off the problem for the time being and snapped up the sample labeled "Patient 2." He broke the seal and swabbed a portion onto a slide, pressed the cover slip to it and slid it under the scope. There was silence for longer than was comfortable, both reluctant to break it. Joble finally pulled his face back from the eyepiece. "It's degenerating."

Hulaksen let out an unsurprised sigh. "How bad?"

Joble lifted his head and made eye contact. "The

element—it's deteriorating. It's dying. And it's taking the rest of the cells with it. I've seen what it does. I know what happens next."

"Which means?" asked Hulaksen.

"It'll take out the entire organism with it. It's just a matter of time. And not much of it at this point. How's he doing?"

"It's been up and down," said Hulaksen. "Right now it's down again. Very down. And getting worse."

Joble nodded, his mind continuing to run in the background. He reached for Chakeena's sample. Prepared it for viewing. Loaded it onto the scope and slid it into view. He focused, shook his head, then zoomed in further. "Doctor, there's really no easy way to say this. The Princess will die soon. Days—if that."

Hulaksen just stared at the monitor, the likenesses of his ill-fated patients staring back at him.

Joble looked up from the scope. "You really think this has something to do with *music*?"

"They do. I mean, the patients were convinced."

"Hmm..." Joble scratched his head, his expression unwilling to soften. "Bit of a stretch. Quite a bit."

Hulaksen did not interrupt the thought process, intentionally allowed Joble to work the problem.

"I've seen sound waves affect cellular structure," said Joble. "Certain frequencies. Not permanently, mind you, but I've observed the phenomenon. I could look into it."

Hulaksen gently shook his head. "Your guess is as good as mine. Maybe better at this point. I'm afraid I'm at a loss. And we're running out of time." He paused, his finger firmly pressed to his temple. "And there's something else. They also felt strongly about the *performer*—that he was also an influence of some sort."

"The performer?"

"I know. I don't know what to think. We've been looking into him. Ryder's his name. Kaiden Ryder. Here." Hulaksen pulled up an image on the screen. "Got it from security records from when he entered the opera house."

Joble glared at the screen, studied the photo. "Anything else?"

"There was a spacial anomaly that night. I can get you the report. It's a stretch too, though. No credible connection."

"Yes, the report would be good," said Joble. "And I suppose I could run some audio tests. It's an angle I had not considered." He continued to glare at the screen, the image of Kaiden tearing at his attention. "What species is he? I don't recognize it."

"I don't know. Seems to be a mix. Humanoid, obviously, but beyond that, tough to say."

Joble remained locked on the image, his interest unusually piqued. His glare deepened as he strained to remain objectively detached. "Can we get him in here? I could run a battery of tests. And we'd have the direct source of the audio—that would be best. Otherwise we're just guessing." He continued to stare at the screen, unable to unfix his attention. "I'd be interested to see what's happening with him physiologically, too. Biologically."

"Well, that's the problem," said Hulaksen. His eyes dropped to the floor. "You see, we've lost him."

CHAPTER THIRTY-TWO

The room rocked as Bronson came to, his impaired faculties providing him with a vague cloud of swirling imagery. As an awareness of his body crept in, it brought with it the feeling of the cold concrete floor on his back as well as a pounding head and overwhelming nausea. He rolled to his side in anticipation as what little remained in his stomach emptied onto the floor, then strained to part his lids to get a fix on his location but was unable.

A muted sound in the background tore at his attention. It was garbled. Indistinguishable. Musical? He returned to his back as the numbness in his clavicle became apparent. It was something he at least recognized—the receipt point of a blast. Thankfully only a stun. Not his first and likely not his last. But who? And why? And just where the hell *was* he? He grappled for more but there was nothing. Only the nausea and dry heaving as he again went unconscious...

It was him as a child on Vietrus aboard a scooter. The wind on his young face, the freedom of a newcomer to life in his heart, and the warmth of his mother's soup in his belly. Genroy, his twin brother and best friend, called out to him:

"Faster, Bronson! Faster!" He poured on the throttle and actuated the thrusters sending the scene before him blurring past.

The speed was liberating. There were dwelling projects to the left and an endless cityscape to the right, his neighborhood now a stream of flicking images as he sped down the surface street. "Race you home!" shouted young Bronson, craning around to search for his brother. "First one to the guard gate is the—

Boom!

A collision tossed him through the air. The force of his shoulder clipping a parked craft sent an excruciating wave up his neck. He tumbled to a stop and flopped to the ground, connecting the back of his head to the awaiting asphalt as...

He opened his eyes to find a dark ceiling above. Strained to lift himself. Gave up. Turned his head in the direction of a distorted figure to the left. He winced, the ringing in his ears overwhelming him. As its volume settled, the figure came slowly into focus bringing with it a familiarity. But that was it, only a familiarity and no more.

He attempted to speak but his throat failed. And it was becoming obvious that he'd been subjected to more than just a blast and a thump on the head. There were drugs involved too, and heavy ones gauging from the effects. Not the good ones. Not the ones like the k-mite. No, these were another breed altogether. The ones like the Service had used on him in their tests. The ones used to push him to the brink of breaking in simulated situations of torture by unfriendly others. The ones they'd used to prepare him for just such a situation as this. And it was also becoming clear that this was indeed *no* simulation, which led to the next question: How had he fared?

As he continued to come to, his memory trickled in bit by bit. He'd been on a mission. He'd been transporting the figure that sat in the corner whose name had still not returned to him. They'd been ambushed. There was a van. A gleaming rifle. And... A sniper. And the *damn* sniper had hit his *damn* target.

A regretful groan emerged as he realized he'd allowed himself and the nameless figure to be captured by whoever was in the *damn van*! He held his head as the sentiment finally materialized into a barely audible statement: "Damn it."

He strained to focus back on the figure but succeeded in only sinking again into the land of seven-year-olds speeding through the surface streets of Vietrus on their scooters...

Kaiden stopped mid-song and deactivated his synth. The glow faded and the warbled hum waned as it powered off and disappeared into its case. He sat forward, nudged Bronson. "You okay?"

Bronson's arm shot to his side and grasped an empty holster, his eye already assessing Kaiden through a cracked lid. A relieved sigh followed. He dropped his arm and twisted toward Kaiden. "I think so."

"You were pretty out of it," said Kaiden.

Bronson wiped his eyes. Stretched his neck. "What happened?"

"They asked you questions. A lot of them."

Bronson wrestled with his wits, his memory still out of reach. "Who's they?"

"I don't know. Whoever these guys are."

Wincing from the pain, Bronson lifted a hand to his head. Then, groggily: "And then what?"

Kaiden gave an indifferent shrug. "You answered."

Bronson rolled to his side. Grunted up to an elbow. "Never would've done that."

"You did though," assured Kaiden. "You told them everything."

Bronson shook his head, still skeptical. "Like what?"

"You said that Magnus brought you in to find me. You said that the Princess was sick. That she had gotten better and then worse. Much worse. And that I had something to do with it."

"Shit," whispered Bronson.

"And you said she was dying."

Bronson dropped his glance to the floor as the reality began to sink in. "What else?"

"I don't know," said Kaiden. "There was a lot. You told them all about a Project Vivicon or something, and also—"

"*Damn* it," sighed Bronson. "Did they torture me?"

"No. They didn't touch you," said Kaiden. "They drugged you. They said, 'You'd give up all the goods after a healthy dose of this,' and then stuck you with whatever it was. Seemed to work. You just started answering everything. Didn't matter what they asked."

"Yeah, I get it," said Bronson. He rolled. Rubbed his head some more, a sense of defeat now firmly taking hold. "Anything else?"

"They said they were hungry but would be back. Seemed happy about what they got. And they said I was next. But I don't know anything."

"Yeah, I know," droned Bronson, his energy slowly returning. "How long have we been here?"

"Not sure. Is it true about the Princess?"

Bronson deliberately evaded. "How many of them?"

"Two."

"How long have they been gone?"

"Not long. Maybe thirty minutes."

The crevices in Bronson's forehead furrowed as his brow drew in tight. "That makes no sense. Something of that strength would have knocked me out for hours."

"It's my synth," said Kaiden. "I don't know why. But it works."

Bronson didn't even blink. Enough testimony had been given as to the power of the device. His mind instead went straight to work. Obviously escape was the priority. And there was always a way, always an advantage. It just had to be looked for. It just had to be... A smirk began to form on his leathery face along with a twinkle in his bloodshot eye. He pushed himself up and leaned on the wall beside Kaiden. Brushed off his boots. Inspected the unlit room. "So they think I'll be out for hours, do they?" He nodded to himself as the smirk grew into a smile. "That's good. That's an advantage."

CHAPTER THIRTY-THREE

"And then he said, 'If you accept the job, there's an extra forty-thousand credits in it for you each,'" said Gluke, holding out as long as he could before bursting into a roar of grunting laughter. He slapped a paw to the table. Shattered a plate of chewed up bones. Let out a guttural belch— filling the space with the putrid stench of vinoh and Vietrusian rhino ribs.

Thyrro kept it going. "To spy on someone? No. Steal something? No." He gave it a second, tapping into what little comedic timing he possessed. "*To ambush and interrogate the great Bronson Decker!*" He let out a howl, slurped at his drink, swallowed what made it into his mouth, and dragged his sleeve along his furry chin to sop up the rest.

They were celebrating, and rightfully so. For success was theirs to cherish. The assignment, though far from flawlessly executed, had been accomplished. They'd captured and secured Bronson. They'd transported him and Kaiden to the secret location. And they'd contacted their employer to confirm completion of the job, at which point they'd been offered a second job *should they choose to accept it.*

They of course accepted, happily filling Bronson with enough truth serum to put down a giant land-hog for a week, then sat and listened to the most famous ex-serviceman "slash" private investigator "slash" many other formidable things provide them and their employer with some of the most valuable intelligence in the Conglomerate. So a couple of drinks and a snack at a nearby watering hole was the very least they felt they owed themselves.

They were still laughing—deep, resounding belly laughs—when the waitress glided up on a pair of bright pink skim-skates. A real beaut: endless legs, slender face, human, her metallic hot pants and matching top clutching at her hour-glass frame in all the right places leaving very little to the imagination.

She tossed her sheeny hair aside and pierced the boys with an exotic stare. "Getcha boys anything else?"

Thyrro subdued his laughter. Looked to Gluke, then to the waitress, his blurry gaze focused on the fullness of her glossy lips. He smiled and said cynically, "Oh, no. We *couldn't*."

"No," echoed Gluke. "Couldn't *possibly*. Gotta get back to... *work*," raising his wooly paws to air quote the "work" part.

They stared at each other for a moment before erupting into another drunken fit.

The waitress smirked, calmly let the boys have their moment, her large copper eyes narrowing to a teasing squint. She cleared the broken plate and shot them a spir-ited wink. "I'll take that as a yes. One more round, comin' up."

Thyrro caught his breath long enough to call out to her as she turned and skated off. "Miss!"

She slowed, hovering the thickness of her skates' repulsion pads above the floor, then turned her head—not far enough for eye contact, but just enough of an over-the-shoulder to let them know she was listening, the smoky daylight streaming through the room backlighting her flawless outline like the halo of an angel.

"Whatcha got in the *back*?" asked Thyrro. "Anything stronger? Anything *good* back there?"

She twisted her slender neck a little further. Leveled a glint from the corner of her eye, glanced down the slant of her cheekbone to the elegant line of her hip. "Oh, yeah. I got something in the *back* for ya all right." Then strolled off in the direction of the bar providing the boys with a swaying view that would all but guarantee her a healthy tip.

And there they sat for the next hour—drinking, paw-slapping, devouring everything before them, and cackling like a couple of pie-eyed teenagers. And when they'd finally had their fill, unable to put down even one more rib or gulp back yet another mug of that which had indeed been stashed in the back, they took care of the bill, tipped the waitress—*well*—and stumbled out of the establishment, wobbling along the streets singing an endless array of Quadladritic oldies.

CHAPTER THIRTY-FOUR

"She *was* a little lean, wasn't she?" said Gluke, still fixated on the waitress from their lunch break. "But still..." He slurped at the thought of her as they arrived at the hideout's entrance.

Thyrro hovered a paw over the bio-lock, struggling to stay stable.

Gluke watched on. Hiccuped. Then: "You just gotta wait till it's in your sights and then go for it. Old sniper trick. If you're waitin' for it to stop we'll be here all day."

"Shut up. I got it." Thyrro wobbled, tipped, caught himself with the wall.

Gluke stepped up. He lifted his paw and waited till the rhythm of the sway was right, then flopped it down on the lock. A click announced his success. "See? Easy." He yanked at the door, the iron hinges protesting with a groan as it yielded to Gluke's sheer might.

It was dark and took a moment for their already impaired vision to adjust. Gluke made his way to an empty desk in an otherwise empty room. He dropped to a chair, sat back, and adjusted his belt, easing up the burden of his lunch. Thyrro followed suit. They took some time to catch their breath, the room deafeningly silent except for a squeaking fan and the panting from their hike.

Thyrro leaned forward and tugged off a boot. Inspected its interior. Spotted the problem. "No wonder." He slid a blade from a sheath on his hip and went to work—carved a chunk of leather from the insole and returned the knife to its home. Then rubbed at his heel. "Gettin' a damn blister."

Gluke glanced at him. Grunted.

Thyrro yanked the boot back on. "Well, whatd'ya say? Wanna do this?"

Gluke gave a nod. "Yeah. Don't know what we're gonna get though. I don't think the skinny one knows any more than he's already said. But, part of the job I guess."

"Yeah," said Thyrro. "Got the recorder?"

Gluke dug in his pocket and removed the device, wiped at a smudge on its face.

Thyrro watched with wavering eyes, grunted, sat up. "That thing's pretty valuable right now, his full confession an' all. You know we *could* just—"

"Don't even think about it," said Gluke. "Not worth it. Not with these guys."

Thyrro belched. Nodded and sat back. "Yeah, probably not." He wriggled his foot in the boot and slid his heel into place, then stamped it on the ground. "Well, let's get to it then."

They stood and lumbered off down a long hallway, led like moths to a light in the distance that hung from a compromised wire above the only door in sight.

When they arrived, Thyrro wrapped his enormous paw around the vintage deadbolt. He swayed, released another belch, and began to slide it open when...

"Wait!" whispered Gluke. "What if he's awake?"

"Not possible. Not with that dosage. He'll be out till morning."

They looked at each other. Considered it. Then, with a better-safe-than-sorry nod, readied their blasters.

Thyrro leaned into the lock and slid the bolt through its sleeve. An awful scrape accompanied it before announcing its completion with a clank. He heaved at the door, activating the interior lights. They peered in cautiously, found Bronson flat on his back, his cuffed hands resting on his belly. And in the corner against the wall, squinting from the sudden burst of light, sat Kaiden, unrestrained.

"See. Just like we left him," said Thyrro.

Gluke grunted an acknowledgment.

Thyrro entered and approached Kaiden. Holstered his firearm. Looked down at him. "Now, we're not gonna have a problem here, are we?"

Kaiden shook his head, avoiding eye contact. "Nope."

"Good," said Thyrro as he knelt at Kaiden's side. "Because while I do this, my friend over there, the one with the wobbly blaster pointed at you, is gonna make *damn sure* there's no problem. Yeah?"

Kaiden nodded. "Yup."

"Excellent." Thyrro yanked at the zipper of his coat and withdrew a leather pack from his pocket. He cracked it open to reveal a row of digital syringes and a number of glass vials containing a hazy brown liquid. He removed a vial and shoved it into the loading chamber of the nearest syringe. A buzz followed as the vial seated itself. He slid the syringe from the pack and removed its shield, swayed slightly, then: "Whatd'ya think, five units?"

"Pfft! That's plenty," spit Gluke. "He's just a tiny thing. Probably doesn't even need *that*."

Thyrro slurred something incomprehensible and

entered the desired unit number into the device. It whirred as the plunger drew back and transferred into its delivery barrel the desired dosage. Thyrro grinned. "Okay, locked and loaded. Let's do this." He leaned over, aiming the gleaming tip at Kaiden's arm, then turned to Gluke. "Damn good ribs though, right?"

Gluke snickered, licked his chops. "Damn right they were."

Thyrro's smile widened, still savoring the snacks in his mind. He turned back to Kaiden's awaiting arm and was about to stab it when...

"Hey!" bellowed Bronson as he sunk his boot deep into Gluke's knee!

Gluke dropped to the ground, dropped his blaster. The weapon discharged, "stunned" the wall—the shot erupting into a flare of molten sparks.

Thyrro twisted to see. Bronson rolled, scooped up the blaster with his tethered hands, got off a shot to Thyrro's chest. Boom! The syringe clanked to the floor and rolled across it. Thyrro fell too, though not so delicately. But it was not enough to keep a Quadladrite of his size down. He sat up, shook his mane, and started to stand as...

Gluke lunged from the other side. Bronson evaded, blasted him. Dropped him again, the force of the fall shaking the room. Gluke grunted as he lifted his head and tried to focus—his lunch break working dead against him now.

Bronson swung to the left. Another shot to Thyrro to buy some time. Another hit. He wrenched his neck to the right, found Gluke working his way up again, then swung back to find Thyrro too already hoisting himself—neither staying down, neither evidently even discouraged.

"Shit." A quick shot to Gluke as Bronson searched the

room racking his brain for a solution, forcing a flurry of calculations to flood his head. His eyes darted, adrenaline surging within, instincts alert for whatever his faculties might provide. And as he waited, letting the process work its magic, the answer finally came to him.

"That!" He locked eyes with Kaiden, pointed an emphatic finger at the syringe. "Your dart!" He swung his fettered arms to indicate Thyrro. "Your target!" Then an even more piercing glare at Kaiden. "*Up* the dose and put him *down!* Now!"

Kaiden saw the syringe, puzzled at it for a second, then got the picture. He leapt up and shot over to it, scooped it up and fiddled with the settings, quickly gauging its weight as the device loaded the added dosage, then drew back his arm and swung it as hard as he could directly at the oversized target.

Thyrro watched the incoming projectile soar toward him, connect, and sink itself into his arm. He let out a laugh, looking down at it in disgust as it introduced its contents into his bloodstream. "Why you little rat! You think that's gonna save you?" He snarled. Plucked it from his arm. Flicked it across the room. "I hate to break it to you my friend, but it's gonna take a lot more than that to..." His eyes rolled. He swayed, tried to fight it, caught himself, swayed some more, then: "...put me down." He dropped to the floor, landing with the force of a giant oak just as...

Gluke lunged again at Bronson.

"Shit!" Bronson got off another shot, entirely aware he was only postponing the inevitable. He considered options. Considered an increased blaster setting. It would certainly stop the madness, but the time it would take to recalibrate would also leave him vulnerable. Though risky, it may be the only way. He quickly weighed it in his mind, but there was really only one answer: Put this thing down for once and for all. Period. He flipped the blaster and flicked the switch, waited, time seemingly standing still as...

Gluke, standing yet again, scoffed at him. "You idiot. Who do you think you're dealing with? I know precisely how long it takes that blaster to recalibrate. And you know what? You don't have that much time. I took you down once and I'll do it again." He brushed himself off, swept his disheveled mane from his face, and marched straight at Bronson, about to smack the blaster from his hands when...

From across the room, like a blowdart of the ancient Vietrusian tribes, a second syringe spun through the air and sunk itself deep into Gluke's neck.

"Bullseye," whispered Kaiden.

Gluke shook his bewildered head, a surge of unrelenting fury building in his chest. "What the..."

The syringe whirred as it emptied itself. The blaster whined as it primed itself. The whine peaked; the weapon blipped. Gluke's eyes bulged from their sockets. "Oh shit."

"Sorry, my friend," said Bronson, "but not today." He stabilized his aim, reveled at the prevailing position he was now in, then pulled the trigger back to its breaking point...

Boom!

Gluke lifted his paws in a futile attempt to shield himself as the blast bowled him over and sent him crashing to the floor. There was a grunt. A twitch. Some sort of a mumble. And then: silence. And this time he did not get up.

CHAPTER THIRTY-FIVE

Dolph paced back and forth the length of his private workplace at Old Ruechestire Square, the tapping of his heals on the tile floor like a metronome counting the seconds to his trial. Grivel would arrive soon and it was time to up the stakes.

Since their last meeting, much had transpired. The intel Dolph had provided Grivel appeared to have been useful. Although there'd been little communication between the two, purposely—in order to avoid blowing any covers— Dolph had reason to believe the ambush had gone as planned since Bronson had not made it back to the estate. But in light of the information he'd acquired from the logs, as well as the most recent details he'd obtained by bugging the doctor—an ingenious move if he did say so himself— Dolph felt it necessary to call a meeting immediately.

There were no samples left at the lab, which was a problem. But he was now in possession of something far greater, and if he played his cards right it could be just what was needed to finally secure his place in the Network. But time was running out. Chakeena and Magnus, whom he'd discovered to be Patients 1 and 2, had both taken ill again and, according to the scientist's findings, would not recover. And on top of that he'd learned that the gene, which now held far more value than even Bronson, would be lost with the deaths of the patients and that they were the only two living hosts left.

The door buzzer squealed. Dolph halted mid-pace, checked the camera. It was Grivel. Showtime. He headed straight for the door, mentally noting how much more calm he felt compared to Grivel's last visit. Yes, Dolph now had some credit. But would it be reflected in the monster's attitude? Would the animal grant him some? The funny thing was he didn't even seem to care, an indication itself of an advance of status, if only in his own mind. He deactivated the verifiers, input the codes, and unlatched the door. "Watch your head," he said to Grivel, matter-of-factly.

The animal ducked as it entered, heaved itself to a sofa near the door and sunk into it, the accompanying odor revolting as ever.

Dolph stayed standing. Partial pride, partial power-trip. He thrust out his chin and erected his posture, waited as Grivel worked out a more comfortable position, eventually lifting the injured leg and resting it on the table before him.

"Well," said Grivel, "what's so important you needed to drag me all the way over to this crap-hole *again*?"

"Yes, of course. Straight to it." Dolph knew he would have to improvise, especially on which parts to give up and which to keep to himself. It would require some quick thinking. But there was also a store of confidence knowing he'd figure it out along the way as he always had. He pivoted, his back to the monster, then resumed his clicking pace of the room. "I trust everything went as planned with Decker?"

Grivel grunted something resembling an affirmative.

Dolph stopped. Pivoted back. A pompous nod. "Well, I've come across some new information pertaining to this Project Vivace. It has to do with the disease and—"

"I do hope your *new information* is *not* that these idiots think there's been some kind of miracle. That this Ryder can heal people." Grivel sighed, his enormous orbs glaring at his ruined knee. "Because if that's what you dragged me down here for, I'm not gonna be very happy. I had Decker interrogated. Got everything he knows." Grivel lifted his gaze and made eye contact for the first time since he'd arrived, locking a laser-like glare on Dolph. "*I know* what I'm doing. Now please tell me you have something more than mere fantasies and fairytales."

Grivel's glare did its job in sobering Dolph. His stance slumped. He swallowed and nodded. "Yes, I have more."

Grivel leaned back, folded his tree-trunk arms, and waited for Dolph to give him anything to justify the inconvenience.

"Well, I don't know about miracles," said Dolph, "but there *were* three subjects who were affected by something."

"Yes, I know," droned the monster. "The Princess, your father, and the politician, who's dead."

"Right. But—and this is all very technical—but here's the deal. There's something that changed in their bodies. Something genetic. Something that's never happened before. Science has never seen it."

Dolph watched for a reaction but there was none. Grivel simply sat and stared. Dolph gulped back the nerves as inconspicuously as possible and continued: "And, yes, it can make them better, but it's only temporary. In the long run it actually speeds up the disease. That's what happened to the politician. And that's what's happening right now to the Princess and my father."

Grivel lifted himself, leaned forward every so slightly. And Dolph noticed. Oh yes, he *noticed*.

"Now, this genetic thing," said Dolph, "that's the important part. And it's valuable for a number of reasons. It's valuable to science because—if they can figure out how to control it, how to manipulate it to suit their needs—it could heal people."

Grivel eased himself back into the sofa's thick cushions.

Dolph gulped again, observing the action. "But I don't want to bore you with that part. That's not what this is about. You see, the thing is—"

"Oh for crap sake!" roared Grivel. "What the *hell is* the thing!"

The response spiked the hair on the back of Dolph's neck and shot chills through his entire body. "Right," he continued, shaken, "the thing is, this genetic, 'thing,' in its current form is deadly but only to the carrier. It's isolated. It's not contagious and so proves no threat to anyone else. But..."—he took a breath and turned up the drama, readying himself for the big bit—"...but it *can be* and *has been* altered to be much more dangerous. Much more deadly."

Grivel came ever so slightly back to life. "Deadly? How deadly?"

"Well, my source said it could take out entire populations, that it even had the potential to cause an *Extinction Level Event*." Dolph purposely halted, waiting to let the statement sink in.

But Grivel did not respond as expected, merely rolled his eyes. "Who's your source?"

"Ah, well... *That* I can't say. But I can tell you that it's one of the top scientists in the Conglomerate."

"Seems exaggerated," scoffed Grivel, scratching at a flea buried in his infested coat. "An E.L.E. is no small thing. Besides, potential and actual are two very different things."

"But it's been done. It's not theoretical. The genetic... *thing*... it's been altered. It took out an entire lab of specimens and caused a lockdown."

"Lots of accidents in labs," said Grivel. "That doesn't mean anything."

Shit! thought Dolph. He was losing him. What else? What could he say that would sway the monster? What else could he come up with that would... And then it hit him: "Well, there *was* something else," continued Dolph. "You see, this scientist was extremely concerned. Went on about a threat level. A Threat Condition or something that—"

"Threat Condition?"

Dolph nodded. "Yes."

"What about it?"

"The scientist assigned one because of the lockdown."

"A Threat Condition was assigned?"

"Yes."

"He said that?"

"Yes."

"He *officially* declared it? Had the power to do that?"

"Yes, that's what he said."

"And it was assigned because of this genetic... *Thing*?"

"Yes."

Grivel went into his head. Took a moment. Gave the statement its due regard. Then looked up at Dolph. "What level?"

"T-Con 3."

"Hmm..." Grivel sat back, attempted to contain himself,

though it was tough now. He stroked his mane. Found another flea. Flicked it off. Then: "You sure?"

"Yes, I'm positive. T-Con 3."

Grivel lifted himself from the sofa and began his own pace of the room. Creaks from the floor rung out as it yielded to his weight. He stopped in front of a map. Stared blankly at it. "A Threat-Con 3, huh? Well, now that *is* something. I'll of course have to verify it first, which will be easy enough. I have resources for that. But if it's true, it *is* pretty big."

"That's what I thought. But there's more."

Grivel turned to him, now all ears.

"Unfortunately whatever it was that caused the lab disaster was destroyed and—"

"Destroyed?" said Grivel.

"Yes, but the scientist did a lot of testing before that and said there were many ways to recreate it if you had this gene thing. Many ways to weaponize it."

"And?"

"Well, there are a few problems. It can only be acquired through a blood sample of someone who is infected with it. And it has to be acquired while they're still alive or it's no good. And there are only two people alive that I'm aware of who have it, the Princess and my father. But—"

Grivel nodded knowingly: "But they're both dying."

"Yes. And there's no known cure. No chance of recovery. And they're dying fast."

"Yes, I see." Grivel raised a paw to his giant chin, ran a claw along it. "This is a problem." He stared at the floor, deep in thought, his breathing loud and uneven.

Dolph waited for a response. For now, he'd done what he could. In his mind, a masterpiece. If the monster wasn't moved by this then how could it even be considered a monster at all? If this didn't raise the blood pressure of this filthy beast, then—

"This is real, right?" said Grivel.

"Yes," assured Dolph. "As real as the intel I got you on Decker."

"And it's no good after they die? No good at all?"

"Completely useless."

"And there are no others infected with it?"

"Correct."

Grivel again nodded in agreement, his matted mane dancing on his shoulders. He pondered the problem some more. Then, finally: "We need that blood."

It was a bold statement and showed he'd heard what Dolph had said and that he *was*, evidently, still a monster. But more importantly—much more importantly—for the second time in as many meetings, Grivel Gromme had used the word "we"—music to Dolph's meddling ears.

A chirp from Grivel's communicator interrupted them. He ignored it. Then a double-chirp. Something important. He yanked it from his belt and clicked his claw on the scraped faceplate. It lit up. He viewed the message. It was short but it was enough to cause Grivel to put a paw through a nearby wall.

Incoming Transmission—URGENT:
    Decker escaped.
    End Transmission

Part Six

PATIENT ZERO

CHAPTER THIRTY-SIX

"...further studies support the following theory. It's as though the introduction of element *JF1Kx* into the specimen in its current state amplifies all biological aspects.

"In the case of an organism, this would increase the entire organism's life potential at the most fundamental level. At the cellular level. But therein lies the problem. Because within the macrocosm that is any organism exist millions or billions of interdependent microcosms, each one seeking to extend *its* own life. And in the case of a disease, *its* potential becomes amplified as well when hosted by an afflicted patient.

"In the case of Patient 1, the gene has given added life to the patient but at the same time has given added life to the disease. It's made it stronger. Substantially stronger. Made it more of what it inherently is—more unstable and more lethal.

"It is this scientist's theory that without the existing flaw in *JF1Kx* there would be a harmonious alignment of all. An organism without conflict in itself or its interdependent components. A truly symbiotic system as a whole whose

life-enhancing factors would far surpass any life-threat-
ening ones. Fix the 'x' in it—the 'corruption' of it, if you will
—and evolution could theoretically be pushed into hitherto
unreachable heights. It is for this reason that—"

A pong from the lab's computer interrupted.

Joble looked up and stared across the room. *He's here*, he
thought, a stir of anticipation tugging at his gut.

The computer ponged again, snapping him out of it.

"End log entry," said Joble.

"Yes, sir," replied the computer.

[End: Log Entry #TX501-29, J. Fedder, DSc]

"I apologize for the interruption, sir," said the computer,
"but Dr. Hulaksen is at the gate."

"Yes, of course. I'm on my way."

"Yes, sir."

Joble stood and proceeded toward the wing leading to
the main entrance. Hulaksen would have with him the one
in question, the one they'd been searching for—the
common denominator in all of this. And maybe even with a
little luck, some help. He of course remained skeptical as
any good scientist prides himself on being. But there was yet
a glint of hope and one he could not ignore. After all, it was
something new, something fresh, something encouraging in
this unprecedented occurrence that had all but come to a
halt.

Hulaksen had gotten Joble up to speed. Chakeena and
Magnus's health had declined again, as predicted, and this
time all evidence indicated they would not recover, also as
predicted. Of course it had always been inevitable. It had
always been merely a matter of time. And just as Joble said
it would, the gene had accelerated the spread of the disease,

as confirmed by their most recent bloodwork. Chakeena had been isolated in one of the many external buildings on the estate, per Joble's orders, and had been tented for reduced contact with others until they knew more. Magnus had taken similar precautions and had round-the-clock medical personnel monitoring him with visitor restrictions put in place.

Kaiden's arrival had brought with it the opportunity to analyze the instrument. Hulaksen had attempted some audio tests on Magnus, but to no avail—or not much at least. For while it had caused a temporary spike in Magnus's brainwaves, it had not improved his physical condition in the least and certainly had not even come close to lifting him from the semi-comatose state he'd fallen into. Yes, he and Chakeena were both now indeed days from death. Maybe hours.

Hulaksen had briefly looked over Kaiden from a medical standpoint, which brought to light many interesting things but which ultimately solved nothing. So with no indication of improvement in sight, and with the clock ticking fast, he'd skipped what certainly would've been a futile trip to the Empress's and instead headed straight to the lab with Kaiden in a last-ditch attempt for an answer.

"Open east-wing gate," said Joble as he arrived at the main entrance.

"Yes, sir," said the computer.

Joble pressed the door's handprint panel. It lit up green. There was a clank followed by the break of an air-seal. He heaved at the vault-like door and stepped outside. It was refreshing and a welcome break from staring down the barrel of a microscope for hours on end. But as welcoming as it was there was still no escaping the severity of the situation or the work that still lay ahead.

A shuttle pulled up and came to a halt, settling to the ground as the repellers disengaged the lift-cushion. Through the tinted window Joble could see Hulaksen paying the driver. And beside him, unmoving, the guest of honor's obscure outline.

The shuttle door opened with a soft swish and Hulaksen stepped out, visibly agitated. He wiped his brow, then tucked the handkerchief neatly back into his breast pocket. "Dr. Fedder," he said, his voice tight and raw.

"Dr. Hulaksen," replied Joble, still fixated on the outline.

They shook hands, exchanged formal glances, then turned to the shuttle and its remaining passenger. "Doctor," said Hulaksen, "I'd like to introduce you to Mr. Ryder."

Kaiden emerged from the shuttle, stepped out and shot Joble a nod. But his attention was quickly drawn to the enormity of the metallic building, the starlight reflections glistening from its featureless surface.

Joble inspected Kaiden with the eye of an expert. He was taller than expected. Thinner too. Long hands. Snow-like skin with an almost olive undertone. And there was something else—something harder to describe. It was an energy about him, pronounced and tangible yet inexpressible at the same time.

Joble purposely broke the silence, eager to get on with it. "Honored to meet you, Mr. Ryder."

Kaiden, still gazing up at the building, turned his head and leveled a curious stare at Joble.

Joble met the stare. Smiled. "Why don't you let me show you around?"

Kaiden nodded and the trio made their way into the structure, the urgency of the evening evident in their every step.

Joble and Hulaksen discussed the cases while Kaiden

followed, still intrigued by the sheer flawlessness of it all—an awe-inspiring environment that was as esthetic as it was antiseptic.

As they moved through the maze-like corridors, Kaiden was reminded of the purpose at hand. This was a science facility. This was for Magnus. This was for Chakeena. And it was life and death they were dealing with.

Joble gestured toward the bio-lab and entered, Hulaksen and Kaiden trailing close behind.

As they arrived at the station, Joble pointed to the rows of stools perfectly lining either side of the chrome counter that extended the length of the room. "This is where I do much of my work," he said. "Please, take a seat."

Hulaksen sat, clearly still preoccupied with his patients.

Kaiden inspected the vaulted ceilings as he settled onto a stool beside Joble.

Joble straightened up the area, then too took a seat. "Well," he said, "if you don't mind, I suggest we jump right in."

Hulaksen nodded.

"Where is everybody?" asked Kaiden.

"The lab's reserved for high-security research," said Joble. "In this case it's just us. Did you bring the device with you?"

Kaiden tapped the projector on his belt. He unclipped it and placed it on the table.

"This is it?" said Joble.

Kaiden nodded.

"Interesting." Joble picked it up and examined the instrument, running a finger along its seamless touch panel and brushed silver surface, the faint etchings shimmering under the stark lab lights. "I have some specimens set aside in the audio chamber," said Joble. "We can run some tests and record the results."

Kaiden's sapphire gaze flicked to Hulaksen as if to seek consent. Hulaksen surfaced from his thoughts long enough to feign an approving smile. Kaiden looked back to Joble. "Yes. Of course."

"Okay. First a few questions. Can you tell me about the device? Anything unique there?"

"Everything, really. It projects a hologram of an ancient instrument but with my own modifications to it."

"I see. And what about its components? Anything unique about them?"

"Yes. The audio generators," said Kaiden. "They're pretty unique. Is there something specific you're looking for?"

"I don't know yet," said Joble. "We're starting from scratch here. The tests themselves are what will ultimately matter. I'm just getting some basic details before we run them. Anything else out of the ordinary?"

Kaiden thought about it. Then nodded. "I tune it differently."

"Differently?" said Joble. "In what way?"

"Well, standard is 440. But I tune to 444."

"That's hertz?" said Joble. "Cycles per second?"

"Yes," said Kaiden.

"I see. And the composition on the night at the opera house? What can you tell me about it?"

"It's in the key of A. The emphasis is on A5, the pedal note. The piece centers on that and its harmonics. A movement from minor to major."

Joble considered it. Did the calculations. "An octave above A4. That would be 888 hertz." His brow furrowed. "Interesting. Have you ever heard of the Pure Tone?"

Kaiden looked up. "No."

"How about the Angel Tone?"

Kaiden shook his head. "Is that important?"

"I don't know. There's lore surrounding it, that it's a healing frequency. No real evidence to support it though. But still, it's an interesting choice given the circumstances. Why the tuning difference?"

Kaiden shrugged. "I like how it sounds. Actually, how it feels."

Joble nodded. Jotted down some notes. Looked back up. Inspected Kaiden more closely. "What can you tell me about your ancestry?"

"I don't know much. Never knew my parents."

"And you've never looked into your genetic line?"

"No," said Kaiden. "What's that got to do with this?"

"Maybe nothing. But the factor of genetics has presented itself in the patients, which makes it potentially relevant. You see, it's not my job to assume. My job is to gather and objectively observe, connect any applicable dots and see where they lead us. We're looking for *anything* that may be of help here. Anything that stands out. Anything anomalous." Joble jotted down some more notes, then looked back to Kaiden. "Did Dr. Hulaksen fill you in on everything?"

Kaiden nodded. "He thinks my music did something."

"And what do *you* think about that?"

"Well," said Kaiden, "people do seem affected by it. But this thing with the Princess and Magnus is a bit of a stretch." Kaiden dropped his eyes to the immaculate floor. "We just came from Magnus's. He's in bad shape. And from what the doctor says, the Princess is just as bad."

"Yes, I understand. I know it's serious," said Joble. "Let's see if there's anything we can do to help." He scratched his head and jotted down some more notes. "I'd like to get a blood sample. If you don't mind."

Kaiden again looked around the lab as if it somehow legitimized the request. "Yes, of course."

Joble worked swiftly, picked up a package and ripped it open to reveal a sterile swab. He wiped Kaiden's wrist, then plucked up the prepared syringe and attempted to insert the needle. But it failed to penetrate.

Joble looked up with a curious stare.

"Might be easier here," said Kaiden. He extended his other arm, drew back his sleeve and pointed to a spot higher up from the wrist, closer to the inside of his elbow.

Joble wiped the area. Noted a tiny tattoo. Some sort of a diagram... And a word. He puzzled over it for a second. Then: "What's 'Earth' mean?"

"Not sure," said Kaiden. "But it's been there for as long as I can remember."

"I see. Well, let's try this again, shall we?" This time Joble went with more force, and it worked.

Kaiden watched as the syringe drew in his blood.

Joble noted the color: still red, like most humanoids, but much darker than anything he'd seen before. A deep maroon with a distinctly black hue to it. He removed the syringe and dabbed the entry point, blotting the excess blood. "Just give me a minute."

Joble placed a drop on a specimen slide and slid it under the lens. He peered into the eyepiece and focused the scope. "Computer, blood sample Ryder 1 loaded onto scope twenty-six."

"Yes, sir," acknowledged the computer.

Kaiden held his arm and inspected the pristine work-station.

Hulaksen remained visually fixed on the activity but was still with his patients mentally.

Joble zoomed in closer and fiddled with the settings as he took in what now lay before his eyes. He squinted, backed off from the scope, shook his head, then went back in—this time much more intently. There was more squinting, more adjustments, and then... A whisper: "What?" He flipped a switch, magnifying it even more, then lifted his head as he leveled an astonished stare at Kaiden.

"What is it?" queried Kaiden.

Hulaksen, alerted by the questions, joined in. "What's going on?"

Joble ignored them both and went straight back down for more. He zoomed in even further. Another appraisal. Another head shake. And then: "Computer?"

"Yes, sir."

"Please scan specimen Ryder 1."

"Scanning." The computer whirred, then wound down and let out a distinct blip. "Done sir."

"Please confirm there is *no* trace of the genetic material *JF1Kx* in the specimen."

"Confirmed," said the computer. "No trace of *JF1Kx* exists in specimen Ryder 1."

Hulaksen stared at Joble wondering where this was going while Kaiden watched on quietly.

Joble took in a deep breath—a long, slow one with an even slower exhale. "Now scan for the theoretical genetic material designated *JF1K* as described in my logs."

"What?" said Hulaksen.

Joble closed his eyes, ignored the question, and waited for the result.

The computer whirred some more, blipped a few times,

then stopped. "Confirmed. Genetic material *JF1K* is present in specimen Ryder 1."

Hulaksen's eyes widened. His jaw dropped. He shifted his gaze to Kaiden, then back to Joble.

Kaiden, completely lost at this point, repeated the refrain. "What?"

"Computer," said Joble cautiously as the sheer gravity of it began to set in. "Please rescan and reconfirm the presence of genetic material *JF1K* in sample Ryder 1."

"But sir, I'm quite certain that—"

"Please rescan," he said, this time with decidedly more demand in his tone. *JF1K only. No x.*"

"Yes, sir," said the computer. More scanning and blips ensued for what seemed like a lifetime. Then: "Rescanned and reconfirmed. Genetic material *JF1K* is present in specimen Ryder 1." The computer paused for a moment before continuing, this time adding a mechanical emphasis on the pertinent points. "*JF1K only. No x.*" And then, as dry as ever: "And if I might add, sir, in abundance."

Joble sat back on his stool. "Holy shit."

Kaiden's eyes drifted between the doctors.

Hulaksen again fixed his gaze on Kaiden, this time much more present to the situation.

Joble stared blankly at nothing, then managed a mumble under his breath. "It's Patient Zero."

CHAPTER THIRTY-SEVEN

"It'll work. I'd bet my life on it," said Joble as he stepped out of a shuttle in the driveway of Magnus's estate, a small chrome suitcase in hand.

Hulaksen held the door for him. "You're sure? Your transmission was cut off. Not sure why. So I didn't get all of it."

"Yes. It'll work. It couldn't have been easier once we got Kaiden's sample."

Hulaksen ducked his head into the shuttle. "Don't go anywhere," he said to the driver, "we'll be right back," then rushed off with Joble under the glittering nightlights of the estate.

Chief Drusher rushed up and intercepted them. Caught his breath. "Anything I can do?"

"I don't think so," said Hulaksen.

The Chief nodded and dropped a hand to the door panel at the main entrance. The door swished open. He stepped aside, made way for them to enter, visible concern residing in his exhausted eyes.

Hulaksen and Joble entered the glass-like foyer, their

steps echoing throughout as they rushed across the marble floor past the grand staircase in the direction of the west wing.

"I spent more time just confirming there was nothing in his blood that was going to be rejected or do any harm," said Joble.

"And?"

Joble shot an astonished look at Hulaksen. "I've never seen anything like it. It was as if the thirst of a thousand years was finally being quenched. Their specimens drank it in like they'd been stranded in a Vietrusian desert for half their lives. It was the final stage they'd required to be complete. It perfects each DNA strand, one to the next. Like a chain reaction. And it's *fast*. Of course I would normally have done more extensive testing if it weren't for—"

"No, you were right to come," said Hulaksen, reaching the stairwell to the sleeping chambers. "I put him on life support a couple hours ago. He's declining quickly."

"And the Princess?"

"Not much better. Kaiden just left. He's on his way to her as we speak. She asked to see him—hasn't seen him since the opera house. I really hope it won't be her dying wish."

"It won't be," said Joble. "Not if I can help it."

Hulaksen nodded in agreement as they ascended the staircase. "I was already here when I got your transmission," he said. "And it was closer too. So we'll go to her next."

They continued their ascent, their shoes clicking softly on the polished steps.

"It's different from a typical case at this juncture," continued Hulaksen. "While the disease is definitely more accelerated, the patients seem to have more fight in them too. They're not giving up as easily. They're stronger, but so is the disease. It's like an escalated battle."

"Yes," said Joble as he reached the top of the staircase. "They're knocking on the door of a higher state but being driven back down by a corruption of that *same* higher state. It's a war. And unfortunately I know all too well which side wins if we don't get it right."

"Then we *need* to get it right," said Hulaksen, indicating Magnus's room with a sweep of an arm. "Right here."

They rushed in, the looming sense of death immediate and pervading. There were two female attendants in protective gear—masks, gloves, stark-white coats.

Above Magnus hung a tangled bulk of hoses. At his side a pulsing transfusion machine, its merciless thumps a rhythmic reminder of the patient's condition. And at the foot of the bed, a blipping monitor, which is precisely where Hulaksen's attention instantly went. He motioned the attendants out of the way and checked the numbers. "Better hurry."

Joble went straight to work. He placed the case on the side table and pushed a hand to the lock. It clicked open. He lifted the lid revealing a row of vials and a pair of syringes. He removed one of them and began to prepare it.

Hulaksen stepped up to Magnus, gently shook him. "Lord Magnus." But there was nothing, only a faint wheeze. Hulaksen shook him again, harder this time. "Magnus. Please!" Magnus slowly parted his lids, a hazy film now covering his syrupy eyes. "This is Dr. Fedder. He has something he's prepared for you. We'd like to administer it with your permission, sir."

Magnus lifted his eyes to find the glistening syringe now full of the reddish-black substance.

"It's been tested, sir," said Joble. "While I cannot guarantee success, it did work on your sample specimens."

Magnus's gaze shifted from the syringe to Joble and then over to Hulaksen.

Hulaksen added emphasis to his stare. "We haven't much time, sir. It's my recommendation that we administer *immediately*."

Magnus gave the go-ahead with a labored nod, the graying skin of his jowls bobbing against his neck.

"Sir, policy dictates I receive verbal confirmation."

There was a moment of silence. Then, hoarsely: "Administer... Please."

Joble instantly sunk the syringe deep into Magnus's neck and depressed the activator. The syringe whirred as it flooded Magnus's wanting bloodstream with the concoction. Once it stopped, Joble removed it and placed it on the table beside its case.

Hulaksen shot over to the monitor, eyes like a hawk on the gauges.

"Will he live?" asked a voice from behind.

Joble looked to the back of the room where Dolph had been sitting, waiting, watching. "I believe so," said Joble. "I *hope* so. We'll know soon."

Dolph stood, stretched, strode over to the bed. "I hope so, too."

Joble removed a lancet from the case. He pricked Magnus's arm. Captured a drop. Then pulled out a magnifying loupe and popped it on his eye.

Dolph, whose attention had not left the case since they'd walked in, neared himself. It was like a kid in a candy store and there sat the sweets. He craned his eyes while Joble inspected the blood sample.

With Hulaksen still glued to the monitor, Dolph took another careful step. Then another. They'd miss a full vial of course, and the syringe too. But if he could just get a small swipe, it might be enough. He removed a swab from his pocket keeping it hid in his hand, quickly surveyed the room. All eyes otherwise engaged. Good. His heart hammered. Hand quivered. He locked onto the target, summoned the courage, then slowly extended his arm toward the syringe, preparing to claim the prize when...

Joble looked up from the loupe. "It's working."

...Dolph yanked his arm back, practically throwing a joint out.

Hulaksen confirmed. "I see it too. Numbers rising."

Dolph stood frozen, the jolt nearly stopping his heart.

Joble snapped up the syringe, wiped it, and returned it to the case. But even with the doctors only inches away, the urge in Dolph was so strong that he actually considered grabbing it and running. Foolish of course, and an act that would defeat the entire purpose of all of his work. So he resisted. Repressed it.

Magnus gave a grunt and stirred as the others watched on and waited, each with their own interest at stake. He coughed. Stirred some more. Wrenched his face.

Joble looked to Hulaksen, whose eyes had drifted back to the monitor.

Dolph, alert to everything in the room, still schemed.

Another cough from Magnus as he strained to lift his head. Hulaksen looked up, moved in closer as Magnus slowly opened his eyes and scanned the circle of spectators, color already drifting back into him. "What is it?" he finally managed, hint of a chuckle: "Someone die?"

Hulaksen exhaled. His shoulders dropped as his stance visibly relaxed. He cracked a relieved smile. "How do you feel?"

Magnus looked up. "Better already." Then swept his gaze over to the monitor. "How's it looking?"

Hulaksen nodded. "Better."

"And Chakeena?"

"She's next," said Hulaksen. "Shuttle's waiting downstairs."

"Well then," said Magnus, a flicker of strength awakening in his eyes, "what're you waiting for?"

CHAPTER THIRTY-EIGHT

"We're in luck. She's in one of the guest quarters," said Gluke, returning from his midnight reconnaissance. He brushed off his knees and caught his breath.

"How's that lucky?" asked Thyrro.

"It's at this edge of the grounds, right around the corner, so it's easier access. Close to the rear entrance. I can't kill the alarms. I checked. Too complicated. So they *will* go off. But this way we don't need to go in too deep. It will be in and out fast. So like I said, lucky."

Thyrro grumbled an acknowledgement and cinched up the slack on his harness.

"There's someone with her though," continued Gluke. "We *could* wait till they leave but—"

"We're not waitin' for nuthin! She dies and we don't get paid!"

"That's what I was gonna say if you'd let me finish!" snapped Gluke in a hushed yelp.

Another grumble from Thyrro. "All right then. Let's go."

They crept around the corner and followed a path concealed by a tangle of slender vines and pale-leafed clusters draped over a veil of ornamental lattice. Reaching its end, Gluke stopped, leaned against the estate's perimeter wall, the wire he'd secured snaking up it like a slithering serpent.

"We enter here," he whispered to Thyrro, "but we'll have to leave through there once we have her." He pointed to a gate looming in the distance nestled next to a guard shack. "We'll have to deal with the guard," he said. "But it shouldn't be an issue. Then straight back to the van and we're outta here."

Gluke tugged at the wire. Still secure. "Okay, follow me." He clamped the cable to his harness, locked it in, and engaged the winch. It groaned as it heaved his enormous body up the wall for the second time of the night. When he reached the top, he unhooked himself and waited. Listened. No alarms yet. Good. He reversed the winch and sent it back down.

Thyrro secured himself and began his ascent, his legs scrambling for some kind of purchase on the slick wall. The winch stopped. He disconnected from it and crouched beside Gluke, together forming a silhouette of two large lumps attempting an inconspicuous position but failing utterly.

Gluke scanned the moonlit grounds then looked at Thyrro: "Ready?"

Thyrro responded with a hoarse whisper: "Born."

Gluke yanked his blaster from its holster and leapt from the wall, landing with a thump and a grunt.

The alarm instantly let out a blood-curdling wail that resounded through the entire estate.

Thyrro dropped beside Gluke, looked for instructions.

"That one there!" shouted Gluke.

Thyrro saw it. Nodded.

They took off toward one of the many structures on the grounds—a smaller one on its own off in the corner dimly lit by the distant lights of the palace. Thirty meters and closing. Twenty. Ten. A shout from the guard shack alerted them.

"You get her!" barked Gluke. "I'll get him!"

Thyrro maintained his pace as Gluke dropped to the ground sniper-style. He took aim, fired. Missed. More shouting ensued as he trained his sights again on the target. He calmed himself and squeezed off another shot. The guard spun from the impact and sailed to the ground, wiggled a while, then stopped.

Gluke scanned the area for any additional threats. Nothing yet, though they were undoubtedly on their way. He lifted his gorilla-like body and stood. His stance alert, he swept the grounds visually, blaster leveled in outstretched arms as he began a slow creep toward the target in a stocking state of readiness.

The patter of feet alerted him. Someone behind him. He spun, took them out in a single shot. Swung back and rescanned the area. Then bolted off in the direction of the structure, arriving to find an open door, some unlucky attendant on the floor, and Thyrro with Chakeena slung over his shoulder squirming in a futile protest.

"Good," said Gluke. "Hold a sec." He peered out from the doorway. Spotted another guard. Sighted him and took him out. "Okay. Go!"

They took off for the gate as the blinding glare of a spotlight exploded onto them. Gluke shielded his eyes, shouted over the wail of the alarm. "Get her to the gate! I'll open it."

Another guard racing in their direction from the now fully lit-up palace fired off a shot. It ricocheted off the gate as Thyrro reached it. He spun, lifted his blaster and took out the shooter. Spotted more off in the distance. "Hurry up! More coming!"

"I got it!" shouted Gluke as he swung into the shack. He scanned the wall of monitors—guards rushing from every direction. He dropped a paw to the gate's control key on the panel, twisted it. The gate jolted and began to part, the sound of scraping metal filling the air as it slid along its tracks. He watched as Thyrro squeezed himself through—Chakeena's fragile fists furiously pounding her gargantuan captor. He held a moment. And when the time was right, snapped the key back and reversed the gate, then blasted the panel and took off, squeezing his enormous frame through the opening with seconds to spare.

The gate let out a grating screech and closed with a clank behind him, as...

Bronson hurled his body into it with all his weight!

A clang rang out as his shoulder connected. He lifted an arm and took aim through the wrought iron bars but was instantly met by the smack of Gluke's paw sending the blaster hurling to the ground.

"Shit!" Bronson rocketed over to the shed. Found a smoking panel and fried wires.

"That was her!" snapped Kaiden, arriving out of breath.

Bronson snatched his communicator from his vest. Scrambled with the map.

"Bronson, that was the Princess! They got her!"

"I know," replied Bronson. "It was them."

"Who?"

"The abductors."

Kaiden crinkled his brow, searched for an answer. "*Who?*"

"The two idiots. Remember? Truth-serum guys? Dart boards?"

Kaiden swung around, strained to see, saw the diminishing figures stumble off in the distance shrouded by the darkness of night.

Bronson continued to work the communicator. He reset the receiver, recalibrated its scanner, and waited as the map frantically searched for the signal.

"What're you doing?" asked Kaiden. "They're getting away."

"Remember when I reversed the bug they had on me?"

"What?" Kaiden thought about it. "Yeah, I guess. But—"

"Well, I had a feeling it would come in handy. And I bet you a million credits I know where they're headed. Now if I could just get this damn thing to lock on."

"I'm coming too," asserted Kaiden.

Bronson shook his head. "Too dangerous. And you'd only slow me down."

Kaiden took a solemn stance and glared at Bronson.

Bronson weighed options while waiting for the signal to lock. He flicked a few more settings, "Damn piece a crap!" then smacked the device with a hefty backhand. A glowing blip sprang to the screen. "Ha! Got 'em!" He looked up, found Kaiden still staring him down—the same unyielding glare he'd employed on the night they first met. He shook his head. Sighed. Then relented: "All right. Let's go."

CHAPTER THIRTY-NINE

"Yeah, she's there all right," confirmed Bronson, his eyes pressed against a pair of night-vision binoculars, the florescent halo radiating from the instrument like a firefly in the night. "Top floor. Last room on the right. Near the staircase. What about the guards? Any change?"

Kaiden, crouched beside Bronson atop a roof of an abandoned factory, peered down at a dozen armed animals scattered throughout the compound below, ground zero for the Underpath Network itself. "No," said Kaiden. "No change. But I still don't see how we're supposed to get to her."

"You let me worry about that," said Bronson. "Remember, you're here as additional eyes. You do only what I say. Exactly what I say."

Bronson magnified his view and scanned the featureless building nestled in the compound's center. It was monolithic in shape, ominous and imposing, wrapped by prison-like walls crowned with rows of laser-spike barbs and swiveling security cameras. "Looks like she's awake. Or coming to at least." He zoomed out. "Someone's headed her way. Tall. Looks like a doctor or something. Wheeling a cart. She's going in."

Bronson's communicator blipped. Without removing his eyes from the binocular's eyecups, he yanked it from his pocket and handed it to Kaiden. "What does it say?"

Kaiden read it aloud: "Bronson, received your transmission. We have an antidote. It works. Lord Magnus recovering as we speak. At Empress's now. Crucial you return with Princess soon. Will remain here until further notice. Friend, if Princess is still alive, she won't be for long. Please hurry. Dr. Hulaksen."

"I should've taken care of those guys when we had them," said Bronson.

"If you had, we wouldn't know where the Princess was," said Kaiden.

"If I'd taken care of them, they wouldn't be around to take her in the first place."

"But you said it yourself, you're not a murderer. Besides, they would've just sent someone else."

"Yeah maybe. But still..." He sighed. Though rarely one to relive the past or experience anything resembling remorse, Bronson was yet feeling it tonight. He'd allowed the Princess to be abducted from under his nose. And worse yet, by two imbeciles he'd had in his very hands and could easily have prevented from ever abducting again.

Now on the verge of death, the daughter of the Empire's reigning ruler lay helplessly hostage to some of the most sinister animals in the Conglomerate, all likely because he'd allowed himself to be captured and jacked up on truth serum. And if that weren't enough, he'd practically served to the enemy on a silver platter the means to manufacture a catastrophically lethal weapon. So if ever there were a time to harbor a little guilt or feel some added pressure, this was it. And his time was running out. "The doctor, or whatever it is," said Bronson, "is hooking her up to something. Taking her blood."

"They're here," whispered Kaiden. "Headed toward the building."

Bronson shifted position, trained his view down to the compound. A guard. Another one. And... The imbeciles. "I see 'em," said Bronson. There was a pause, then a head shake. "And Grivel Gromme too. Shoulda known."

He pulled back from the binoculars and looked at Kaiden. "Okay, here's the deal. You're gonna stay here. I'll head down to the gate. You watch for me. When I signal you, hit this." He handed Kaiden the communicator and indicated a pulsing switch.

"No, I'm coming too."

"Not this time. I need you here to pull this off."

Kaiden looked to the compound, then back to Bronson: "But what about—"

"No buts," snapped Bronson. "No time for that. You read the transmission. I'll go down. And when I give you the signal, you hit it. Not before, and not after. And as soon as you hit it, you throw it as far as you can in that direction, away from the compound, and then get the hell outta here."

"And then what?"

"I disengaged the transmitter on the bug they had on me after we escaped from them, so they don't know we're here. This will reactivate it. It will alert them of its location. And if I know Grivel, he'll order every single one of those guards after it. Like immediately. You understand?"

"Sure," said Kaiden. "I guess so."

"Listen, they'll open the gate to come find me. They'll follow the signal to wherever the transmitter is. This buys us time. I can enter the compound while it's open and retrieve her."

"And what do *I* do?" asked Kaiden.

"You head straight back to the craft and wait. I'll come to *you*. Then we get her back to the doctor as fast as possible. Got it?"

Kaiden nodded tentatively. "Yeah, I got it."

CHAPTER FORTY

The telepath stood at Chakeena's bedside with its attention firmly fixed on the now half-full vials of blood, its large gray eyes distorted behind the thick goggle lenses.

Chakeena's breathing had shallowed and was practically imperceptible. Bruises and open wounds had formed and had begun to fester. There were branching patterns of bulging veins tracing down her arms and up her neck. And her face, now blueing from want of oxygen, had taken on a stiff and waxy veneer.

The telepath tilted its oblong head, glanced down to the monitor, studied the gauges—all having now dipped to their lowest readings. Though the sporadic pulses in them indicated the presence of life, they were indiscernibly slight at this point.

A rustle of movement grew in the hall, the tramping of heavy feet underlying the contentious echoes of voices growing closer and louder until...

Grivel clomped through the doorway, his godawful scent preceding him. He lumbered across the room, stopped beside the bed and took Chakeena in. "So this is her, is it?"

"Yup," said Thyrro, trailing behind.

Then Gluke. "As promised."

Grivel moved in for a closer look. Sniffed her. "She alive?"

Yes, thought the telepath. *Barely*.

"Hmm." Grivel worked his way over to the vials, the muffled thump of the machine's unhurried rhythm pushing carefully measured pulses down the tubes into the failing body. "And this is what all the fuss is about?"

"Yup," said Thyrro.

"As promised," said Gluke.

Grivel looked to the telepath, pointed a crooked claw: "The blood is good?"

It is good, thought the telepath.

"And if she dies?"

The telepath turned to Grivel. *Death is imminent. The body is failing. That which is extracted before she expires shall remain viable.*

"Can we go faster?"

No. It would kill her.

Grivel grunted. "Hmm. Vicious cycle."

The telepath looked to Grivel with a lifeless stare, gave him what he was looking for: *They got her here in time.* Then went back to work.

"Yeah, okay." Grivel turned to the idiots. "Lemme see 'em."

Thyrro and Gluke both eagerly lifted their transaction devices.

"A hundred thousand each," said Grivel as he prepared the transactions and authorized them. Then, cynically: "*As promised!*"

The telepath suddenly stopped, turned and locked its goggled gaze onto Grivel. *He is here.*

"Who?" said Grivel.

He, thought the telepath. *The threat.*

Grivel scowled. "The what"?

Thyrro's communicator blipped, interrupting the exchange. A light blinked. He fiddled with it, his fingers far too fat for the task.

Gluke's eyes went alert. "What is it?"

"Hang on a sec." Thyrro fiddled some more, regained the lock. "Looks like Bronson's signal just went live."

"What! Where?" asked Gluke.

"Just a sec," said Thyrro.

Grivel glared at the idiots, growled, his paw unconsciously moving to his wounded leg. Then, under his putrid breath: "Decker. Bronson *damn* Decker."

The telepath maintained its lock on Grivel and upped the emphasis: *He is here.*

"Here?" said Grivel.

Another blip from the communicator. "Damn," said Thyrro. "He's here. Outside the compound. North. A hundred yards or so."

"What? Why that slippery little snake!" Grivel bared his fangs, exposing the odor and accumulated filth to the others in the room. "Find him!"

Thyrro looked to Grivel. A silent pause, his expression dripping with reservation. "But what about—"

"Oh you'll get your damn credits!" barked Grivel. "Don't worry! Just go!"

"You're not coming?" asked Thyrro.

Grivel shook his mane. "Not a chance. Precious cargo and Decker bent on retrieving it? That's a lethal combination no matter how you slice it. And all I got between it and him is a world-class pack of boneheads?" He tugged at his communicator, slipped it from his belt. "Tell ya the truth, my money's on Decker. But maybe it'll buy me some time."

Grivel went to work, composed an order to capture Bronson or keep him from entering the compound *if anyone wanted to see tomorrow!* He transmitted it, then looked back up to the idiots: "I let you get away with one screwup. But I won't let you get away with another. You got it?"

They nodded and stumbled off, their bickering like buzzing insects as they disappeared down the hall and into the stairwell.

Grivel stepped up to the window. Watched the guards below as they received the order. Composed another transmission with the alleged location and an additional order that half were to go with the idiots and the other half were to stay and stand guard. He sent it, waited, stared at the yard below with vacant eyes as he considered the situation. His anxious claw tapped on the communicator, the clicking unwittingly in sync with the pump's thumping.

He dropped his gaze to Gluke and Thyrro as they scrambled from the building and across the compound below. There was a lot of pointing and yelling, the whines of blasters being charged, and then the alarm.

Everyone scattered like ants.

He is coming, thought the telepath.

"Yeah I know," droned Grivel, hate thick in his voice. He put a paw to his chin, gears still grinding in his mind.

The telepath flipped a switch on the pump, slid the needle out of Chakeena's arm, and carefully secured the vials in their case—Grivel way too absorbed to notice.

"Okay," he said. "Got no choice. Gotta do it." He looked up. "Disconnect her. I'm taking it. It's too valuable to risk Decker getting his hands on it."

It is already done, thought the telepath as it snapped the

257

case shut and handed it over. *It was time. To continue would have put it at risk.*

A dull tone sounded from the monitor as the gauges bottomed out.

The telepath locked eyes with Grivel. *She is dead.*

Grivel displayed an indifferent look. "Oh." Then took the case and fondled it while considering his next move.

A flurry of shots from the yard jerked his attention back. Shouts and thuds of unlucky recipients flopping to the ground followed.

Grivel slid the case under an arm, pocketed his communicator, and unholstered his blaster. "All right Decker, let's see whatcha got." He clomped across the room to the door, checked the hall, then took off inelegantly galloping toward the stairwell—the yelp of the alarm incessant in his ears.

He reached the stairs and the deadline for a decision. Down would surely be a date with Decker. A no-brainer. And up would get him nowhere. Or would it?

The ongoing blasts from below and the thud of another body going down prompted a decision. Grivel snatched the communicator and sent off another transmission, this one ordering a getaway craft to extract him from the roof. He smiled, a pompous nod. Then: "Up it is."

The alarm suddenly ceased. The staircase creaked under his weight as he began to scale it. More shots from below urged him along, one ricocheting off a rail next to him. He shielded himself from the blaster flares and continued his ascent.

Reaching the top, he placed his entire store of weight into the door and hurled it open, then exited to the roof and thumped across it. He dropped behind a rail and took cover, sending off another transmission to the craft—a *much* more emphatic one this time.

A firework of flames lit up the night and streamed across the roof, taking out a portion of the guardrail at his head. "Damn it!" More flames. Then an explosion, the blast vaporizing the remainder of the rail.

He rolled behind another one, craned to see, straining to put an eye on the shooter.

It went quiet, an uneasy silence as he stilled himself, watching, waiting, knowing all too well what would come next.

And then, through the wisps of obscuring smoke—like an apparition approaching from a curtain of fog in the night—appeared a silhouette he knew all too well headed straight at him and closing quickly, blaster raised and readied.

"Decker!" shouted Grivel. "You're wasting your time!"

Another firework lit up the rooftop, begging to differ.

Grivel shielded himself from the blast, ducked and held for a moment. "Damn him," he said to himself. He reloaded, rolled into position, and fired, missing by inches. Then another one—this time a hit!

Bronson's arm gave way, his blaster toppling to the rooftop.

Grivel quickly got off another shot as he again evasively rolled.

Bronson shielded himself from the ricochet and, as Grivel was reloading, sprinted across the rooftop and leapt at the monster, the collision knocking the wind out of its enormous chest.

Grivel compulsively coughed, gasped for a breath, wheezed in a lungful of smoke-filled air, his paw remaining locked on the case like an iron vice.

Bronson scooped up a section of the guardrail and swung it, connecting with Grivel's blaster paw. A crunch followed, then the clanking of the blaster as it bounced off an aluminum air vent.

A hum from above seized their attention. It was the escape craft—large and looming as it descended toward them—music to Grivel's ears and future freedom from Bronson's annoying antics. "Ha!" gloated Grivel. "That's my ride." He twisted to stand.

Bronson dove at the monster, collided and wrapped an arm around its neck, squeezed with everything he had as he kicked at the case.

Grivel wriggled. Squirmed to escape. Sunk an elbow deep into Bronson's ribcage.

Bronson's arm instinctively shot down to his torso allowing Grivel to shake him off.

The craft's hum increased as it hovered above, dark and menacing, now mere jumping distance from the roof.

"No time for this old friend," shouted Grivel. "It's been fun. But I gotta go now." He lunged up and leapt for the craft, scrambling to heave himself aboard as it began its instant ascent.

Bronson pulled a second weapon from his boot—his beloved varmint-annihilating blaster. "You got it all wrong, Gromme," he said as he trained it on the monster. "You see, it's not you I want." He loaded a round into the chamber and zeroed in on the target, holding fast his aim. "It's your pretty little case." The blaster blipped. He squeezed off a shot. A burst of light spewed from the muzzle and streamed straight at the target, taking out the case's handle and part of Grivel's paw.

Grivel yanked his arm back. Roared!

The case plummeted to the roof, landed with a bounce and a crack.

Bronson flipped the blaster's settings, again took aim, and waited for it to charge as the craft began its getaway.

"Bad news, Gromme," shouted Bronson. "Gonna have to end this here and now." The blaster's whine peaked. It blipped. "But I'm sure I'll see you again soon enough." He squeezed the trigger, sailing the blast precisely at the case— a stream of liquid fire trailing behind it.

Boom!

The flash connected with the case, showering forth a cascade of blood that formed into a tornado of maroon mist twisting in the escape craft's wake.

Grivel let out another roar, shaking his bloody paw at Bronson. "Damn you, Decker!"

The craft tipped and turned away, the hissing sound of its boosters filling the space as they engaged and lifted the craft into the black of the night, Grivel's grumbles ebbing in the distance as they drifted away.

Bronson maintained his focus on the target, squinted an eye, then took aim and squeezed off one more shot—just for good measure—erupting what little remained of the case into a wash of bloody flames.

CHAPTER FORTY-ONE

[A Few Minutes Earlier]

Bronson looked up from his location below and signaled Kaiden. It was go-time.

Kaiden triggered the communicator and tossed it as hard as he could in the indicated direction, then took off straight for the staircase with Bronson's orders cycling in his head. He reached the first step, stopped and activated the repulsers on his belt, and shot off down through the stairwell.

Nearing the ground floor, he redirected the repulsers and slowed to a stop at the doorway. There were booms of blasters ringing and the yelp of an alarm, as predicted. He poked his head out to check the surroundings. All seemed clear. *Good.* He shot off!

As he rounded the corner, the gate came into view as well as a number of laid-out bodies. He reduced his speed and peeked into the compound. Took in the ominous structure. Then launched himself in its direction as a rogue blast crackled through the air overhead. He dove and skidded on the concrete, shred his shirt and scraped his arm. Then another shot. "Damn." Maybe it *wasn't* rogue. He rolled to evade. Took cover behind one of the bodies. Took a moment to gather his wits, tough with the continued yelp of the alarm.

The glistening of an abandoned blaster caught his eye. He quickly scanned the area for hostiles. Scooped up the weapon and sailed off across the compound until the building's wall at last stopped him dead in his tracks sending a concussive blow rippling through his body. He pressed himself against the wall. It was stable and somehow comforting in all the chaos. But another blast from behind quickly ended that.

He dropped to avoid the shot, gashing an arm on a torn handrail. A stream of blood gushed forth. "Shit." He looked to his arm and reconsidered his actions. Maybe it was wrong to have followed. Maybe he should've stuck to Bronson's orders. But the shots echoing from the building prompted him to forge forward.

As he scanned the compound, he spotted an entrance. Ten meters at most. Definitely doable. All he had to do was not get killed. He took a moment to center his thoughts, reminding himself of the reason for it all, then jetted off along the length of the building and straight into the smoky stairwell, blurting an involuntary "yes" as he dropped to his knees and took cover.

The moisture issuing from his arm had increased. He tore off a chunk of his shirt and wrapped his arm in it as he caught his breath, then tightened the tourniquet and checked again for others. Another guard on the floor. The echo of a battle above. He lifted himself and had just started his ascent up the stairs when the alarm suddenly ceased. The silence was followed by the creak of a door. *Top floor?*

Roof? He took a chance and took off, sailing up the staircase, his heart hammering in his chest as the distance between him and whatever awaited above closed.

Reaching the top, he soared into the hall and halted himself to a stop at the targeted door, standing as still as possible as he listened. The blasts from above resumed. Then thumping on the roof and Bronson's muffled voice—but nothing from inside the room.

This was it. It was time. He disengaged the repulsers and allowed his feet to gently settle to the floor as he steeled himself for whatever he was about to witness, then heaved a silent sigh and leapt through the doorway.

Time stood still as he took in the scene and attempted to process it. For there before him—colorless, motionless, blood draining from her wrists—lay Chakeena. And at her side a slender figure cloaked in white utterly unmoved by his presence. The figure disposed of a bloody ball of gauze, then turned and locked an empty stare on Kaiden with its goggled eyes. *It is too late*, it thought, then nonchalantly went back to work, wrapping a set of tubes with horrifying machine-like precision, inhuman and absent in its every action.

Kaiden dropped the blaster and rushed over. Tapped Chakeena tentatively. "Princess. It's me. Kaiden." He grasped a shoulder and lightly shook her. "Princess." Then a more frantic shake. "Princess."

The telepath placed the neatly wrapped tubes in their case, snapped it shut and turned back to Kaiden. *It is too late. She is dead. Minutes ago.*

"No," he whispered. "This is wrong. Something's *wrong.*" He looked down, took Chakeena's hand. It was like ice and already stiffening, encouraging him even more to accept the truth of it. And as the grief for someone he barely knew unexpectedly crept into his throat, he grappled for an answer—the dreams, the visions, the irrepressible urge—all of it leading to this unfathomable moment.

He looked back up to what was now undeniably a corpse, forcing him to confront that she was indeed dead no matter how hard he rejected it. He released her hand. Shook his head. And as he hovered over her—struggling with the unthinkable, the notion of hope now all but entirely extinguished—a single drop of his blackish blood trickled down his arm, slowed to a near stop at the tip of his elbow, lingered a moment, then gave way to gravity and landed squarely on her bloody wrist.

The telepath instantly ceased all action as if mentally jarred by the occurrence, swung toward Kaiden, eyes gaping at him from behind the bulky lenses, its inaudible response jolting through the psychic neurostream: *No. It cannot be.*

Kaiden ignored the reaction, completely oblivious of the exchange that had just taken place. For in that instant his unadulterated gene had been introduced into Chakeena's bloodstream and the imminent merger had begun. Slowly at first, one chromosome to the next as each awoke, then another, and another, speeding up faster until it reached the cellular level, her body gulping in the life-giving cure as every cell encountered transformed into its perfected self. It continued to gain speed, building, surging, Kaiden's DNA now a biological juggernaut coursing through her and propagating like wildfire as it wholly satiated the previously unquenchable.

Still unaware of the unstoppable event that he'd set into motion, Kaiden remained speechless. The telepath, *all too* aware, thoughtless.

Muffled blasts from above seeped in through the ceiling followed by curses and an explosion. Then more curses, more blasts, and one final explosion that ultimately quieted it all.

Silence inundated the room. Time again stood deafeningly still.

The grief in Kaiden's throat worked its way to the surface. He closed his eyes and surrendered, at last about to accept the atrocity that lay before him, when...

The sound of a single breath broke the silence. It was shallow, soft, but perceivable.

Kaiden's eyes snapped open. He gazed at the lifeless face, waiting, watching, wondering, himself now finding it difficult to breathe. And then...

Another one—the inhalation of one who a moment ago was undeniably dead.

The telepath, its face now as agape as it was capable of being, lifted its goggles and glared at Chakeena, then swept its stare over to Kaiden.

Kaiden stared back. "You said she was dead."

She was, thought the telepath.

The monitor ticked. The gauges twitched. The telepath moved in, its piercing attention on it all.

"Princess?" said Kaiden.

Give her a minute, thought the telepath.

Another breath ensued. Then another—deeper this time as the hands of the gauges at last lifted and began a low, slow dance.

Kaiden squeezed Chakeena's hand. The telepath squeezed in even closer.

The breathing continued, more rhythmic, more consistent until finally—like a lone ray of sunlight cresting the horizon of a distant planetary dawn—the monitor's faceplate lit up. A blip rang out and the gauges surged.

The telepath turned to Kaiden, closed its lifeless eyes,

knelt and bowed its oblong head. *It is you. You are He*, it thought. *The Nadishia Wanai Ka Ré.*

"What?"

The telepath lifted its eyes, locked onto Kaiden with a deep, reverent stare. *The Nadishia Wanai Ka Ré—He who is not without.* It bowed its head once more. *Nönnac Alim, you grace me.*

"I don't know what you're talking about," said Kaiden. "I'm no—"

But a raspy whisper cut him off: "Kaiden?"

He gasped, turned his head, met the eyes of what could only be described as an angel.

Chakeena squirmed, struggled to speak, attempted to moisten her pasty mouth. Then, softly: "You're here?"

"Princess?" He gaped at her. "I don't understand. I thought you were..." He looked back to the telepath, searching for some sort of an answer.

You are He, thought the telepath. *He who is not without.*

The corners of Chakeena's mouth curled and, as energy permitted, grew into a glowing smile—quite possibly the first real smile of her entire life. "Come closer," she said.

Kaiden moved in.

"Closer."

He brought his face to hers, careful of her delicate frame.

She grasped his arm and squeezed, tears pooling at her eyes and streaming down her cheeks as she lifted her mouth to his ear—a gentle whisper from a gentle soul as the final surge of the gene reached her already awakening heart. "It's you. It's *always* been you."

She dropped back to the bed, stared at Kaiden with her inky eyes.

He stared back, wrestling with the sentiment as he strived to reconcile what he'd just witnessed and all that had led to it—the prescient vision that started it all now loudly echoing that very same sentiment in him, that it had indeed always been *her* as well. He turned to the telepath, still amid its own awe of the event, when...

Gluke burst through the doorway, blaster drawn and instantly on Kaiden!

Kaiden swung around. Found Gluke and the tip of the blaster's muzzle. Instinctively blocked Chakeena.

"What?" said Gluke. He stood and gathered himself, swept the room to confirm no hidden threats, then swung back to Kaiden, scratching his head. "You? The skinny one?"

Out of breath, Thyrro clomped in behind Gluke and scanned the scene. "What?" He looked to Gluke. "The skinny one?"

Gluke shot his partner an impudent glare. "That's what *I* said!"

The telepath stepped forward and made itself a barrier between the weapon and Kaiden.

"Get back!" blurted Gluke, his blaster now fixed on the telepath. "Now!"

The telepath stood its ground, stared the blaster down—a still, unconcerned stare—then shifted its deadpan gaze back to Gluke. *You know not what you risk.*

Gluke pressed a thumb to the blaster's safety and flicked it, bared his rotting fangs. "I'm warning you. I won't say it twice."

The telepath stood firm, unyielding certainty deep in its dull glare.

Gluke lifted a brow and shrugged. "Fine. Have it your way." He tugged back on the trigger, the discharge instantly flaring like the spit of a dragon from the muzzle's mouth as...

The telepath calmly raised a hand and sent forth a subsonic burst. *No.*

The space in the room rippled as warped wave-rings radiating from her hand surged forth, arresting the blast midair and bowling the idiots to the floor. They landed in a succession of thuds. There were groans, some fidgeting, and then, nothing.

Kaiden stood speechless, staring at the telepath. Then turned to Chakeena.

The telepath looked to Kaiden and again lowered its head, reverence emanating from its entire being. *Nönnac Alím, you grace me.*

The silence was broken by the tramping of steps in the hall growing louder as they neared.

Kaiden and Chakeena's focus shot to the door—eyes wide and aware.

The telepath did not move, did not blink, remained firmly in its worshiping stance before Kaiden and merely thought: *He is here*, as...

Bronson burst into the room and slid to a stop! He glared at the scene, the telepath now centered in *his* blaster's sights.

Without lifting an eye, the telepath slowly raised a hand in the direction of Bronson and, keeping its head dipped to Kaiden, its body still submissively bent, merely thought: *No.*

CHAPTER FORTY-TWO

"Please let them in and show them to the drawing room," said the Empress.

An aide in ceremonial attire dipped her head with the required courtesy and said, "By your command," then turned and signaled an awaiting steward with a flourish of her hand.

Chakeena, enjoying one of the many hors d'oeuvres being offered, was mid-conversation with Dr. Hulaksen and Joble. But her eye was sharply on her mother and her attention on Kaiden, who'd yet to make an appearance.

The Empress had gathered everyone for a celebration. And it was certainly an appropriate name for such a gathering, for there was much to celebrate. Chakeena and Magnus were alive and had never felt better—*literally,* never in their lives—with shiny medical results to support the claims and unprecedented discoveries coming in by the hour.

Joble's findings were even more dramatic. Tests indicated no trace of the element's flaw anywhere in them—the "x" was simply gone, leaving their entire cellular structures altered and complete. From a genetic perspective, they were perfect. From a more practical standpoint, Magnus had the strength of a twenty-year-old. His mental clarity had surpassed anything he'd ever experienced. And no sign of the disease at all, or any other ailment for that matter. As for Chakeena, she'd put on weight—healthy, much-needed weight. Her skin radiated. She had an overall increase of well-being, a newfound interest in others, and the cleanest bill of health of her life. And her vitality had skyrocketed.

It was not yet known how the antidote would ultimately play out. Joble had tested it on others afflicted with the disease, but it had not healed them like it had Chakeena and Magnus. In fact, the subjects had rejected it, which came as a surprise. He'd assumed it would've worked with everyone's physiological deficiencies—disease or no disease —since *it was,* genetically, the missing piece. But it didn't, bringing to light yet another anomaly in and of itself.

Could it be that the "x" had somehow assisted the process, somehow prepared the way for the antidote? A genetic "primer" if you will. As illogical as it was to think that you'd need the broken factor introduced before the unadulterated one would take, it was the only difference he'd found and so served as the current theory. Of course with no "x" remaining he would be unable to prove it. The disaster had taken out his lab samples, and Bronson had taken out the rest. And just how it had even come about in the first place yet remained a mystery, despite subsequent attempts to replicate the initial anomaly with Kaiden under similar conditions.

Part of Joble resented Bronson for what he'd done, but another part was forced to support the decision. It was the right thing to do given the situation, the potential weaponization of the element being far too great. But Joble knew he would never stop trying to reproduce the positive side, the life-giving side of that which he'd had a hand in achieving. An accomplishment that was more of a miracle than anything else. A miracle that now stood before him embodied by Chakeena—very alive and vastly enhanced.

"Empress," said the aide, re-entering the drawing room, "I present to you Lord Magnus Vasudum Rue, Sir Dolph Vaviliun Rue, Lieutenant Bronson Cannon Decker, and Mr. Kaiden Ryder."

The Empress chuckled. "You may, but you needn't be so formal. After all, this is a special day and these are my closest of friends."

"As you wish, your Excellency," said the aide, bowing again before quickly departing.

A grin sprouted and blossomed into a wide smile on Chakeena's ivory face. "Will you excuse me, please?" she said. But before the doctors had a chance to answer she was off in the direction of the arrivals.

She swung up to Magnus, embraced him, cherishing him, not taking for granted the fact that he too had barely made it back from the brink of death.

"Chakeena," said Magnus. "You look wonderful."

She nodded in response and released him.

Hulaksen and Joble approached as the rest in turn said their hellos, leaving only Kaiden and Chakeena now facing each other.

Chakeena beamed at Kaiden. "I'm so glad you made it. How *are* you?"

"Good," he said. "Tired. There's been a lot of testing."

"Yes. I heard." She looked down to the floor, uncertain of her next move, then looked up and relented to the urge, wrapping herself around Kaiden and burying her face in his chest.

Kaiden tensed at first but soon settled into it.

"Ladies and gentlemen," announced a butler, "lunch is served. Please find your way to the Grand Veranda and take a seat."

A pair of servants in silken robes heaved open the ceiling-high doors to reveal the sprawl of the estate lawn exquisitely backdropped by a blanket of stars and boundless space. On the lawn sat a table adorned for lunch, the scarlet sunlight glistening on the silverware, its meter-high centerpiece bursting in a spectacular assortment of Vetrusian flora. And at the lawn's edge, a kenneled area where Boomer was attending to his own meal.

The guests made their way to their seats and took them. Chakeena sat between Kaiden and Magnus. Opposite them sat Bronson and the Empress, resuming their conversation from the drawing room, with Dolph settling quietly beside them.

Chakeena and Kaiden discussed the night of the concert and when they'd first met in the officials' area. Bronson had engaged the Empress with another anecdote from his serviceman days. Dolph was engaged too, though much less so, his attention covertly fixed on his father.

Ever aware of propriety, Chakeena politely excused herself from her conversation with Kaiden and turned to Magnus, a giant smile gleaming from her. "And how are *you* feeling?"

"It's still taking some getting used to," said Magnus. "I feel like a young man again."

Chakeena giggled. "Well, I can't speak to that, but I *am* still getting accustomed to it as well. Every time I turn around there's something new. Something different." Her ebony eyes drifted to Kaiden. "Something amazing."

"Yes. Nothing short of a miracle."

Chakeena lowered her voice. "*He's* the real miracle."

Magnus grinned and nodded. "Yes, my dear. He sure is."

A line of waiters filed out to the veranda, the swish of their robes announcing their arrival. They aligned themselves at the side of each guest and simultaneously placed the first course on the table. "Sautéed Vietrusian root stalks," said the head waiter, his statement steeped in regal enunciation.

The conversations around the table resumed as the waiters formed a line and departed.

"One of my favorites," said Magnus.

"Mine too," said Chakeena. She took a whiff, savoring the scent, then waited for the others to dig in before lifting her fork and gracefully securing a bite. She took a taste. *Oh no*, she thought. *A little overdone. How unfortunate.*

Magnus nodded. Then, under his breath: "Yes, unfortunate."

"Pardon me?" she asked.

Magnus kept his head down and discreetly clarified. "Oh, I was just agreeing with you, my dear."

"I'm sorry?" she whispered. "Agreeing with what?"

Magnus shot her a confused look. Then another whisper. "Just that they *are* a little overdone."

Chakeena halted like a caught criminal. She looked to Magnus, her defenses immediately up as if her deeply instilled etiquette was under attack. "Why I said nothing of the sort." She paused, took note of her tone and internally de-escalated, then shook her head to Magnus apologetically. "I'm sorry." She discarded it as coincidence and continued with her lunch, noting to herself: *But I did think it.*

Magnus turned to her. "You *thought* it?"

Chakeena again froze, queried the question with wide eyes. *Two* coincidences? Two as precise as that? She carefully placed her fork on the table and raised a napkin, dabbing her generous lips, now utterly absorbed by the exchange. She contemplated the events of the week, considered all that had taken place, all that had transpired. And as she did, an answer began to come to her. *Could it be?*

Could what be? thought Magnus.

Chakeena locked eyes with him, still adjusting to the idea of it. *It's like the telepath*, she thought to herself.

Magnus stared back. At first he questioned his own sanity. Her mouth had not moved; he'd deliberately watched it this time. Uncertain what to say next—or *think*—he sat back, swallowed a mouthful of roots, and shook his head in disbelief. Was it possible? At this point, why not? After everything else of late, after all the other unexplainable events, all that had been revealed, why not this too? "Remarkable," he finally said to himself. He carefully lowered his voice even more and confessed to Chakeena: "My dear... I think I'm hearing your thoughts."

"Me too," she said softly, as if hearing herself say it made it real.

Holy shit.

The inaudible interruption yanked their attention across the table where they met the uneasy stare of Dolph.

"What is it, Son?" said Magnus.

Shit! Dolph thought, again. "Nothing, Father." He tried to swallow. Inhaled some food. Coughed—too now feeling caught, his wits arrested by the question.

"Son, are you okay?"

"Yes, of course. It's just..." He fumbled for something. Anything. "...would you please excuse me? I have to... I mean, I have a—" He dropped his fork. Squirmed. Continued to cough. Then stood and scrambled off toward the palace.

Magnus and Chakeena glared at Dolph as he disappeared into the distance, then looked to each other and, in perfect sync, shifted their gaze over to Kaiden.

Oblivious of the occurrence, Kaiden continued with his lunch. He went for another forkful, stabbed a stalk and was raising it to his mouth when he glanced up and caught their stares... *What?*

CHAPTER FORTY-THREE

[A Few Days Earlier]

A blip from Dr. Hulaksen's communicator rang out. "He's here," he said. "At the gate. I'll go get him."

Dolph, seated in silence at the back of his father's room, gave a measured nod. "I'll wait here."

"Yes, of course," replied Hulaksen, already hurrying off.

Two attendants donning medical garb—masks, gloves, stark-white coats—watched over Magnus, the indications of urgency in their every move.

At the foot of the bed was a blipping monitor. Above it, a tangled bulk of hoses. And beside it, a pulsing transfusion machine busily removing affected blood and replacing it with an unaffected stream in an attempt to keep Magnus alive. But while it had helped to delay his demise, it was very much temporary. For as quickly as the unaffected batch entered his system, it was almost immediately contaminated by the host—a desperate attempt at best and ultimately unsustainable.

Dolph stood and sauntered up to the attendants, the

click of his boots echoing throughout the room's glass-like walls. He mopped a patch of sweat from his neck with a gloved hand and turned to them. "I'd like a moment with him—alone."

They looked up, looked to each other, questioned the request with their eyes.

"I don't know if I'll get another chance," he said. "I'll just be a minute."

"Of course, sir," said one of them reluctantly. They bowed in unison and obliged, turned and drifted across the room and into the hall, their hushed conversation marking their increasing distance until it faded to nothing.

Dolph approached Magnus, looked him and the situation over, looked back to confirm he was alone, then went straight to work...

He removed a leather case from his vest. Unlaced it. Revealed a clear vacuum tube with an attached needle assembly. He quickly sorted through the web of hoses above the bed, singled out the one he wanted, and pierced it with the needle, then squeezed it to the assembly and punctured the vacuum's seal. The blood oozed into the hose beginning its glacial journey to the awaiting tube. It was thick, dark, and—most importantly—*affected*.

His heart raced as the device captured gulp after gulp of the coveted treasure. It was hard to believe it was actually happening. But it *was*. And soon he would have in his possession the means to not only acquire the respect that he deserved from his unsavory peers, but also the... He caught himself. Forced off the badgering thoughts. Cautioned himself against overconfidence. After all, he was far from out of the woods yet. There were still a number of things that could go wrong to soil the plan, an entire array of obstacles to overcome before he could achieve his ultimate end.

Yes, for the time being he must remain careful, rational, aware, and...

The sound of the attendants' padding footsteps pressed into his world, growing louder by the second.

The tube was only partially full but it would have to do. He removed the syringe, packed and pocketed the tube, and quickly sealed the insertion point with a narrow strip of adhesive, as...

"Sir Dolph," said one of the attendants as she arrived at the doorway. "May we enter?"

He spun around, wiped his brow, attempted to subdue his heart rate. "Yes, of course," he said. "And thank you."

"It is our pleasure," said one of the attendants, bowing her head as they returned to Magnus's side and continued their monitoring.

Dolph crept across the room and exited, a hand fondling his vest as he entered the hallway. He exhaled, strolled over to the window to check on Hulaksen, peered down and found the doctor greeting the guest in the driveway, the vantage point providing a clear view of the item in question and the doctors' conversation easily within earshot.

Dolph watched on from above as Joble grasped the chrome case at his side and released his safety belt. "It'll work," said Joble, stepping out of the shuttle. "I'd bet my life on it."

Hulaksen held the door. "You're sure? Your transmission was cut off. Not sure why. So I didn't get all of it."

"Yes. It'll work. It couldn't have been easier once we got Kaiden's sample."

Hulaksen ducked his head into the vehicle, said something to the driver, then rushed off with Joble under the nightlights of the estate.

Chief Drusher intercepted them, gasping to catch his breath. "Anything I can do?"

"I don't think so," said Hulaksen.

Drusher nodded, opened the mansion's door and made way for them to enter, as...

Dolph turned and headed back to the bedroom, seating himself again in the back of the room. His stomach rolled as he considered what would come next. Part two of the plan was to acquire the antidote. Maybe he could, maybe he couldn't. And who knew if it would even work. But if he could get some it would certainly be icing on the cake.

As for part one—the crucial part—it was done! He'd successfully secured a fresh batch of the *JF1Kx* element, the potential means to an unlimited weapon and unimaginable power, possibly one of the most valuable commodities in the Conglomerate. And on top of that an all-but-guaranteed rise in stature, and maybe even a place in the High Council of the gloriously devious Underpath Network.

He double-checked his vest for the tube, reassuring himself it was real. A smile formed on his face as the acquisition was confirmed—but he quickly suppressed it and recomposed himself.

Joble's voice emerged from the hall as he and Hulaksen reached the top of the stairs, his words echoing of truth in more ways than one: "...They're knocking on the door of a higher state but being driven back down by a corruption of that same higher state. It's a war. And unfortunately I know all too well which side wins if we don't get it right."

EPILOGUE

As Chakeena glided through a lush, green field and gazed up at the cobalt sky above, taking in the scents and crisp air of the peculiar planet, the sound of a young voice from behind yanked at her attention. She looked back to find the face of a little girl, then watched the scene fade as she slowly emerged from the depths of the dream...

Chakeena opened her eyes, blinked, was met with the same glossy face now inches from her own as it came into focus.

"Mommy!" said the girl. "We're almost there!"

Chakeena beamed at the girl as she took her in, her auburn locks dancing on her shoulders, the ice-blue eyes round and wide full of spirited life. "How exciting!" said Chakeena. She kissed the girl's forehead, sat up and peered out the port-side window of the *Odyssea*—the transport vessel they'd been traveling in for the past many months.

The accompanying flotilla scattered haphazardly at their side came to view along with a blanket of hull lights sparkling like stars in the night delightfully dotting the expanse of jet black space.

In the windows of the ships could be seen the passengers otherwise known as "The Chosen." But in truth they were chosen by no one. Rather, victims of circumstance. For it had eventually been discovered that Chakeena and Magnus were not the only *Mortiferum* hosts to have attended Kaiden's performance, the performance since designated by Joble as "Anomaly One." No, there had been more. Many more, in fact, all also carrying within their DNA the *JF1Kx* element, Joble's "genetic primer," which did indeed turn out to be the missing link he'd hypothesized. And after sufficient time had passed to monitor the progress of Magnus and Chakeena in order to ensure there was no relapse of disease or latent adverse affects, the antidote was produced and distributed to those hosting the element yielding uniformly astounding results.

The news swept through the Conglomerate like wildfire. But even though it was practically impossible to view as something other than a miracle, some still did. In fact by many it was received with skepticism and controversy while others either demanded treatment as their inalienable right or rejected it as a form of heresy. It ultimately divided the population. Uprisings ensued. Many and varied uprisings. But unknown to the general public was the fact that those denied a dose were not even remotely candidates. For all attempts to replicate the results on a broad scale had been ultimately unsuccessful.

The genetic corruption, the "x" in the element—the link required to bridge the gap between the desperately wanting and the perfected DNA in all known species in the sector—had remained as elusive as ever. Only Anomaly-One hosts carried the key and were receptive. Only they and no others were able to bask in the glory of its results. Those administered the antidote who did not already possess the "x," disease or no disease, simply did not survive. It was too much for their system. At first a slight rejection and some non-optimum symptoms. But soon after, typically within weeks, each of the trial's participants tragically died. Yes, the only way to safely introduce the antidote was to first have the primer in place. And the primer could not just be forcefully injected into their systems or transferred from one to another either. That had also been tried and people had died. The Anomaly, true to the word's meaning, was unique in that it somehow, in some mysterious way, had caused the element to form. And without the way paved by it, the antidote would overwhelm the entire organism and quickly cause its demise.

This was where the heresy came into play. This was the point of that contention. For the antidote, the literal lifeblood of the "initiated," Kaiden's blood, or any derivative therefrom, became considered the work of witchcraft and the killer of all things sacred. So rather than being welcomed with open arms by the remaining population, The Chosen were ultimately ostracized.

As for Kaiden, he was forced into hiding and assigned round-the-clock security. Yes, quickly did he fall from a sort of savior to an adversary, giving rise to the ensuing witch hunt. And on top of that, facts were falsified. Fueled by the Network, their twisted "truths" were distributed far and wide on the media feeds, the lies further dividing the population. Those still afflicted with *Mortiferum*, though lacking the "x" marker, were led to believe the antidote could save them as well, and that The Chosen and their "leader" were merely holding captive their treasure for reasons of greed. This in the face of the unafflicted being led to believe the disease itself was the enemy, that it had mutated in its hosts and had put the entire Conglomerate at risk in a new contagious form. All of it equally untrue.

With the discovery of The Chosen came an abundance of the element, rendering the batch Dolph had secured far from the last. But that did not stop him from presenting it to the Network. And neither did it stop them from weaponizing it and using it to serve their sadistic schemes. Oh yes, they unleashed it all right, though never to the extent of extinction—at least not before the flotilla's evacuation or to the knowledge of its passengers.

Months of sector-wide research revealed that Kaiden's planet of origin, which had over the course of a thousand years finally risen from the barbaric state from which it had begun to its current enlightened state, thrived as a society. They had continued to ascend in every aspect of life, advancing in ways theretofore unimagined. And knowing the planet would not only support the genetic blueprint of The Chosen, but also openly welcome them into their world, it was the obvious choice for relocation. So, after years of preparation, they escaped.

It was not known whether The Conglomerate would survive. For it to do so would require advances on many fronts—medical, spiritual, environmental, educational, political, and for far too many, moral. For if it did not advance in these areas and other areas, it was certain its fate was sealed. As for the passengers of the flotilla, theirs too was sealed, though much more hopefully. For them it was a new sector, a new planet, and most of all, a new start.

"There it is!" blurted Keena Rose. "I can see it!"

"Me too!" cheered Paul. "Dad, look! It's just like the pictures!"

Kaiden smiled, nodded, fatherly pride swelling in his heart. "You're right, Son. It is."

Keena Rose chimed in. "It's The Big Blue Marble!"

"No," protested Paul. "That's not it. It's called *Earth*. Remember?"

Kaiden grinned and pulled them both in closer as they gazed at the gleaming planet in their fore. "Actually, you're both right," he said. "It *is* called Earth. And it's *also* called The Big Blue Marble." He smiled, admiring their beaming faces, their eyes eager for the coming explanation. "But more importantly," he continued," there's something else you can now call it too." He wrapped his arms around them and squeezed their little bodies tight as he shifted an adoring gaze over to Chakeena. "From now on, you can also call it *home*."

NOTE FROM THE AUTHOR

Thank you for taking an interest in my book. I sincerely hope you enjoyed it.

Anomaly One was a labor of love and a very personal project for me. It was initially prompted by the loss of my mother many years ago. But shortly thereafter, life managed to get in the way and it wound up sitting on the back burner for more than twenty years before I finally jumped in again to finish it up.

Feedback so far as been extremely positive and very much appreciated. As you may know, reviews are important to authors, especially independent ones. So if you did enjoy the book, please consider leaving a review. Nothing longwinded or anything like that is necessary—just a line or two about your experience would be great. It would be very helpful and would mean a lot to me.

Thank you again for reading *Anomaly One*.

- Rick

ACKNOWLEDGMENTS

I'd like to thank my wife, Marlan, and daughter, Mila, for their undying support as I ventured into and forged through this sizable yet satisfying undertaking. I love you both with all my heart.

ABOUT THE AUTHOR

Rick Krusky is a publicist, entrepreneur, and emerging author. Rick was born and raised in Calgary, but relocated to Los Angeles in 1987 where he currently resides. For more information on Rick, visit: rickkrusky.com.